EAST WIND

By

Jack Winnick

Fireside Publishing Company
Lady Lake, Florida

Published by
Fireside Publications
1004 San Felipe Lane
Lady Lake, Florida 32159
www.firesidepubs.com

This is a work of fiction. Names, characters, places, and incidents are either the product of the author's imagination or are used fictitiously, and any resemblance to actual persons living or dead, events or locations is entirely fictitious.

ISBN: 978-1-935517-55-9

This book is dedicated to the tens of thousands of intelligence officers who toil anonymously, day and night, to defend the free world from those who would destroy it. These men and women, citizens of America and our allies around the world, risk their lives continuously in order to protect ours. Whether they belong to the CIA, FBI, MI5, MI6, Mossad or other agency, these people have foiled countless plots aimed at ending our way of life. In most cases, their courage is not made public until long after they have left this earth. Without their thankless bravery and energy we would have long ago succumbed to the forces of darkness.

Jack Winnick

ACKNOWLEDGMENTS

Many people other than the author are responsible for bringing a jumble of thoughts into a printed work. I would first like to thank my editor, Ms. Joan West, for her constant encouragement, suggestions and attention to the details that elude most of us. This book would never have made it to press without her efforts.

Then, of course, most importantly, my sweetheart and constant source of energy, Gisel, gets all the credit for whatever positive results come from the publication of this work of fiction.

Every author, myself included, owes their success to the countless others who have preceded them. In my case, it is the authors of modern espionage novels who are responsible, starting perhaps with Graham Greene, for the genesis of this one.

EAST WIND

Jack Winnick

Prologue

December 9, 2013

Ed Cooper leaned back in his new ergonomic chair, hands behind his head, and stretched his legs comfortably as he gazed out his floor-to-ceiling window at Santa Monica Bay, twelve stories below. It was an exceptionally clear day, for the coast of Southern California, and he could see the entire outline of Catalina Island to the south, and well beyond Malibu to the north. Two huge oil tankers moved across the horizon; one rode high in the water, one low, waiting its turn to off-load its supply of crude. There had been a lot of tankers lately, and Ed felt that each one added just a bit to his already hefty portfolio. The decision to buy crude oil futures had been a risky one, but had paid off handsomely, as their price had escalated along with the terrorist threats.

Ed also thought about his decision to rent this condo on the "Marina," as Marina del Rey was affectionately known here in Los Angeles. Situated at the far west end of the city, directly on Santa Monica Bay, it was the ideal place to live and work. Marina del Rey was the largest man-made harbor in the world, having been carved out of the marshy, inhospitable shoreline more than half a century ago. The area had undergone tremendous growth in the past fifty or so years. The developers had steadily beaten back the environmentalists, and towering structures now enclosed the entire harbor, and well beyond, far inland.

It was costly and prestigious to own or even rent a condo in one of the buildings on the marina; his small one-bedroom went for $7000 a month. He could have gotten one for less, but he'd

1

opted for the "ocean view." It had been well worth it, he mused, as he again let his gaze slowly pan from right to left. The sun had not yet reached its zenith on this bright December morning, so that he hadn't closed the electronically-operated sunshades that blocked out the intense glare.

To his right; on the beautiful, curved, walnut desk that had been a present to himself, just to the right of the 24 inch flat screen computer monitor, stood Ed's favorite picture of Ellen and the girls, Chelsea and Kirsten, smiling happily in the New England summer sunshine.

The marina office/apartment had been a compromise he and Ellen had reached. Ed would spend the "cold months," from October to May in Los Angeles, while Ellen kept her position in the fashionable Hockney School in New Hampshire. The girls had long been of age, and moved into the City to pursue their careers in the fashion magazine industry. Ellen visited Los Angeles during the three-week Christmas break, and Ed spent the summers with her in New Hampshire. The property had belonged to Ellen's mother and to her ancestors before her. Situated on a small creek, frozen over most of the winter, but painted with wildflowers all summer, Ed was happy to spend the summer months there, weekending in the City once in a while, visiting the girls, and going to the theater.

But northeastern winters didn't suit him; he preferred the warm California sun, the heated swimming pool on the third floor, the tennis club on the first, where he and several other men in their fifties played three afternoons a week. He had made good friends of his tennis partners; in fact, it was Lane Wharton, a former broker who had moved out from New York after hitting it big in commodities in the late '90s, who had suggested buying the crude oil futures. It had become a private joke between them whenever they met after an upwards move in the price of crude following a terror threat: "Hey, them Arabs ain't so bad."

The condo maintained a well-equipped gym; Ed had kept the flat stomach and toned muscles of his college days with his disciplined exercise regimen. Yes, this situation suited him perfectly.

Ed rose from his chair and went into the small kitchen, where a pot of coffee was brewing; the aroma itself gave him pleasure. As he lifted the pot to pour a cup, an intense light filled the room, his arm suspended in air, a piece of stainless steel trim traveling at 600 miles per hour pierced his chest below his left rib cage, ramming through the aorta on its way to the other side of the room. Less than a microsecond later a shower of glass and concrete tore his skin completely from his face and body. A large piece of his cerebellum splattered on the family portrait as the main blast of blazing hot air and debris vaporized what was left of Ed and the room. The tower itself and the rest of the marina and complex followed a split second later, as a 300 mile wind leveled the buildings within a mile of the detonation.

The world ended for Ed, his ergonomic chair and his ocean view.

Chapter 1

January 2013

Uri looked out at the sun setting over the Mediterranean. Just a few rolling clouds disturbed the otherwise tranquil scene. A light onshore breeze felt pleasant on his sun-bronzed face. His thoughts went alternately between two scenarios: how wonderful it would be if he could live here, in relative comfort, on the shore just south of Tel Aviv; and how certain his death would be if he returned to talk with Elieazar. If Danielle were here, the choice would be simple; without her—well, without her why bother wondering about a choice.

Danielle had been insistent: the test raid was to be his last. He had done more than his share; now other men, younger men, could take up his burden. His thoughts returned to that last raid. She had known nothing about it until his return from Lebanon, three months ago. From his squad, he was the only one who had escaped. At forty-one, he knew he was getting too old for this kind of field work. Yet, he was one of the few members of the Metsada, the Special Operations arm of Mossad. He spoke fluent Arabic, having learned it as a child, playing with the neighbor children, before the last Intifadeh. He had been assigned as squad leader in the ultra-secret Kidon, responsible for carrying out captures and assassinations in the neighboring Arab countries. The very existence of Kidon had been denied at all official levels of the Israeli government, much like the "Delta Force" in the U.S.

The latest mission in Lebanon had been aimed at Hakim el-Fazikh, a Hezbollah operative known to have led raids against schools in those Israeli settlements located just a few kilometers south of the border. Despite the most drastic precautions, Hakim had led six-man teams into the school grounds during Sabbath evening services, the most recent time posing as traveling ultra-orthodox Jews, desperate for a place to rest and pray. Once inside the compound, they held the youngest children captive, forcing the guards to relinquish their weapons. Then they calmly slaughtered both the children and guards, leaving just one child to transmit the story.

Though terrified, this child, the ten-year old known only as Yaakov, under hypnosis, remembered one detail about the leader of the killers. On his right hand, he bore a crescent-shaped scar, between thumb and forefinger. As Uri read the report, he almost missed this key piece of information. Then his mind raced back to his childhood: one of the Arab children in his circle of friends had shown the others his ability to endure pain, and had cut a small semi-circle in just that spot.

"You see," he had boasted, "a true warrior does not fear pain, he endures it without crying." His parents had been aghast at this mutilation of the body, strictly prohibited by the Sharia, the Muslim law, but he had told them it was an accident.

The scar had remained, at least into their teens, when Uri lost track of him. As soon as he read of the identifying scar, Uri notified Elieazar; he was sure Hakim was his childhood friend. Despite Uri's age, Elieazar felt he was the man for the job: eliminate Hakim and as many of his murderous gang as possible. A crack team of five Metsada veterans assembled under the highest security, with Uri as the head. Uri had an idea of where Hakim might be hiding, a place they had often visited as children, just across the Lebanese border, in an area of rocky slopes and caves.

All the team members had grown facial hair similar to that worn by the Bedouins roaming the area, with their grazing goats. These Bedouins were tolerated by both Lebanese and Israeli militia, and allowed relatively free access to the region on both sides of the border. The plan was simple: it mirrored the scheme Hakim had used. Pretending to be Bedouins in need of a place to sleep, they carried no obvious weapons, only rings with tiny poison-tipped needles hidden inside. On contact, the ring opened and the nerve toxin poured into the victim. Paralysis came within five seconds, with no warning.

5

The team reached the caves at twilight, bringing with them a herd of ten goats to help with the ruse. The goats bleating as they roamed the rocky hillside, Uri led the men in apparent disarray up toward the caves which he suspected harbored Hakim. After three stops at uninhabited caves, an Arab suddenly appeared from nowhere, dressed in filthy, tattered fatigues, armed with an AK-47 and two sleeves of cartridges. He demanded they halt and lie flat on the ground. His dirt-covered clothing matched the color of the tan soil. Even his head covering seemed to be one with the craggy features of the landscape. His face, aged by sun and wind, was heavily creased; a scruffy beard hid most of his features. His eyes, however, were piercing in their blackness. It was a face that had not seen laughter in many years.

Showing his empty hands, palms outward, Uri said the traditional Bedouin greeting to strangers, "As-salamu alaykum."

The sentry, unimpressed, motioned again with his rifle for them to prostrate themselves. Following Uri's lead, the team lay flat on the rocky ground. Another sentry, taller than the first, solidly built, also carrying an AK-47, slung loosely over his shoulder, appeared from a cave directly above them. He too was humorless, suspicious, and lacking in the hospitality usually shown by the Bedouins. The two of them carefully searched the meagerly-clothed strangers, finding nothing but water casks and hunks of dried goat meat, not even a knife to use as a weapon.

"Where is your herd?" the second sentry demanded. Uri pointed out the scraggly herd of goats scattered along the hillside. Apparently satisfied, they led the five shepherds, one guard on either side, to a large cave above them and to the left. Two other armed Arabs were cooking dinner, a pot of unrecognizable meat in a gray stew.

"You may spend the night," the first sentry said, "but then forget where you were."

As they had practiced, the team bowed in obeisance, then rose and kissed the Arabs on both cheeks, placing the poisoned rings on their necks. The four men stiffened as one, not quite realizing what had happened. One however, emitted a short cry just before he fell, paralyzed, to the floor of the cave. In less than a heartbeat, two more Arabs burst into the chamber, AK-47's at the ready. Uri and Hakim recognized each other instantly. The second Arab, a bald, muscular man, clearly Hakim's chief lieutenant, was unknown to Uri.

Hakim's lieutenant, carrying one AK-47 with another strapped around his shoulder, immediately opened fire on the five Kidon members, felling all of them. In the split-second it took for Hakim to register Uri's presence, Uri was on him. He remembered Hakim's near-useless left arm, and with his right hand, twisted it violently behind his back, grabbing the man's rifle with his left. At the same time, he placed Hakim directly between himself and the lieutenant. Facing his leader, the lieutenant paused. In that instant of indecision, Uri placed five rounds into his torso, spinning the Arab into a bloody spiral of death, while at the same time, in a blur of practiced motion, stinging Hakim with the deadly poisoned ring. The terrorist who had mercilessly killed so many innocent women and children looked with helpless hate into Uri's eyes as he slumped to the floor of the cave.

Uri knew what he had to do now. He must leave a message for the Hezbollah terrorists who would come upon this scene. Even before checking on the condition of his men, Uri took the curved knife from beneath Hakim's robe and sliced open his abdomen, slimy organs spilling from the still-living corpse. He knew Hakim was still cognizant of what was happening; Uri wanted it that way. It was not only that his childhood friend had betrayed him so ruthlessly; he also wanted to leave a chilling scene for Hezbollah to discover. Raw recruits did not expect such savagery from the Israelis, even though they themselves were known to do far worse to the women and children they abducted from the kibbutzim near the border. Kidon did not officially exist, and the government would disavow any knowledge of the action.

He poured the hot gruel from the cooking pot directly into the open wound. Death would come within thirty agonizing minutes. Then he moved to the other four paralyzed terrorists and calmly slit each of their carotid arteries, blood spurting onto the cave walls. Only then did Uri look to his men. Two had been killed outright from the burst of rifle fire. Avram, the youngest member of the team was still alive, but had lost a lot of blood.

7

"Avram," Uri said, "can you help me move them?" Avram nodded weakly. Together they struggled to bring the entire team outside the cave. Leaving Avram, Uri hurried down to their staging point, about a hundred meters downslope, where they had buried a small reconnaissance radio. He signaled for helicopter assistance; the GPS would pinpoint their location. Then he hurried back to Avram, but it was too late. Uri did not take time to grieve; he had done that many times before. Instead, he went back into the cave to look for any maps, codes or documents the terrorists might have had with them. He found only a few scrawled notes in Arabic, and even though he had a good knowledge of the language, he was unable to make sense of them. He did notice the repetition of a single word that seemed oddly out of place: "Opera." Hakim had never shown the slightest interest in the arts of any kind, let alone opera. He would pass the notes on to Elieazar; perhaps the decipher teams at Mossad could make sense of them.

In just a few minutes, the familiar whup-whup of the rotor blades brought his attention back to the bloody scene. He hoped the cost in lives of these good, decent men had been worth it.

When he returned home, Danielle could tell that this mission had etched more than the usual grief on his prematurely-lined face. He told her what he could; she could fill in the blank spots. That was when she had given him the ultimatum. After two days with no answer from him, Danielle packed up her things and left. Now, two months later, Uri still felt the hollow inside him. He had tried several times to contact her. He called her parents' house in Haifa, but they said she didn't want to talk to him.

Then the message came for him from General K at Mossad. Uri was to come in at once to the headquarters building near Tel Aviv. The exact location was a closely guarded secret. The rumor had been spread with great success that it was in the beach city of Herzliya, north of Tel Aviv. Uri smiled as he realized how effectively the "public relations" office had been in keeping the nosy press and tourists away from the true location. Once tourists got to Herzliya they found enough to do in the beautiful resort location to distract them from worrying about Mossad.

As Uri approached the headquarters building, he speculated about the reason for his summons. *Another raid inside Lebanon, that must be it,* he thought. Well, that wasn't going to happen, not again. He had lost too many young, eager men, boys really, in the last one. On the other hand, General K—no one knew his full name—would not be the one to handle such dirty affairs; Mossad left that to the Metsada command. And Metsada never used the Mossad headquarters for meetings with agents.

Such a meeting as that would have been arranged with a series of unique telephone messages, leading from one location to the next, until finally he would have been met with an anonymous source carrying his instructions. Uri would just have to wait and see.

He pulled into the dirt-covered parking lot next to the plain sandstone building that served as Mossad's headquarters. No name plate announced the occupants. There was only a simple sign that said "Domestic Affairs" over the door. There were no armed security guards patrolling outside the door, no concrete barriers. The security here lay in anonymity. Reporters were warned in no uncertain terms, if they should ever be admitted here, to forget where they were. So far, the approach had worked perfectly.

However, armed guards were stationed invisibly in tall buildings at the perimeter of the small complex of government buildings. They kept watch on Mossad Headquarters around the clock, and were ready to instantly blow to smithereens any unauthorized or suspicious vehicle or personnel. "Retirement Offices" and "Vehicular Registration" read some of the signs on the adjacent sandstone buildings. As far as Uri knew, they might very well be authentic.

The outer door opened into a tiled foyer where an armed guard sat reading yesterday's Ha'aretz. Uri was aware of the multiple cameras that sent his image not only to the guard towers, but also to an armed detail behind the innocuous-looking mirrors around the foyer. Uri showed him his picture ID, getting only a cursory glance from the guard, and was buzzed into the inner hall. General K's office was on the second floor, overlooking the small government complex that housed Mossad as well as some truly domestic offices, such as welfare and the like.

9

He was shown immediately into General K's inner office, where four other senior officials sat, attired in the standard Israeli garb of plain shirt open at the neck, and tan slacks. There were no introductions; they got right to business: "You remember those notes you picked up in the cave?" General K asked Uri gravely.

No formalities here, Uri thought. He nodded, wondering what in the world was going on. He had never seen an assemblage like this. He almost always had gotten his orders, if not from Metsada, then directly from Elieazar.

"Colonel Mandel will fill you in. It's big." The General motioned to a portly man with a shock of white hair, an unlit cigar hanging from his mouth.

Uri had heard of Mandel but had never met him. He knew he had something to do with the decipher team, probably headed it.

"We've spent the last two months on these damn things," Mandel barked. He spoke Hebrew with a distinctive Brooklyn accent. Uri had heard that as a young man at the end of World War II, Mandel had been in the U.S. organization called the "Office of Special Services" (OSS). He had stayed on as it became the CIA and had immigrated to Israel after the six-day war in 1967. Although he was unknown outside of Mossad, Uri had heard nothing but glowing praise for the man.

He had, for example, been one of those who had warned the Army of the coming Egyptian attack on Yom Kippur, in 1973. His warning had gone unheeded, with near disastrous results. The Egyptians had overrun the Israeli positions along the Suez Canal and taken back all the Sinai before they were finally stopped and sent packing. But it had cost Israel dearly in lost soldiers. No such mistake would be made again.

Mandel sat back in his swivel chair and ran his hand through his thick, white hair. "Did you look at those notes at all?" he asked Uri.

"I didn't have time to study them, but, yes, I looked them over."

"You read Arabic, don't you?"

"I do, but I'm not a cipher expert," Uri replied, wondering where this was headed.

10

"Did you notice frequent use of the Arabic word for 'Opera'?"

"Yes," Uri said, "but I didn't have time to make any connection with Hezbollah."

"We've been at it for two months, looking at all kinds of translations and codes, but we just picked up on something yesterday. 'Opera' is a new software package that allows simple construction and access to web pages."

Uri looked at him dumbly. "Web pages?"

"Computers, email, messages...We figure they are communicating with each other right under our noses, using innocent-looking web pages. They're using chapter numbers in the Quran to set the code..." He got up from his chair and strode impatiently across the room. "Never mind," he said, waving his hands, "We don't have time to teach everyone all the code work. The important thing is, these notes you found...they refer to web pages. Those we've been able to trace so far are all in English. Very clever, they got by everybody; our CIA contact in Jerusalem tells us Langley wasn't even up on it." He suddenly looked directly at Uri. "You worked with him a while back on the joint operation with the Americans," he said. "'Jordan' he goes by, remember?"

Uri remembered Jordan well. Shortly after 9/11 the CIA had requested that Israel cooperate in a top-secret antiterrorist program; Uri had been the main contact. The two primary target countries of the terrorists were to share all information, but without public knowledge. The bulk of the American public did not want to have the animosity of the Arabs toward Israel plopped onto their backs. Most American politicians handled American-Israeli relations with kid gloves.

"What does this have to do with Opera?" Uri asked.

"The web pages we've been able to find so far, all look like college homework, very clever. But the scary thing is, most were set up in the U.S. It looks like there's something cooking for a Hezbollah operation there. You're headed to Washington tomorrow. Your contact there is FBI, but she's well-trained, a computer whiz and..."

11

"Hold on a minute," Uri interrupted. "*She?*" Uri was used to women in the armed service, Israel was equal-opportunity when it came to defense. But there were few female agents in Mossad, and none in the action wing, Metsada.

"Yes, she, and not only is she well-equipped in internet communication, she's the one who broke the web page business and she speaks fluent Arabic," Mandel added, "unlike most of the FBI or CIA. You're going to love her. Get packed, you're going commercial."

Chapter 2

June 2013

Lara threw her pencil at the waste basket and let out a grunt of frustration. She had had it with Deke Trotter. This was the last time she was going to suffer his chauvinistic, condescending and paternal lectures. Lara Edmond was 31, intelligent and fed up. She took a sip of her now tepid coffee and took one of her famous walks around the small office. Jim Turner, one floor down, had told her he knew whenever she had a chat with Deke. He could hear her "trot" around the linoleum floor.

She and Jim had gone through the FBI anti-terrorist training program together. They both had opted for analysis rather than fieldwork. Lara was too attractive and Jim too heavy; both would stand out like the proverbial sore thumb. But she liked analysis; she had been an avid reader since she was seven or eight. She had started on an old set of Nancy Drew mysteries her grandmother had saved in their old Ohio farmhouse, and gone on to devour anything she could find on the glamorous, cloak-and-dagger days of World War II.

William Stephenson was her favorite of the WWII spies. When she learned of all "Intrepid," as he was later known, had done to outwit the Nazi spy machine she absolutely fell in love with him. At fourteen, she had been devastated to hear of his death. Outrage was not too strong a word for her feelings about Kim Philby and his cronies, as she learned of his treachery against his native country, England. Philby, from one of the "best" families in England, had avoided capture for decades as he continued to hand over secrets to the Soviets. Breeding, she realized, is no way to determine patriotism.

13

Lara's family was not wealthy, but they had given heavily to fight for their country. Two of her father's uncles had died in France in 1944; one of her own uncles had been lost in Vietnam. Though she was opposed to the U.S. role in Vietnam, she was proud of Uncle Bert's service. He had died five years before she was born, but she never tired of hearing of his exploits. She'd have been just as proud, she thought, if he had been opposed to the war and been jailed for protesting; it was the honest commitment to something he believed in that rang true to her.

"What about Philby," her brother Bob argued, "He was just following his belief in communism."

"No, he was playing a game, seeing if he could outsmart both MI5 and MI6. He didn't care how many of his countrymen died to satisfy his ego," she replied. Bob laughed; he wasn't interested in politics or commitment; just sports, beer and girls. But he loved to tease her.

Bob was as large and rawboned as Lara was petite and trim. Both had inherited the blond hair and blue eyes of their mother. But while Bob was happy living his life in the small Ohio town where they were born, Lara had more far-reaching plans. She had set out to go to college with the help of a scholarship, and to prove herself to be the best in whatever she attempted. She had enquired about a career in the FBI as she approached graduation, and had quickly been taken into the program.

Now it sometimes felt as if she herself were just playing a game after seven years of anti-terrorist training, including an ultra-secret year at Quantico, that even Jim didn't know of. He knew she had been gone that year, of course, but FBI agents often disappeared for a while, even those not in the field.

Just as in college, Lara had been at the top of her class; in the preliminary training program she was always the first to decode the exercise messages, those pretending to be intercepted from enemy field agents. In her teens, as she was reading of Intrepid's adventures, she also learned of the breaking of the German enigma codes. That huge breakthrough, mainly at Bletchley Park outside London, had done more to shorten the war in Europe than any other single event. Even more lives could have been saved, she learned, if the stiff-necked, block-headed generals, including Montgomery, had had the sense to listen to their code-breakers.

At Quantico, she had amazed her instructors with her seemingly intuitive way of unraveling their carefully encoded messages. Doubly, and even triply imbedded codes fell to her methods. She had an advantage over almost all the other trainees: she was more computer-literate. Furthermore, she had used her spare time to learn passable Arabic through an online language course. The FBI had enormous computer-based resources, more than any one person could utilize. In that maze of bureaucracy, ten different independent computer teams had been established, none knowing of any of the others. This occurred when pots of money appeared at the end of the fiscal year; Bureau managers would seize the chance to augment their stations by applying for a million bucks or so, for vague advanced computer-based listening and decoding programs. To the bean-counters who doled out the year-end dollars, all of these sounded like good ideas, and none of them cared to spend the time and effort to see if there was any redundancy. So there were the ten independent teams, all bright young people, working away, oblivious of the others.

Because of her computer skills, coupled with her placement in the Bureau, Lara had gotten permission to access all these programs on a "C5," a temporary classification that allowed her to "evaluate and append," shorthand for terminating duplicate programs. She had found a bonanza of decoding tools, produced by the ten independent sources. They each had come up with clever ways to identify and decipher messages, especially those sent through international email. After the horror of 9/11, the emails sent and received by known terrorists were sifted for clues. The analysts were surprised to find that almost all their instructions, crudely coded, had been transmitted in English rather than Arabic.

Among all the government agencies involved with international terror, the NSA, the National Security Agency, was in charge of monitoring all email traffic; they were in fact, in charge of monitoring *all* electronic traffic. The conclusion arrived at was that the terrorists would assume that the Arabic messages would be subject to much more scrutiny, and so were communicating some crucial notes in English. Those English communications, however, were being sent in some unknown format through unknown media.

Lara was able, after the fact unfortunately, to unravel the crucial messages sent from the al Qaeda leadership to Mohammed Atta and the others, by using a combination of several of the FBI decoding programs. It had been a sore spot with the FBI directorate that there were so few Arab-speaking agents available on the anti-terror squad. Lara's discovery had made her the "Golden Girl," and put her in her current position as Special Agent in charge of primary electronic terrorism traffic. This meant she had the responsibility for the identification of suspicious electronic traffic, without the authority to do anything about it.

The NSA did not abandon this crucial part of the nation's eavesdropping easily. They had to be assured, as did the Department of Homeland Security, that they would be alerted to any suspicious traffic immediately. Since the NSA was prohibited from any field action, Homeland would normally then take on any "cloak and dagger" indicated by the information. But because of Homeland Security's overwhelming tasks of overseeing the nation's ports and airports, this one area of field activity was grudgingly left to the FBI.

That authority at the FBI fell into Trotter's basket, and he was overburdened, she knew, and under equipped, she felt, for the job. Trotter was old school; he believed more in the field agents than the analysts to sniff out prospective threats. He had had some successes post-9/11, and that had kept him in his position. His agents had uncovered two separate al Qaeda cells in New York City, close to setting off terror bombs on the subway. The arrests were kept out of the media; the Agency didn't want to panic the subway-riding public. This motive overcame the urge to take the political credit for the coups.

But Lara now had access to all the email traffic floating around cyber-space. The FBI had for over three years, been able to monitor all telephone and email traveling between the U.S. and overseas. Though the enormous volume of traffic didn't allow the Bureau to analyze every message, certain keywords and phrases triggered immediate attention. "Israel," "destruction," "Allah," and "martyr," of course rang alarm bells, especially when detected in the codes that had been broken. One of the teams whose work Lara had been privy to had deciphered a code, in Arabic, that mirrored one of the early Nazi codes. It was one that Field Marshall Rommel, the "Desert Fox," had used to communicate with his allies, the Saudis, back in 1941. It was not widely known in the West, especially in the U.S., that the Arabs, while courting the British, were actually working with the Nazis to bring the entire Middle East under Axis control.

All communication in Arabic was suspect; electronic traffic to or from Pakistan, Afghanistan, and Iran was scrutinized daily. Most of the U.S. public believed that the interception had taken place only at Langley. Project Carnivore, set up in the year 2000, later dubbed "Magic Lantern," had been mothballed after severe negative public reaction to spying on private communication. After that fiasco, the president had given the agency tacit approval to use NSA technology, and their blank-check budget, to set up a huge ultra-secret listening post, costing over a billion dollars, in the top three floors of an innocuous-looking science building on the Georgetown University campus. A whole team of young agents, posing as graduate students, monitored both telephone and emails flowing between the U.S. and the Middle East. More than five billion transmissions a day were filtered through several levels of analysis. Traffic in Arabic or Farsi got automatic transfer to the Arabic and Persian staff. There were known hot-spots in Iran and Pakistan, almost certainly al Qaeda cells. Communication to and from these cells had already triggered the arrest of twenty-nine suspected terrorists, who were being held secretly in federal prisons.

Traffic in English was a tougher situation. The sheer volume, coupled with the possibility of imbedding the messages in levels of code, made the job seem insurmountable. That's where the "computer-meisters" that Lara had access to had proven invaluable. Their programs detected patterns in messages that had certain syntax errors that Middle Easterners were prone to. Misuse of pronouns and conjunctions were easy tells. The use of an extra "a" or "the" was a dead giveaway, and they had been able to get enough information against five Iranian students to get them deported. After tracking their emails for six months, to and from Iran, and checking on their status in school, agents found they had not been attending classes, and had not even registered for the current semester. That was enough for INS to boot them out.

So when Lara came to Deke with another set of curious emails to and from Lebanon using words like "freedom" and "flight," she expected to get at least a positive reaction, if not outright glee. His section had been under intense pressure to come up with something the bureau chief could use in the constant inter-office competition. Instead he had just shrugged and put her report on top of a stack of papers on his credenza, a place that was known as the graveyard. That's when she had stormed back to her office in frustration. As she made her third stormy trip around the desk, she saw a large shadow on the floor, and looked up to find a youngish man in a gray pinstripe suit standing calmly in front of her.

"Agent Edmond?" he asked, stone-faced.

"Who are you?" she replied, though she had a pretty good idea.

"Fredericks, Homeland Security. We're taking over the electronic surveillance of the college students."

"On whose orders?" she barked angrily, her face reddening. She knew full well who would have ordered something like this. Since the Bureau had merged anti-terrorist activity with the Department of Homeland Security, there had been not cooperation, but competition. Turf and glory came with newsworthy hits. While early successes had been covered in secrecy to aid future investigations, political pressure made it necessary to advertise any arrests. Now the head of Homeland Security was pulling rank to grab what was clearly a coup in the making.

She stormed into Trotter's office, but instead of receiving the usual unconcerned reception, he welcomed her with a grim visage, "I was just about to call you. You're getting a new partner." While she stood there, somewhat unraveled, he continued, "An Israeli, part of a secret wing of Mossad we're not supposed to know about. Anyway, they've picked up on some transmission among the bad guys, the real bad guys, and it looks like an operation is headed our way. He's an expert on Hezbollah, speaks Arabic, you're going to love him. He'll be here tomorrow."

Chapter 3

June 1999

The gathering at the Mosque had been talked about for weeks. No one seemed to know who the special speaker was, or where he was from. So it was a large, eager young crowd that gathered after the Friday prayers. Walid was only 16, but he had heard from his older friends that someone was coming who could and would make a difference in the Shia communities world-wide. A hush came over the crowd as a large entourage of white-cloaked men made their way slowly to the podium. From inside the group, suddenly appeared the turban-clad form of the great man himself, to an audible gasp from the crowd.

Sheikh Hassan Nasrallah, a younger man than Walid expected, somewhat plump, with a full black beard, strode forward and raised his hands, palms outward, to the eager throng. He smiled as he looked around the crowded mosque, but it was his eyes that drew Walid's attention; they were so confident and full of inner peace. This was clearly a man on a mission, a mission with which he was supremely assured. The assurance he exuded was not lost on the supplicants.

Nasrallah was one of the most famous people to ever grace the village. He was known as the leader of the Hezbollah, which had formed as the most effective fighting force in the Lebanese civil war that began in 1982. Hezbollah, or "Hizbollah," as it is known in the Arab world, the armed "Party of God" in Lebanon, was originally made up of followers of Ayatollah Khomeini, the Shia leader who took over Iran in 1979. The vast majority of funding for the Hezbollah fighters came from Khomeini's "Revolutionary Guard." Their goal was to establish a strict Shia nation in Lebanon, similar to the theocracy in Iran.

Nasrallah had taken over the reins in 1992, when an Israeli helicopter gunned down his predecessor and mentor, Sayyad Abbas Musawi. Musawi had spent his formative years in a Shiite village in Iraq, part of an area that was under the influence of the Iranian clergy, where he came under the hypnotic power of Khomeini. Even before Khomeini's ascension in Iran, Musawi was espousing his radical philosophy to the Shia in Lebanon, and creating havoc in that unstable nation with the kidnapping and murder of Western-leaning dignitaries. A deeply religious Shia, his followers included many Sunnis, and even, surprisingly, many Lebanese Christians.

Walid knew that Sheikh Nasrallah was determined, in addition to creating a radical Shia nation out of the remains of Lebanon, to throw the Zionists out of Palestine. Hezbollah's successes in harassing the Israeli troops and terrorizing the Zionist border villages were a source of pride to Walid and his friends. For example, Hezbollah troops masqueraded as harmless shepherds while setting up rocket launchers in the hills near the Israeli positions. Then, during the night, they bombarded the area with their notoriously inaccurate rockets, randomly injuring a few soldiers and civilians. They sometimes dressed Lebanese Arab boys as young Jewish students on a school outing, getting into the Israeli compounds, where they then blew themselves up becoming martyrs and a few Israelis became bloody bits of flesh and bones. All in all, a good trade.

Walid and his friends were constantly reminded, in school and in mosque, that the Shia were the offspring of the Prophet himself. If the Most Blessed Ayatollah Khomeini could rid Iran of the Shah and his American warlords, and Hezbollah rid Palestine of the Zionists, why could not Pakistan claim back its rightful share of the Indian peninsula, Kashmir and beyond? Hezbollah, as everyone in the region knew, had taken over the terrorist role in Lebanon when the "Palestine Liberation Organization," the PLO, had been driven out by the Israelis in 1981. But the peace deal, brokered by the Americans, failed to address the threat posed by the remaining terrorists, mainly Sayyad Abbas Musawi's Hezbollah. They were now free to cause chaos in the once-liberal Middle-Eastern nation. Hezbollah soon became the equal to Islamic Jihad, Hamas, and the other radical, violence-oriented militias. It seemed more than logical to Walid that this bold, mesmerizing Sheikh who now stood before them in his village was the answer to his life's goals, goals which had lain dormant until now. More than logical, thought Walid, in that he felt as if he were divinely inspired to take up the Sheikh's cause.

As if listening to his very thoughts, Nasrallah echoed them to the crowd. "It is time," he said, "for the Shia to regain the world that the Prophet claimed for us. Rise up and join us, all you young people, and help bring the Prophet back to the fore."

On and on he went, mesmerizing the youthful audience with that calm gaze, forceful voice, and most of all, the supremely self-assured manner. Here was a man who had humbled the mighty Israelis and their international Zionist benefactors, most notably the Americans. Walid felt a sense of empowerment, as though his whole life's purpose had suddenly appeared.

The Sheikh went on for over an hour. His manner of speech had a hypnotic quality. Walid had heard of charlatan preachers, no matter what the religion, who could repeat the same sanctimonious religious phrases time after time, but with a metronomic cadence. The effect on the audience is always the same, their eyes glaze over and they appear ready to do the master's bidding. In spite of knowing this could happen, Walid resisted believing this was happening with this great Sheikh.

When the hypnosis was complete, several of the Sheikh's aides roamed among the crowd, looking for acolytes. The aides were distinguished from the rest of the crowd by their identical white robes, each fastened with a small pin bearing Nasrallah's likeness. These aides knew what they were looking for: Young naïve boys with the same eager, accepting look seen in the faces of the Hitler Youth during one of the Fuhrer's rallies in the 1930's. Nasrallah's aides had been trained by studying the crowds in those old films; there was a certain look in those fresh, young faces as they enthusiastically stretched their right arm toward the Master of the Third Reich.

They found Walid easily enough. He eagerly signed his name, and in the column marked "expertise," put down "engineer," although he had only just been admitted to the Technical Institute, though a year ahead of schedule.

Walid returned from the mosque in a kind of trance. He felt reborn, as if his life's true calling had been revealed to him. He barely felt his feet touch the ground as he returned home. His father, who spent most of his time at his exporting facility in the outskirts of Karachi, not far from the border with India, was home for a few days. At dinner, his father, Aman, immediately noticed the change that had come over Walid. Usually, Walid finished his meal and retired to his room and his technical books. But tonight, he sat at the table, relaxed and seemingly content.

"What has happened to you tonight, my Kaka?" His father teased him. He knew Walid had outgrown the moniker used for small children. But tonight he sat there and just laughed easily at the joke. Aman stroked his mustache and thought to himself that indeed his son had found some sort of maturing influence in the past week or so since he had last been home. Perhaps a girl? No, he knew Walid's strict adherence to *Sharia* would not have altered in such brief a time.

"Are your studies going well?"

"Yes, father," Walid replied, "I am certain I want to be an engineer."

"And the exporting business?"

There was a pause as Walid thought how to reply. He didn't want to hurt his father's feelings. "I'm not sure I'm cut out for that. I want to study more about computers."

"Well, my son, there are opportunities in the firm for that," his father said quickly. "We have to update our system of inventory, billing and so on."

"Of course, Father, I'll keep that in mind."

That seemed to end the conversation for the time being. Aman did not want to pressure his fine young son. He had three years yet at the Technical Institute before even entering the University. Aman would be happy to pay Walid's tuition, if it came to pass that he were admitted. It would be a glorious thing for the family to have a son in the world-famous NED Technical University in Karachi. Once he finished his education…There was plenty of time. Aman relaxed and enjoyed his tea.

Walid's sense of contentment and purpose slowly faded in the coming weeks as he waited for further word from the Blessed Sheikh. He became restless with his studies. He hoped the meeting had not just been a dream.

The message came for him three weeks after his epiphany. A young mute appeared at Walid's house with a brief note on plain, white paper. Before Walid could even digest the note, the mute had disappeared. Walid was to be interviewed by one of the Sheikh's men. He was to appear at a local school, or *madrassah* as it was called. By the time of his appointment he had heard from several of his friends that inquiries had been made around town as to his character and commitment to *Sharia*. Apparently he had passed this test, because his interviewer was quite detailed in his questions. "What kind of engineer do you intend to be?" he asked at one point, clearly recognizing that the 16 year old was not already practicing.

"Computer," Walid quickly replied. The interviewer paused, appraising him carefully.

"Come to the *madrassah* Saturday, after morning prayers," the interviewer ordered. That was the end of the interview. Walid noticed the man had not told him his name.

Saturday at the *madrassah*, Walid arrived along with five of his classmates. They were ushered into a small classroom, where a man totally cloaked in black coarsely gave each of them, in turn, their instructions: Walid was to finish college in Pakistan, then arrange for graduate study in the field of Computer Sciences in Los Angeles. During his coming years in Pakistan, he would attend weekly "prayer meetings" with his mentors from Hezbollah. His devotion would be severely tested, he was warned; there could be no deviation from the path designed for him. There was no further word of where this path would lead; Walid must be patient. "But," the man in black said to him, "The Most Blessed Sheikh Nasrallah has chosen a very special role, indeed, for you." He placed one hand directly on Walid's shoulder and looked him straight in the eye as he spoke to him. "You will be at the forefront of a great adventure. It will be many years and you must prepare carefully. In America, you will appear to abandon many of the

24

Shia laws, but in your heart you will remain devoted. Are you willing and able to do this thing we ask of you?"

Walid nodded, a sixteen-year-old asked to make a lifetime decision, his heart beating wildly.

"You must say the words, young warrior."

"I am willing and able," Walid replied in a hoarse whisper.

"Fine. You will know me only as Ghalib. I will be the source of further instructions to you." He gripped Walid firmly with both hands, and for the first time, smiled at him. Ghalib apparently liked what he saw in this jihadi.

Walid left this meeting feeling very strange, as though overwhelmed by a powerful presence. As he walked home he recalled the story of the Christian warlord, Ibn-e-Hatim, in Arabia in the time of the Prophet. Ibn was very wary of this man Mohammed, who was converting multitudes of the masses and threatening the Hatim Empire. Ibn had gone and heard the Prophet speak it is told, and he felt overcome in the same way that Walid felt now.

The Prophet Muhammad saw Ibn and said: *"You are looking at the present poverty and helplessness of the Muslims. You find that the Muslims today are living in distress. They are surrounded by crowds of enemies and have no security of their lives and properties. They have no power in their hands. By God, the time is not far when such a vast wealth will come to them that there will be no poor among them. By God, their enemies will be vanquished and there will exist such a perfect peace and order that a woman shall be able to travel from Iraq to Hijaz alone and nobody will trouble her. By God, the time is near when the white palaces of Babylonia will come under the hands of the Muslims."* Ibn embraced Islam with perfect faith and sincerity and remained faithful to the end of his life.

So the 16-year-old Walid embraced the teachings of Sheikh Nasrallah in the same way, feeling an inner peace born of a new sense of purpose. The next Friday, when his father took him to prayers at the mosque, Aman noticed Walid's calm demeanor. "You are doing well in your studies?" he asked the young man.

25

"Yes, father, I definitely want to go to NED when I graduate. And then to UCLA in America, for graduate studies after that."

Aman looked at his young son with wonder. He had never shown such resolve. "I will pay your tuition to NED, and if, when you graduate, you still want to go to America, well, we'll see." He still had hopes Walid would change his mind about coming into the export business.

Walid just smiled. "Thank you, Father; as you say, we'll see." But in his heart Walid knew where his future lay.

Chapter 4

February 2013

She was a pleasant enough person, he thought, and certainly attractive enough in her Western way, but her fate had been sealed two years ago. Ghalib had been firm in his instructions: find a mate who would seem perfectly suitable for a young man in the corporate world in America. But she must be sacrificed, not as a martyr, but as a necessary, disposable entity. He thought as always of the incredible pleasures waiting for him afterwards, most notably the virgins ready to grant his every wish.

Walid looked in the mirror over the small sink and was satisfied at what he saw: a trim young man of 29, dark complexion, but not sinister-looking, even to Western eyes. He had shaved all facial hair, contrary to the instructions of the Holy Quran, but necessary in his holy calling, as Ghalib had reassured him. To avoid all suspicion, Walid could not be seen as overtly religious, but rather as an Asian immigrant eager to assimilate into Western society. He wasn't really all that religious, not compared with most of the others. He attended services at the local Mosque every Friday and performed the morning prayers, mostly from habit, but many times skipped the other four, being at work or in transit. Being Shia, he was allowed to consolidate the five prayer times into three sessions, but still, here in America, he had grown slack.

There was no getting rid of his Pakistani accent; most Americans thought he was from India, judging from his appearance and submissive behavior. His computer skills had

27

made it simple to find menial work for the two-year period of preparation. His original student visa had been easily converted to a work permit, once he convinced his employers to certify that his skills were "essential and unique." Americans, he found, were much more concerned about their own profits than anything else. If he could do a job, and do it well, a job that an American would either snub or demand a higher wage for, they would sign any form necessary to keep him on the payroll.

In Karachi, he had been well-schooled in computer technology. He had been accepted almost immediately by the Computer Sciences Department at UCLA for his master's degree. The courses, he found, were simple, and the tasks he had to perform to get his tuition paid plus $2,000 a month as a Research Assistant were ridiculously easy. He merely had to do some programming for his professor, who had multiple grants from the U.S. government, grants concerned with topics that would be laughed at in Pakistan. For example, one of them dealt with the probability of an artificial disease being spread by domestic cats. He found it hard to believe that the government could waste millions of dollars on problems that didn't exist. It was later in his tenure that he found out that the person at the National Institutes of Health who had handed out this grant was one of the professor's former students, paying him back, in a sense, for the financial support he himself had received as a student.

Walid was surprised to find that the great percentage of the graduate students in the engineering college were foreign born, like himself. The faculty had to obtain grants and write research papers to try to further their careers, and there simply weren't enough native-born students to fill the posts. Walid, being naturally extroverted, fit in well with the masses of students from Asia and the Orient. They would have lunch together, often do homework together, and spend their spare time watching American movies. These were mainly subtitled in Hindi, a language most of them knew well enough to allow them to learn the colloquial American English being spoken in the films. It was a common way for foreign exchange students to become familiar enough with English to get along in America, where, of course, no one used Hindi or any other Asian language.

Professor Kartal, a Turkish immigrant, was Walid's major professor and mentor. He was delighted to have a student from NED, one of the most distinguished universities on the Indian subcontinent. With a student of Walid's capabilities, he knew he could just turn him loose on a computer-related problem, and wait for the results. A great way to satisfy the research sponsors and generate a few research publications, the authorship of which he would share with Walid.

Professor Kartal, whom the students called "Bobo," but not to his face, of course, was a large man with a stupendous appetite. He seldom shaved or showered, and his office was littered with the remnants of fast food, in or out of their Styrofoam containers. The main attractions of his office, however, were the staggering heaps of papers, journals, unanswered mail and student reports. There was literally, no place to sit. The giant piles of haphazardly stacked paper defied gravity, it seemed, they were so tall. Trying to find something among these piles of waste paper was useless. Kartal depended on the graduate students, or his thin, harried secretary, Marcia, who was constantly shivering in her lank, gray, knit sweater. Walid finished his work in less than two years, presenting "Bobo" with a polished thesis ready for publication in some obscure journal or another.

Getting his job after graduation was even easier than getting his degree. A small start-up company in the San Fernando Valley had needed someone to keep their computers clean of the increasingly annoying "viruses," as they were called, that cost the company hours of valuable down time. Hearing of the opportunity, he emailed his friend Rashiv, back in Karachi, a coded message, asking for some specific help. Rashiv knew what he wanted; he was part of a team that implanted viruses in the computers of U.S. companies known to be on friendly terms with India, one of Pakistan's chief enemies. Vcomp, the company Walid was applying to, had no such ties with India, so they had not yet been victimized by Rashiv and his compatriots. On getting Walid's request, Rashiv sent an innocuous-looking email to Vcomp, apparently requesting sales information. When the secretary in the Valley opened the attachment describing the phantom company's needs, the virus went directly to the operating system, rendering the company's sales directories inoperative.

The next day was Walid's interview. The interviewer had been up all night, along with several of the staff, trying to find and flush the virus, but without success. On hearing of the problem, Walid said he had seen similar situations and might be able to help. He was left alone for about an hour at one of the company's workstations, knowing of course, exactly what to look for and how to resolve it. He took a full hour to give his performance more credibility. After that coup, it hadn't taken long to get the papers signed for his visa and to begin working. The salary, relatively small, by U.S. standards at $45,000 a year, assured him he would not be replaced before the "time" came.

He met Sarah, a girl with lustrous dark hair and brown eyes, during his first week at work. While at the canteen, a small lunchroom shared by several of the small companies in the building, he had seen her buying some yogurt. "You must be from the Middle East," he offered gamely.

"No, I just like yogurt," she laughed. By her reaction, Walid could tell she was not put off by his approach. They sat down together and began a simple conversation. In an instant, an hour had passed, and they both had to get back to their jobs. But the next day, there she was again, at the same time. Their relationship had begun. Within weeks it had turned intimate.

Although from a Jewish family, Sarah herself had nothing to do with the religion. In fact, she and most of her friends were opposed to anything smacking of U.S. imperialism, including the occupation of Palestine by the Zionists.

Walid pretended a lack of interest in the topic, and offered nothing when the subject came up. He was just a guest in the country, a poor Pakistani trying to survive in the U.S. He did, however, often tell of the miserable conditions in his home town, with many of his family barely surviving. Thank Allah he was now able to help. The truth was actually far different; his family was one of the wealthiest in his community, having established a lucrative exporting business immediately after the partition from India after World War II.

Sarah was immediately drawn to his poor Muslim status, an example of the grief her country was causing around the world. It wasn't long before the friendship turned to romance, a relationship that brought her family, who held the traditional view of the Zionists, no end of misery. Even though they didn't go regularly to pray in the synagogue, they were members of a congregation and gave liberally to the Zionist cause.

Sex with Sarah was a wonder, one he hadn't even considered when he embarked on his mission of martyrdom. In Pakistan he had been celibate, as demanded by his family. He and his friends, all male, of course, mused privately about intercourse and all the acts associated with it. They had gotten hold of some Western magazines, unknown to their families, and gazed in rapture at the unclad female form. They talked endlessly about the virgins awaiting those brave enough to enter martyrdom. A virgin himself the first time with Sarah, Walid was actually grateful that she was so experienced. Sarah and her friends had been openly promiscuous since their early teens. His virgins in the afterlife, he dreamt, would be as grateful to him for the expertise he was gaining now, despite it coming from a Jewess.

Walid had been instructed to maintain a normal social life, including the sexual relationship; he was to look as much as possible like a normal young man, eager to assimilate into his new adopted country. Sarah loved going to parties with her intellectual friends, and she insisted he come along. The conversations were mainly political.

"Why is this country always at war?" was the inevitable starter. They were at Josh Green's house, his parent's basement actually. Josh's father, Mort, had given him a "so-called" executive position at his used car-parts operation in Van Nuys. When Josh had graduated UCLA with a degree in political science, there seemed no real place to go. He was tired of college so graduate school was out. He made some-half-hearted attempts at job applications, but failed miserably on the interviews. Finally, his father became exasperated seeing him lie around the house all day, listening to his I-Pod, and watching videos; so he created a position called Vice-President for Customer Relations. Josh was supposed to handle any complaints that came in from the network of car parts stores that bought from Mort's warehouses. After a few weeks, Josh found he could just leave the job to his assistant, Valerie, who had been doing it herself for twenty-five years. She knew all the customers, all the complaints and all the remedies. Josh seldom even went in to the office any more.

The Green family had immigrated to the States around 1900 from Eastern Europe. Their name at the time was Gurion, which had come from the German word, "gruin," (green) but Josh's great-grandfather changed it to "Green" to "fit in." Josh had heard that they were related somehow to the first prime-minister of Israel, David ben Gurion, but that was ancient history.

Josh heard the remark about the country being at war and immediately chimed in. "Sure, as long as there's somebody to oppress, we'll be the first ones in the door. Oil, copper, coffee, you name it, the U.S will be there to exploit the resources and screw the natives." He took another hit off the marijuana joint being passed around. There was typically no drinking at these get-togethers, but marijuana was usually available. Walid never smoked, and by now no one even offered it to him. Sarah, however, joined in freely, both the smoking and the conversation.

"Look at Israel," she said, "millions of Palestinians thrown out of their homes and left with nothing."

Walid smiled inwardly, thinking, *With enemies like this, who needs allies? These friends of hers have been inducted well by the political science and other liberal arts faculty on campus.* Further, the campus was peppered with fliers advertising rallies and meetings for the Palestinian cause. The Israeli side had given up trying to debate the issues, as they were always shouted down by the overwhelming Arab presence.

David Grossman, a small, thin boy with severe acne scars tried to enter the conversation. Walid knew he had a serious crush on Sarah, but she seemed oblivious. David knew full well how the Arabs had gotten the most from the more liberal elements of the American press; even many of the Jewish journalists took the side of the Palestinians. In actuality, the Arabs living in Palestine prior to the U.N. partition had been allowed to stay, or were paid well for their property if they chose to move to the Arab side of the border. "The Israeli Arabs are very well treated," David lamely entered, but his efforts went in vain. Walid suspected his main goal was to impress Sarah. "You know," David continued, "there are millions of Arabs living in Israel as citizens, and even members of their parliament, the Knesset. But essentially all the Jews who had been living in the Arab countries were forced to leave, several hundred thousand; many times the number of Arabs who were displaced."

"Then why are the Israelis always starting these wars," Josh answered almost immediately. "Every ten years or so they invade the Arab countries. Ever since the Israelis took the Palestinians' homes away from them and forced them into the desert with nothing but the clothes on their backs they've been starting wars to get even more land from the rightful owners."

David got excited that someone had actually paid attention to him. "That's not true; the Arabs have started every war: 1948, 1967, and 1973. Then the PLO and their suicide bombers after that. Besides, the Arabs living on the Israeli side of the boundary actually do better than those on the Arab side, or in Jordan or Lebanon. A lot of them actually commute in to work, too."

"Oh, right, and where did you read that, the Hadassah Handbook?" That got a chuckle from most of the half-stoned crowd. Josh went on: "And how come the U.N. is always condemning Israel for their beating up the Arabs? Are you saying they just make that up?"

David really got worked up now. He knew how the United Nations and the "Human Rights" groups like Amnesty International did the Arabs' work for them. "Have you ever heard of "Moynihan's Law?" Everyone just sat there silently. They were used to poor David's diatribes.

"It's named after Senator Daniel Patrick Moynihan, who said that at the U.N., the number of complaints about a nation's violation of human rights is inversely proportional to their actual violation of human rights. Or something like that."

Josh and the others really didn't want to argue; they were more interested in the pot.

Walid sat silently and listened; he knew how it would come out. He knew that David was essentially correct. He had found out the facts after he came to the States and read the news reports in the library. It was a far different picture from what he was told in his *madrassah*. Not that it changed his mind about the right the Muslims had to the entire region. Nor would it affect the others; they had been taught well in school, to despise the foreign policy of the U.S. as imperialistic and oppressive. No amount of pleading the facts could reverse their indoctrination.

Josh noticed Walid's pensiveness: "Hey, Walid, what do *you* say, man, you must have a real good idea of what's going on, you come from there, right?"

Walid reflexively broke into his mild-mannered grin: "You know I don't have any political opinions. That's why I came here: to be a computer nerd."

To his relief, the others laughed good-naturedly. After his job was done, his role would be found out; he had no doubt of that. Until then, however, he wanted to avoid any political talk. He knew the FBI had its eyes and ears out, looking at the activities of Muslims, both foreign and domestic, especially those with connections to countries with predominantly Shiite populations.

Walid, however, had found it relatively easy to blend in with the students and the populace in general. Politics were a hot issue, on campus and in community meetings. He felt that the political meetings dealing with the Middle East were overwhelmingly pro-Palestinian; even the letters and editorials in the Los Angeles Times were surprisingly liberal. Even among the large Jewish population there was widespread antipathy toward the "war on terror." Arabs and other Middle-Easterners were met with acceptance. His task was proving to be far easier than he had feared. He hoped that "Hossein," whoever and wherever he might be, was as ready as he was.

Walid's mind drifted back over the last few years, his indoctrination into Hezbollah, and the progress the Shia revolution had made. The victory of Hezbollah in the brief 2006 conflict in southern Lebanon had made Sheikh Nasrallah famous throughout the world, and not just the Muslim world. Rare victories against the Israelis, act to propel military and religious leaders into instant stardom. Nasrallah's face now appeared on billboards and computer screens throughout his homeland; his voice issued forth as cell phone ring-tones. He was truly an international hero.

Nasrallah had criticized the other Islamic movements. He was especially harsh in his criticism of Osama bin Laden. He had been quoted as saying the Taliban and al Qaeda, bin Laden's organization, are the "most dangerous things that the Islamic revival has encountered," saying, "It is unacceptable, it is forbidden, to harm the innocent." After all, the sneak attack on the American's World Trade Center in 2001, had caused a tremendous shift in the world view of the Islamic struggle, the Jihad. And it had brought about swift retribution against the jihadis of Afghanistan; tens of thousands had been killed by the American bombers. But when asked about suicide bombings in Israel, he explained that such actions against Jews fall outside the normal boundaries. In the mosques, *madrassah*s and tribal areas of Pakistan, it is Nasrallah who had become the hero of increasing sections of the Muslim youth. Osama bin Laden and the Taliban have now been replaced in the eyes of the Islamic Jihadists. Pakistan's frontier provinces and tribal areas now echo with tributes blaring from illicit radio stations; these same stations once heralded the anti-Western exploits of bin Laden. In between recitations from the Holy Quran, these radio stations proclaim the heroism of Nasrallah:

"Nasrallah made us proud as Muslims, and respected by the rest of the world. bin Laden made us hated by the rest of the world and viewed as criminals and terrorists."

"'Nasrallah led us from the front against Israel, the US and the UK. Bin Laden concealed himself in the caves while sending hundreds of Muslims to jail and death."

"Nasrallah united the Shias and the Sunnis in a joint jihad against Israel and the U.S. Bin Laden made them kill each other first in Afghanistan and Pakistan and now in Iraq."

Pakistani jihadi organizations like the *Lashkar-e-Tayiba,* the *Jaish-e-Mohammad,* the *Harkat-ul-Mujahideen* and the *Harkat-ul-*

Jihad-al-Islami, all members of bin Laden's International Islamic Front, were greatly concerned over this praise and support for Nasrallah at bin Laden's expense.

Walid and his cohorts in Pakistan were aware that bin Laden's agents had been telling their followers that the Jihad needs both bin Laden and Nasrallah. They referred to what they describe as the "sacrifices made by bin Laden" for the Muslims of the world in general and of Afghanistan and Pakistan in particular, saying that the Muslims cannot defeat the conspiracy of the U.S. and Israel against Islam without bin Laden's leadership.

The JEM, HUM and HUJI had been in the forefront of the anti-Shia campaign and still refused to make any major statement of support for Hezbollah. They criticized Israel and the U.S., highlighting what they described as the "heroic resistance of the Muslims of Lebanon," but refrained from identifying them with Hezbollah.

Then, as news of how Hezbollah fought the Israelis in the summer of 2006 in Lebanon appeared, there was an electrifying effect on much of the Muslim youth, Walid learned. Hezbollah's resistance against the Israelis was compared to the Afghan *mujahideen's* resistance against the Soviet troops in the 1980's. "The Afghan *mujahideen* took eight years to defeat the Soviet troops," they say, "but Hezbollah took hardly four weeks to defeat the Israeli troops."

Walid smiled inwardly as he considered how his own heroism was soon to be proclaimed around the world. He recalled the tales of the medieval Muslim hero, Rakan, who fought off the Christian crusaders and other enemies of the Prophet. True, Rakan was probably allegorical; he was now the "Superman" of a new Muslim comic book treasured by the kids in Pakistan. Westerners laughed when they saw these comics as indicative of the backwardness of the culture.

Yet most Westerners had no idea of the heroism of one of the greatest warriors of all times: the man known here as

"Saladin," sultan of Egypt, Palestine, Syria and Yemen in the 12th century.

Walid might well be the Saladin of the 21st century, he fantasized. He often saw himself as the great mounted warrior, with his famous peaked helmet and flashing sword. Not only would he find Paradise on the other side, he would forever be remembered in this world as he who delivered the crucial blow that would re-establish the Muslim Empire, "Walid the Magnificent."

Chapter 5

Summer 2009

Hossein ventured out onto the long, mist-laden pier, as he had so many times before. The native Alabamans had long gotten accustomed to seeing him out among the shrimpers in the early hours. To them, he was just another of the "furreners" that had invaded the coast in the last twenty years or so. At first, the immigrants, mostly from Southeast Asia, had sought work on the local fishing boats, using the skills learned in the Mekong Delta and similar places. But now, having saved their money diligently, many had purchased boats of their own and had taken over much of the fleet.

Hurricanes, pesticide runoff and other environmental factors had slowly and irrevocably eroded the catch more than tenfold since the seventies, and now the new laws limiting the number of boats as well as the take, had put an end to the fishing careers of most of the locals, some of whom had generations of Gulf fishermen in their family histories. Some had packed up and left for work in the factories, but others had seen the opportunity to service the new Asian fishermen, who they saw could survive on the smaller incomes quite well. They still needed provisions, tackle and so on, so those who had been fishermen now became the landlords and storekeepers, actually making more money, and working much more pleasant hours. The immigrants were happy with this arrangement: even though they could have set up their own markets and dispensed with the locals, it quickly became clear that good relations more important. Early on, several Vietnamese shrimp boats had mysteriously burned up while at dock. Now, with the new economic balance in place, there was an unwritten calm.

Hossein fit in easily with the Vietnamese. Even though he was Iranian, once out in the sun, he seemed, with his dark skin, to be just another one of "them." Lo Nguyen, who liked to be called "Wen," grew especially fond of Hossein, who learned enough Vietnamese to converse easily with Wen's crew. Hossein had shown up ten years ago, seemingly hungry and eager to work on the boat for the lowest of wages. He had worked hard, sometimes being the first one to clean the boat at 3 A.M., staying until all the catch was off-loaded after dark. While the Vietnamese, and even the townspeople, didn't know exactly from where Hossein had come, they didn't pry, and he had become accepted in both communities, his name being morphed into "Seine," a type of fishing net that hung vertically in the water, typically used to catch minnows or other bait.

It was two years before Hossein asked to take the small skiff out into the Gulf, to do some pleasure fishing, he said. Most of the crew had enough of the Gulf during the six-day work week, but they were happy to see Hossein getting in some fun, even if it was fishing. For the first year, these excursions were as innocuous as they appeared. It was only later that the true value of the plan came into fruition.

Soon Hossein had accumulated enough money to buy his own shrimp boat, and hire some of the other men to crew for him. He also began repairing engines in a hut he bought and refurbished, down near the pier. He was quite adept at engine repair and was soon augmenting his shrimping returns with other income.

Actually, Hossein had left Iran in 1996, armed with a B.S. degree in mechanical engineering from Shiraz University. He had already known his plans for the future. Hezbollah had recruited him five years earlier, even before he had started at University. He was to get an advanced degree in nuclear engineering in the United States, but not at one of the top-ranked programs. He could probably have gotten a graduate fellowship at MIT or Berkeley, but he was to keep a low profile. Nuclear engineering in the U.S. had long been out of favor as a major with incoming graduate students, so that foreign applicants, especially those with high standing in their undergraduate classes, were eagerly sought after.

The government had plenty of grant money for these programs, so much so that many fellowships went begging each year. He had applied to five Universities, and had received offers of financial support from three. He chose North Carolina State, mainly because it was relatively close to Washington, D.C., a city he had always wanted to visit.

He found the work needed for the Master's degree program easy, with plenty of time for him to peruse the library. His research topic dealt with nuclear reactor safety; but his personal research topic was much more interesting. His status as a research assistant gave him all the opportunity in the vast library he needed to launch his private program. Much material had been declassified since the cold-war era; he found it time consuming, but rewarding, as he slowly gathered the expertise needed to put together a small fission, or "Atomic" bomb. The geometries of the first U.S. bombs, used against Japan, "Little Boy" and "Fat Man," were shown in several of the declassified documents; however, the precise amounts of fissionable material were not. It took him more weeks of digging to get those numbers, both for the enriched-uranium bomb, "Little Boy," and the plutonium device, "Fat Man." The choice of fuel was not up to him; others would have to arrange the purchase. But he would be ready when the time came, no matter which fuel was obtained.

There were other details about constructing a bomb, of course, the shape and size, for example. These would be determined primarily by the fuel. But there were other matters not so easily found in the open literature. Exactly how does one trigger the bomb? And how can one be sure the chain reaction proceeds long enough to produce a significant "event?"

He finished his Master's work in 1999; his major professor desperately wanted him to stay for a PhD, but Hossein insisted he must return to Iran and help with the domestic nuclear power program. He returned to Iran for a few months but his purpose was far from domestic. His first stop was back in his village in northern Iran. There he met with his family and renewed some old bonds. His childhood friend, Ahmad, had not gone to college, but had stayed in the village working in his family's business, making kitchen utensils.

He and Ahmad had been close throughout the required middle school; then Ahmad had tired of books and wanted to earn a living. One thing they had shared was a deep belief in the radical Shia precepts they had learned in their religious school, the *madrassah*. Both wanted to do their share in the upcoming battle with the West.

Ahmad greeted him warmly; they spent a week going over old times. Then finally Ahmad got down to business: "have you learned what we have long talked about—the weapon?" Hossein just smiled; he had waited patiently for the opportunity to see what Hezbollah had in store for him. "Yes, old friend, I am ready for Jihad," he said.

Ahmad looked at Hossein for what seemed like eternity before he said, with an intensity he had never shown before, "Come to the Mosque after evening prayers on Tuesday, and dress warmly."

Hossein was totally puzzled but did as his old friend instructed. Tuesday night, as it grew dark, Hossein arrived at the front door of the Mosque, dressed in his warmest American parka. Although he felt he was alert to his surroundings, he never heard the men who grabbed him, covered him with a blanket and bundled him into a waiting car. They drove off, Hossein still cloaked, unsure what he should do; he knew better than to struggle. His few questions went unanswered. It seemed like hours, but in actuality in less than forty-five minutes the car came to a stop and he was roughly taken through a doorway, undraped and told to wait.

Hossein looked around a barely furnished room, perhaps fifteen feet square, the walls made of mud and brick. He was standing on a dirt floor; nearby were a table, four chairs and five straw-filled sacks that probably served as sleeping mats. A home for a family of shepherds, he thought. A candle flickered weakly on the table. The room smelled vaguely of domestic animals, sweat and human waste. No fire burned in the hearth, and it was chilly, even through his parka.

Ten minutes passed, then a single man entered, dressed entirely in black, his face covered except for his eyes. Those eyes Hossein was never to forget; they seemed to burn with an inner glow in the bare, semi-dark room. "Do you believe?" the man said simply.

"Yes," Hossein replied.

"And are you ready?"

"Totally," he lied.

"What are your needs? We must have at least five devices."

Hossein was ready for this request. He patiently explained how much uranium fuel was need for each bomb, and in what configuration the fuel elements must be supplied. He realized he was uncertain of the exact construction, but hoped his self-assuredness would carry the day. The strange man listened in silence, recognizing the extent of the ability and zeal of the young man in front of him.

"And if we cannot provide exactly what you ask, what then?"

Hossein was taken aback by this question; he had not expected to be challenged. "I will produce devices from whatever material you can get for me. It is Allah's will that it be done."

The man in the black cloak studied the young man carefully, then nodded and said, "You shall have your fuel, you will hear from Jamal." He strode out of the room without another word, leaving Hossein to try to gather himself back together. Who was this man, and could he really provide the promised goods? And who was this Jamal? Before he could move, the blanket was on him again, and he was hustled back to the car and returned to the Mosque.

"Do not turn around for one minute," one of the men said as they deposited him exactly where he had been earlier. Hossein did as he was told, standing with his back to the street as he heard the car drive off. Suddenly Ahmad appeared with a big smile on his face. "Do you know who you just met?" he said, still grinning. Hossein just shook his head, he had no idea. "That was none other than Fa'iz himself," he said to a dumbfounded Hossein. He knew to whom Ahmad referred: "Fa'iz" could be none other than the great one: Imad Fa'iz Mughniyah, the greatest of all the jihadi. He was revered in all of Hezbollah; in fact all of Islam, as far as Hossein knew. He was the mastermind of the great U.S. Marine barracks bombing in Beirut twenty years ago; the killer of 241

Americans. Mughniyah himself was worshipped as the single force that drove the warmonger Ronald Reagan and all his armies out of Lebanon forever, like so many whipped dogs, whimpering, their tails between their legs. Oh, the joy that was felt throughout Islam on that glorious day! Hossein and Ahmad, along with most of the village, had danced openly on the street as the word spread. Not until September 11, 2001, when Osama and his brave al Qaeda martyrs struck the imperialists in their heartland, would such open jubilation be seen.

Mughniyah was responsible for many other wonderful acts of Jihad against the West, especially against the Americans. Several diplomats and CIA agents had been disposed of, airlines downed, and journalists abducted for ransom. All had been the handiwork of Mughniyah, though he seldom took public credit, in opposite manner from bin Laden. If Hossein had had any doubts, they now vanished. This man would keep his word; he would have his uranium and become one of the greatest martyrs of all time.

With the proper forged documents, he was off to Alabama, to begin his new life as Gulf fisherman and chief architect of Hezbollah's Jihad in the United States of America.

Chapter 6

February 2013

The wind blew especially cold this time of year, Alex thought, as he blew on his hands, vainly trying to get some feeling back in them. Just walking from the jeep to the hut stung his face and hands, so that he felt unusually clumsy trying to open the simple latch. Finally, he stumbled into the sparsely furnished hut, just a room, really, but anything to get out of that damn wind. He found a pile of yak dung in the basket next to the rudimentary fireplace, and threw a few chips onto the stone floor. He got out his lighter, and briefly tried to start a fire, quickly realizing he needed some paper underneath the dung. His hands were still trembling with the cold and exertion of the arduous journey from Irkutsk. He was getting too old for this, he realized. But he couldn't say no to this kind of money. The Arab better be on time, he cursed silently to himself, just as the three-day old copy of Pravda he had found in his jacket pocket, blazed with a cheery orange glow. Jamal had been explicit, the courier would arrive within two hours of sunset. The edges of the dung started to smoke, then smolder and quickly caught fire, sending blue sparks up the chimney.

Alex moved one of the two wooden chairs in the little room in front of the fire and sat down heavily. He would be glad to get rid of his packages; the strangely-shaped grey metal parts gave him an eerie feeling. He had placed them as far from himself as he could in the vehicle. The UAZ-469 was a poor imitation of the American Jeep, but it was all he could get without going through more proper channels. It rattled, the heater didn't work very well, and the wind blew through the rough canvas top. But he had made it here to the top of the pass, and hopefully he would soon be rid of the sinister metal cargo. And, he reminded himself as the fire warmed his face, a whole lot richer.

Viktor Viktorovich had been the one who warned him of the danger of carrying the strange metal objects. Alex had a pretty good idea what they were; he didn't want to know more. Each piece was shaped like a wedge, a quarter of a ball, so that when four were placed together, the ball would be resurrected. Though each individual wedge was small, less than twelve centimeters in length, each weighed more than four kilograms. Uranium, he knew, was the only metal that was that dense. Many years ago, in his youth, during the glory days of the Soviet Union, he had helped construct one of the ill-fated power plants at Chernobyl. He remembered handling the fuel elements, the surprising heft of the individual slugs of uranium. But they hadn't needed the extraordinary caution with those slugs as he had been warned of with these sinister pieces he was carrying.

Each of the twelve pieces was in its individual crate, surrounded by six centimeters of paraffin, and one centimeter of lead, inside its wooden outer container. The enrichment, he realized—the ratio of the deadly 235 isotope to the more stable, abundant 238—was the key. He was no nuclear physicist, but had learned enough at the power plant to know that the fuel they were using was only enriched a few times over the naturally occurring uranium, maybe to two or three percent. These he now had with him, he reasoned, must be far more unstable, meaning they were probably enriched to weapons grade, eighty percent U- 235, or even greater.

Viktor had held a high post in the Soviet military, Alex knew. At the time of disarmament, back in 1991, Viktor had been in charge of the facility at Sverdlovsk. He could possibly have had access to some of the warheads as the ICBM's had been disassembled. Was that possible, and did the small amount of uranium comprising the wedges he was carrying really have the power of a nuclear weapon? It seemed beyond belief, yet here he was, about to trade them for two million U.S. dollars. It was the only answer, he reasoned, but he couldn't force himself to dwell on the awful consequences of what he could be conspiring in; his share of the transaction overwhelmed any sense of guilt.

He heard the vehicle before he saw it. It was already past dusk, yet the driver had on only a set of dim fog lights. A small French-made utility vehicle slowly made its way to the cabin. The driver was alone, a squat, dark-haired man with a heavy beard guarding a face without the hint of a smile. Typical Arab, Alex thought, but at least he's on time. The image of the money soon to come into his hands warmed his thought.

"Assalam-o-alaikum, Adaab, Tasleemat," came the gutteral call from the Arab, a phrase Alex barely recognized, but knew must be a greeting of some kind. Alex held up his hands, palms outward, the international sign of friendship.

"English?" Alex asked, figuring that was as close as the two could get to common understanding.

"Yes, of course, hello, brother," replied the Arab, a hint of a smile finally creeping into the bearded features.

Warily, they hugged each other, each keeping an eye on the other's hands. "Come, it's warm inside," Alex offered. The Arab nodded, rubbing his ungloved hands together in the cold wind. The French truck must have a decent heater, Alex thought to himself. He considered, just briefly, the chances of getting the money and the truck, leaving the Arab with the Russian jeep and the fuel elements. Practicality replaced greed quickly, as he remembered the duplicity the Arabs were known for; more than one of his friends had been eviscerated by the fedayeen in Chechnya. "I can brew us some tea, but that is all my stock," Alex offered, as he removed his heavy gloves.

"I must start back, I have to drive many miles tonight," the Arab said bluntly. "Do you have the parts?"

This was the tricky part, Alex realized. He knew the Arab would gladly take the fuel elements and keep the money. "I have twelve with me," he replied. "We can deliver thirty more within the month, as soon as I bring them the money."

"Yes, that will be fine. The same price per unit would make it, let's see, five million U.S?"

An Arab who didn't want to haggle, Alex thought to himself, that doesn't sound right. But he followed through; this was better than expected and he could rake off even more than he had anticipated. "Sure, five million, same place, say in three weeks?" He held out his hand to the Arab, who shook it with a warm smile.

"Alright, let's make the transfer, it's cold out there." The Arab headed for the door. "They're in your jeep, is that right?"

"Yes, of course," Alex replied uneasily. "But the uh…"

"The money, what was I thinking," said the Arab, smacking his hand to his forehead in a manner common in the mountains. He strode out to his truck, returning immediately with a small suitcase. "Take a look," he said, opening the case to reveal packets of hundred dollar bills neatly stacked inside. "Two hundred packets, one hundred bills per pack."

Alex stared in greedy disbelief at the staggering pile of money. "Alright," he said, "let's go out to the jeep." He led the way to the jeep, opening the rear door, exposing the sinister packages.

"May I open one," the Arab asked innocently?

"Sure, if you don't mind a dose of radiation. I'll stand back here." Alex took a couple of steps away. "But make it fast. Let's make the transfer and get out of here."

The Arab pulled a small instrument from his parka, Alex reached into his pocket for his revolver at the same time. "Don't worry," the Arab said laughing, "it's a scintillation counter, just checking to make sure what you've got here." With a small screwdriver he pulled open the end of one of the packages, pulled loose some of the containment and held the wand over the exposed metal. Immediately the instrument buzzed angrily and a needle rose to about midpoint on the scale. Some red numbers appeared on a digital display. The Arab smiled, and replaced the paraffin and cover. "It's the real thing, alright," he said, "let's get started. Each of them took one parcel at a time to the Arab's truck. In just a few minutes the job was done. "Goodbye, my friend, see you in three weeks." He extended his hand to Alex.

This was going too easily, Alex thought warily. Keeping his left hand on his pistol, a 9mm OTs-21 Malysh ("Kid") hidden in his jacket, he extended his right hand to the Arab. The Arab seized it, bringing Alex off balance, as he pulled his seventeen-centimeter Shafra from his belt. Alex jerked out his pistol and fired three quick rounds; but the Arab had pulled him just enough to his right to make the shots pass wildly into the night. Simultaneously, the razor-sharp Shafra sliced across the right side of Alex's neck, severing the carotid artery. Bright red blood spurted into the snow as Alex fired his remaining two rounds impotently into the air. His last view was of the smiling Arab plunging the knife through his windpipe, nearly decapitating the Russian.

Leaving the body in the snow, the glazed eyes looking into space, Khallad went back into the hut, closed the suitcase, and returned to his truck. The money was real enough; he hadn't known how complete a check the Russian would make. But the outcome had never been in doubt. The plan was to get enough uranium for three bombs, and he now had it. The Russians could never have been counted on for more help than this. Hossein would have his fuel; the bombs would be made, and the world would see the wrath of Allah.

Chapter 7

September 2013

Hossein had set up the shop two years ago, a place to work on his engines. He had slowly acquired the metal-working tools needed for the job he had set out upon. To avoid any suspicion, he had watched for used equipment to go on the market. He now had a large engine lathe, capable of handling material up to thirty inches in diameter. In addition, he had a vertical mill, radial drill, upright drill, and horizontal and vertical boring mills. Khallad had been totally generous with the funds, and the locals were not all that curious. Down near the waterfront, many of the boat owners worked long into the night making necessary repairs. He had learned in his youth how to work on gasoline and diesel engines, and he was good at it. He would often repair, even totally overhaul engines for the Vietnamese. It was good cover, giving him an income in addition to that he got from his shrimping.

His first goal was the most important. It was back in Iran that the basics had been worked out. When at Shiraz, as an undergraduate, he had recognized what would eventually be needed: a fission bomb that would let the Americans know once and for all they were dealing with people who meant business. Jamal had told him that the uranium would be obtained from sources that he needn't worry about; just let him know how much was needed, and in what configuration. Apparently, Mughniyah hadn't totally believed Hossein at that meeting long ago. At that time, Hossein didn't yet have the expertise to know exactly how to construct a bomb. He would gain that knowledge in his graduate school days in America.

He often recalled his short meeting with Sheikh Imad Fa'iz Mughniyah so many years ago. It seemed so recent, he thought to himself. That was because he had "replayed" it over and over in his mind. Immediately after the meeting he had gone to his computer and recovered all he could find on the great man; his face and his voice. There was precious little in the way of actual speeches, but what snippets he was able to watch left no doubt in his mind as to the identity of the man in the hut. He had indeed come face to face with Fa'iz himself.

Hossein desperately wanted to contribute to the destruction of the West. Each act of martyrdom, shown on television in all its vivid bloodiness, served to make him ache to be the Muslim avenger of all times. Over and over, he viewed the individual acts of heroism: train bombings in Madrid and London, café explosions in Tel Aviv, all leaving heaps of "innocent" bodies in the streets, all having the desired effect of instilling fear in the minds of the Westerners. Just imagine the aftermath of his handiwork…

He had begun his task with the basics of how the Americans' "Little Boy" bomb—the one they dropped on Hiroshima—worked. The idea was that sub-critical amounts of enriched uranium had to be brought together with such force that they stayed as one piece long enough for the chain-reaction to get going. Once enough uranium was together, the neutrons that resulted from individual atoms fissioning would be more than sufficient to trigger an accelerating succession of reactions among the remaining fuel. In this way, in just milliseconds, enormous energy would be released. Just how much he didn't yet know. But he was mechanically adept enough to start dreaming up schemes to bring two or more pieces of material together with tremendous force; enough so that the resulting heat from the initial reaction would not immediately blow them apart.

The Hiroshima bomb was constructed like a gun; one that shot a small mass of uranium into a larger mass at the other end of the "barrel." But this arrangement would not, he reasoned, be easily made into a sphere, the best configuration for criticality.

The obvious answer was to have two halves of a ball confined within a container, surrounded by gunpowder or something more powerful, but maintained at a safe distance from each other prior to detonation. Then, when the gunpowder was ignited, the two halves would be blown against each other, the outer container hopefully holding them that way for a precious few microseconds as the fission occurred.

Hossein had put together a simple experiment using two small hemispheres of iron he cut in the shop. He built an outer enclosure of iron, with a thin aluminum diaphragm to keep the pieces separated. Then he packed the remaining space with gunpowder, along with a blasting cap. He took the device out into the hills a few miles from campus, led an ignition wire out to a safe place and set it off. There was a sharp blast from the gunpowder, and Hossein raced excitedly back, hoping to see the two hemispheres fused together. To his disappointment, pieces of the assembly were scattered over several meters, the two halves of iron far apart.

Dejectedly, Hossein went back to his room. Some martyr he was going to be, he couldn't even assemble a rudimentary bomb. A few days later it came to him: the two pieces could not come together because the air space between them would have been compressed, forcing them apart. He just needed to allow that air to escape during the explosion.

Hossein hurriedly constructed a new prototype, this time drilling small channels in the two iron hemispheres. Back at his spot in the desert, he ignited the gunpowder and saw the result. Sure enough, this time there was one distorted piece of iron, fused wonderfully together. He had his design.

He had worked out the advanced plans from the knowledge gained at the NCSU library. He now knew what critical mass was necessary, once he had confirmation of the quality of the material Jamal had obtained. It had been important to know the ratio of the 235-weight isotope to the more abundant 238, the "enrichment." Every country in the nuclear weapons game had the means to take naturally occurring uranium and separate the 235 from the 238, at least to some extent, and make a much more powerful ingredient.

The reported value of bomb-material enrichment, he had read, was 90%. The U.S., Russia, England and France had all produced that material. If he were able to acquire this grade of fuel; that is, if Jamal were able to, then he was ready. Fifteen kilograms was minimal for criticality, he knew that, and that was for a perfect sphere. Just a few milliseconds of criticality and he would produce a 20 kiloton explosion; that is, one equivalent to 20,000 tons of TNT.

The thought of it made him shiver with anticipation. He dreamt of the ecstasy that the Most Blessed Sheikh would feel when the images of thousands of dead and dying Americans flashed across television screens around the world. Mughniyah would replace bin Laden as the next Muslim hero. He, Hossein Souriani, would be recognized throughout history as Mughniyah's right arm of vengeance.

He reassessed his needs: Attainment of "critical mass" required that a large number of neutrons, the sub-atomic particles emitted by the fissioning U-235 atoms scattered outward, be reflected back into the ball of uranium. His studies in the library had proved invaluable. The highly poisonous, light metal, beryllium, had the qualities he needed; it reflected neutrons with a high efficiency. By searching industrial-metals catalogues, he found he could purchase beryllium-copper alloy in sheet form that would suit his purpose. This high strength material would form the layer surrounding the uranium; its strength would keep the mass together, and its neutron reflectivity would maximize the explosion. Hossein found it amusing that the discovery of the useful properties of beryllium was made by none other than J. Robert Oppenheimer, the Jew who helped build America's atomic arsenal. Now his discovery would help purge the Jews from the Muslim holy land.

In the real bombs, instead of gunpowder to blast the pieces of uranium together, he would use Semtex, the malleable Czech plastic explosive used so successfully by martyrs around the world. Though export of Semtex was now highly controlled, Jamal had gotten hold of several kilograms from the network in Libya, and there would be no problem smuggling it to wherever the bombs were to be assembled. The Semtex would be formed by hand, like putty, around the set of uranium pieces and the beryllium neutron reflector.

Hossein calculated that the amount of Semtex that could be inserted inside the devices was more than adequate to smash the pieces together. He would have more than twice the amount of Semtex in his bombs than was used to bring down Pan Am 103.

But he also needed an "initiator," something to generate some "slow" neutrons to start the chain-reaction. This turned out to be relatively easy. The element polonium-210, when in contact with beryllium, emitted enough neutrons to initiate the fission of the uranium. He would just have to make sure the polonium and beryllium didn't contact each other until the implosion occurred. This was easy enough with his arrangement of the uranium segments. So Oppenheimer's beryllium was going to be a dual-function performer!

Polonium-210, as it happened, was a relatively commonly-used material in the world of nuclear physics research. On the internet, he found he could buy radioactive polonium from a U.S. vendor quite legally (no license required), and have it shipped to a P.O. Box. He used a U.S. Postal money order to pre-pay for it. The government was turning out to be very helpful.

He knew that a young man named Walid, also in deep cover in the U.S., in Los Angeles actually, where the first lesson was to be taught, had put together the communications network. The idea was deceptively simple: while they knew, or at least suspected, that the FBI would be monitoring email, the ever-widening world of websites was a golden prize. By crafting websites that looked like they were part of schoolwork—homework, tests, and so forth—they could be somewhat brazen in their transmissions.

Hossein had heard from Jamal that Walid had come onto these websites while working on his degree. Professors as well as students would post homework and exam solutions on ill-defined sites that were untraceable, as well as unnoticeable.

Walid had set up fake courses, such as "Architecture 203" with no university identification. Here, in English, they could communicate back and forth under the guise of "Problem 2-3," and so on, using a rudimentary code based on Chapters from the Holy Quran.

It was on these websites that deliveries were set. After Jamal had arranged the successful purchase of the fuel elements from the Russians, Hossein was notified that the construction could begin; the elements would be delivered in a month.

Hossein was puzzled when he learned of the shape of the fuel elements Jamal had obtained from the Russians. Instead of the hemispheres he had expected, they were quarter-spheres. The total weight agreed closely with his calculations, but he would have to revise his design to accommodate the shape and size of the fuel elements. No air-escape channels were drilled in the Russian fuel; he puzzled over that for a while, then realized that in a sophisticated device, the engineers could evacuate the air from the fuel chamber, eliminating the problem he had encountered.

Delivery was to be made in the established manner: for two years now they had sent "packages" to Hossein by boat from Cuba, dropped twenty miles offshore in the Gulf. The packages were constructed with flotation devices that kept them just at water level. Tiny, low-power signals, with a range of only one hundred yards guided Hossein to his target. He would pick them up early in the morning on his shrimping runs. It was a plan that worked to perfection. He had retrieved all the fuel elements and had already obtained much of the hardware, some of which would have been suspicious for him to order from catalogues in the U.S.

Now he was sufficiently along with the construction to alert Jamal of a target date for delivery of the first complete device to Walid. This delivery was complicated. The device was going to weigh over a hundred pounds, even though he was using a very simple remote-controlled triggering mechanism. He smiled as he recalled purchasing the components from a scrawny little bespectacled young man, a boy really, at a Radio Shack outlet in Mobile. He scrupulously avoided making such purchases over the internet, even though that would have been quite a bit easier and faster. But he did not want to leave an electronic trail, should the U.S. authorities somehow sniff out their activities. On the other hand, with scores of hobbyists building all sorts of electronic toys, a remote-controlled trigger was not at all suspicious.

Hossein had been given pretty much free rein with the design, and also the means of delivery. He knew that the various arms of the "Homeland Security" force were equipped with both neutron and gamma-ray detectors. His device could be detected from as far away as about ten meters. So transport by truck, plane or commercial ship was unsafe; roads, airports and ports around Los Angeles, as well as other major cities, were under higher surveillance than was generally known. But Hossein had devised a fool-proof scheme. He had visited Los Angeles, and seen the huge man-made harbor called Marina del Rey. There was no commercial shipping here, only pleasure craft. Hundreds of sailboats and yachts went in and out with virtually no inspection. Walid had kept track of amateur sailboat races, especially those that went as far as Ensenada, just across the border into Mexico.

Hossein's prize was to be hidden deep in the keel of a California-based sloop that would be purchased, with cash of course, after the race to Ensenada, to be housed in a slip in the Marina. It would be indistinguishable from the other two or three hundred craft sailing back after the long weekend race. Even if the Coast Guard were to get nosy, a near impossible chance, the depth of the keel under the water line would act as an effective radiation shield. Now he had to finalize the transport of the completed package to the waiting sloop in Ensenada harbor.

The Mexican crew had been assembled under the guise of transporting cocaine into California. They had been well-paid to ensure their faithfulness to the task. This had been left to the able hands of Khallad, whom Hossein had met some years ago in Lebanon, and in whom he had complete confidence.

The path was somewhat circuitous, but avoided the curious eyes of the U. S. authorities. A full six weeks had been allotted for the journey.

Chapter 8

June 2013

The flight from Tel Aviv to Washington had been uneventful. Uri had become used to picking up and leaving at short notice—"Unfortunately," he mused grimly. He was picked up at the huge Baltimore-Washington airport by a military helicopter that whisked him in just thirty minutes to a heliport inside a complex of government buildings. From there a limousine took him and his meager luggage to a nondescript building inside a guarded perimeter.

His escort told him, "Tomorrow you'll have to get formal documentation, but we can get in today with a temporary pass." He slid a card through a slot in the door, and then placed his palm on a stainless steel plate. He heard a chime somewhere in the background, and the escort held his eye in front of a tiny lens, apparently a retinal scanner. The door slid silently open and a guard handed Uri a plastic shield on a chain, which he placed around his neck. "This is good only with escort, for today," he informed Uri, as he looked him over summarily. Obviously Uri, in his standard Israeli garb of short sleeve shirt, open at the neck, did not meet with the standard FBI agent image.

"Let's head up," his escort told Uri sharply. "They're expecting us." Uri noted his name tag identified him as Tad. He looked like a standard Ivy League recruit. Maybe second-or third generation Bureau. Stepping out of the elevator, Uri found himself in a sea of blue-suited, trim men and women. The entry hall was quietly humming with activity, but with little wasted motion, and none of the water-cooler chatter he had seen in other U. S. government offices. This one appeared to be all business.

Tad led him down to the end of the hall, to a door marked simply, "Trotter." He knocked once, receiving a curt, "Come," in reply. Opening the door he saw a middle-aged man, in blue suit, of course, behind a government-issue desk, and a surprisingly young woman seated in front of it. She was also dressed in conservative blue, but her eyes startled him with their intensity. He felt an immediate stirring, but did not reveal anything.

"Uri Levin, meet Special Agent Lara Edmond. I'm Deke Trotter," the man behind the desk said to him, rising and offering his hand. Uri nodded briefly to Lara, then took Trotter's hand. His handshake was firm, Uri was glad to find. The chain of command here was obvious, and he didn't want to be working for a dead fish. He sized up Trotter, as he did whomever he met. The man was in his early fifties, nearly bald, and slightly overweight. He met Uri's gaze with a sincere smile; he was a man who was used to meeting people and instantly earning their trust.

Lara just sat and looked at Uri with what could be construed as mild amusement, in his out-of-place attire. So this was the famous Uri, the field agent of the Mossad who had accumulated a lengthy array of kills. She appraised him as discreetly as possible, whenever he wasn't looking at her. She had noticed what appeared to be a physical interest on his part, when he first noticed her, but she was very used to that in this mostly-men's world. His face and arms were deeply bronzed, which she would expect, considering his background. Large hands, and surprisingly thick forearms richly covered with hair, showed beneath the short khaki shirtsleeves. The hair on his head was black, curly and thinning in front. He reminded her of a young James Caan from the early Godfather movies. When he happened to catch her looking at him, his eyes twinkled and he gave her a little "caught you" type smile. She did her best to appear unruffled.

Trotter brought them back to business. "This website thing the bad guys have going has put us back to square one. Did you get some briefing on it?" This last was aimed at Uri.

"Yes," he replied, "but just the basics. I was shipped off without much background."

"Lara spotted it first. She's been heading the teams trying to track the emails. I can't give you all the details, but one of her

57

guys was accidentally looking up something unconnected with the case on the web, when he noticed some strange syntax on what was supposed to be an Engineering Economics class posting:

"failing to meet economic goal will be cause extreme harm after original date."

He immediately began searching under keywords of "economic," "goal," "extreme," and "harm." He got more than a million hits, most of them dealing with international drug and food problems. But then we began screening, thanks to Lara here, using a program that isolated typical non-English-speaking syntax.

"But I'm getting ahead of myself," he said, nodding to Uri. "Do you remember getting some documents from a raid on a bunch of Hezbollah a few months ago?"

Uri nodded ruefully; he remembered that raid all too well. But what help could those meager pieces of paper have been, he wondered.

Trotter smiled at Uri's bewilderment; he obviously hadn't been briefed. "You recall seeing the word 'Opera' in those scraps? Opera is a relatively old website management program. It can be configured to use something called 'proxy servers.' That makes finding the website originator more difficult. It's also got a password-managing tool called 'Wand' that is integrated into the browser."

Trotter could see by Uri's expression that he might as well have talking Swahili. "A proxy server is a computer that allows clients to make indirect network connections to other networks," he went on. "A client connects to the proxy server, then requests a connection, file, or other resource available on a different server."

Now even Lara was looking amused at Uri's near total lack of understanding. Trotter gave her a look that said "Why don't you try to give him a quick lesson?"

She broke in, "Basically, it's a way to both hide the source and the content of the webpage you construct. That wasn't the original intent of the Opera people, but it can work that way if you're inclined in that direction: to keep anyone not on your home team from figuring out what you're broadcasting."

"As a field agent, I don't often become involved with the internet. Can you be more specific?" Uri said.

Lara appreciated his candor. She told him simply, "The web's just a bulletin board where anybody can post anything they want, and everyone else in the world can go there and read it. But you need the exact 'address' to get there. And that's the trick. Our bad guys figured out a way to obscure the address so nobody else can go there. Or at least we couldn't until you gave us that tip about Opera."

"So we did contribute a little," he said, easing back in his chair a bit.

"You bet," she said. For some reason she felt she was going to enjoy working with this guy; he was so lacking in the pretension she found so off-putting in most of the male agents.

Trotter took command again; Uri was at least on the same planet now: "We called on these Opera fellas, up in Cambridge. Told them we needed some information on how their system worked. By 'we' I mean a couple of the young guys working for Lara. The Opera folks were fine with that, but they weren't too happy to talk about their individual clients; apparently a lot of their income comes from companies who want to send information to all their troops, but to nobody else. But we played the Homeland Security card and made vague reference to the Patriot Act, and they caved pretty quick."

"You mean you know who the Hezbollah agents are here in the States, and what they're up to?" Uri was clearly astonished now.

"No, not quite, but we're getting there. At least we know how they're hiding their webpages, and with the syntax clues, we're able to filter most of them out from the rest of the trash out there in computer space. Now we need to find out what their code words mean."

Lara broke in again: "Do you know the story of how the Japanese naval code was broken in 1941?" Uri sat there a moment and thought.

"You mean the water supply trick?" he said finally. "I remember something about that."

"Yes, that's what I'm talking about." she replied happily. We knew the Japanese code, JN 25, but we needed a reference to certain key words they were using. We had broken the code and knew they were planning an operation on some island, but weren't sure which one. They referred to it as 'AF' but that's all."

Uri noted that she used the word "we" as though she had been part of the operation more than seventy years ago.

"So, on a hunch, we sent an unguarded message that the installation on Midway was short of water. Sure enough, the Japanese picked it up and sent a coded message that 'AF' was short of water. That's all we needed to send the battle fleet out to Midway, and the rest is history."

Her pride in the code-breaking of the U.S. in the Second World War was clear. Uri hoped she recognized that the grunts, the agents out in the field, under threat of death and torture every day, were just as important to the success of any mission; but he said nothing. Instead, he followed her point: "So, you mean we need a target or two, to calibrate the code. I hope that doesn't mean we have to have a terrorist event here in the States before we know what they're up to."

"We've got several irons in the fire, but this looks pretty good. Of course, there are ways we can attack without an event..."

"It looks like you guys are off to a good start," Trotter interrupted. He stood as an obvious sign this meeting was over. We've got a nice apartment set up for you not too far from here," he said to Uri. "I suggest you get settled in and then tomorrow you can get started."

Chapter 9

June 2013

Uri showed up at Lara's office the next day at eight A.M. sharp. His apartment was just what he needed and nothing more. He had gotten a good night's sleep, adjusted pretty well for the time change, and had a hearty breakfast at a local pancake house. This idea of a chain breakfast restaurant was new to him, but he could see why it was popular: fast food, cheap prices and lots of calories. People around here were quite a bit heavier than at home, he noticed.

His new ID and pass were waiting for him at the front desk. They permitted him to use the elevator, but only certain floors were available. *These Americans are very security conscious*, he thought, *even within their own facility.* He arrived at Lara's, and now also his, floor and walked down the hall to the office. His first impression of the office was that it was far larger than he had imagined. Three large windows looked out onto the street below. A circular conference table sat in one corner of the room, a small bar and hot plate filled one wall, and two walnut desks faced each other in front of one of the windows.

Lara was once again dressed in a business-like white blouse, knee-length blue skirt and short jacket. He again noticed the shapely calves and firm-looking thighs, at least from what he could see. He quickly averted his eyes, but she was too quick to miss his obvious interest. "I've gotten you your own computer. It's hooked into the system," she said, indicating the desk directly across from her own. "Just log on using whatever name you want; 'Uri' is fine."

He sat down and typed in his name. "Now hit enter and we're on our way," she told him. The screen showed a page with Lara's name at the top. "I've got you patched into my screen for now, so you can see how this works. I'm going to head right for one of the suspect web pages." Uri watched as she entered an FBI browser that mirrored the commercially available ones. "I can type in some key words and the program will find any web pages that match them," she said, typing in "economics harm date." Immediately, Uri's screen filled with a list of "hits" that numbered over a million, according to a message at the top. Most of the acquired items had to do with the economic harm done by raising interest rates at an early date. But then Lara switched over to a more selective screen that their interaction with Opera had opened for them. Instantly the hits narrowed to just a few dozen. "These now have been filtered by checking for typical Middle-Eastern syntax errors, like misuse of 'the,' 'a,' and 'an.' I go to bank and cash check,' for example."

"But that's the case with a lot of non-native English speakers."

"Right, that's where our work comes in. We've got to find which of the suspect sites are actually originating from campuses, and whether any are terrorist-connected. Most of the visas granted to Middle-Easterners are for student-type permits. But then we've found that a good percentage of these guys don't even enroll where they're supposed to."

Uri couldn't control his surprise. "You mean there are potential Hamas and Hezbollah operatives in the U.S. and you don't know where they are?"

"I'm afraid so. That's why we're tracking down these web page entries. But look at what we find most of the time." She hit one of the entries, underlined in blue. Up popped a grossly pornographic site so sickening Uri had to turn away from the screen. "Sorry," Lara said, recognizing Uri's lack of familiarity with what had been lurking on the internet. "These sites aren't available in most Arab countries; in fact, magazines with pictures of women are absolutely taboo."

"Yes, I'm aware of the crazy ban they have on popular culture in general," he said. "So you mean as soon as these guys get here, to the U.S., they get obsessed with looking at girls on the computer?"

"I'm afraid so. But the real problem for us is to figure out which of these pages are really threatening. The bad guys could easily be hiding behind the porno messages."

"Wait a minute," Uri said. "What about the email traffic? Aren't there a lot of messages going back and forth in Arabic and Farsi?"

"We've got that covered. There's a special team operating openly, as well as in secret, snagging all the email traffic, and all the Arabic email is translated by our Arab-speakers."

"You mean *all* the emails from around the world every day are intercepted and analyzed? How is that possible?"

"It seems incredible, I know, but these teams of computer jocks were set up a few years ago—right after 9/11—to develop programs that would sniff out suspicious emails, especially in Arabic." She didn't mention that she was the one responsible for coordinating the effort. "Then when we got word of your captured documents, we really focused on the English-language web pages."

"But how can you possibly intercept all the electronic traffic, let alone sort it? Aren't we talking about billions of messages every day?"

Lara paused a moment, then replied, "I can't give you all the details, but let's just say there's over a billion dollars worth of hardware, another billion in software, and I don't know how much more in personnel involved. Even I don't know how much..." She stopped when she realized what she had just admitted.

"*Even* you?" Uri said, looking at her with astonishment. "What, you mean you're in charge of this whole business?"

Lara reddened slightly; Uri was the first outsider to recognize her role in the electronic warfare game. "I don't think they knew then how far this thing was going to go when they assigned me to it. But after all the computer teams were coordinated, even the macho guys saw we were on the right track."

"And you're a qualified field agent, too?" He was clearly impressed; he understood why she had so sumptuous an office.

"Want to see me take you down?" She said, laughing at his look of shock.

"No, we even have some women in Mossad who could do

63

that, if I wasn't ready for them. But I believe you."

"You're in some special branch of the Mossad, aren't you, what's it called, 'Masada?' "

" 'Matsada,' he corrected her. But there are things I can't tell you either." So the Americans knew about Matsada, but maybe not Kidon; he hoped not.

Just then there was a knock at the door. "Come on in," Lara shouted. She knew the knock; it was Jim Turner from downstairs. Jim was the only male in the branch she fully trusted not to hit on her. When he met her in the hall, or in the cafeteria, his eyes never traveled up and down her attractive figure, even after they had passed. She had learned the trick, as did most women by the time they reached college age, of peeking in a mirror or glass door to see if the man turned around to watch her walk by.

In her early days here, Jim had invited her over to his house a couple of times for dinner with his wife and two children. Jim and Betsy, with their two teenage daughters, were the ideal American family. They lived in a modest house just outside the Beltway. It was obvious to her, from watching the couple together, how much he loved his wife and family; it reminded Lara of home.

Jim always treated Lara as an equal, a colleague, and they shared details of many of the cases they worked on. Jim often asked her opinion, not just on computer matters, where she was the local guru, but also on matters related to the various field agents they both worked with.

"Jim, this is Uri Levin, from the Mossad. Uri, Jim Turner, Special Branch also."

"Yes," Jim said to Uri, "we've heard a lot about you guys, all good. We're hoping to learn a few things." Jim smiled warmly and grasped Uri's hand with a firm grip. He was a large man, too big for a field agent, but could more than hold his own if it came to a physical brawl. Uri liked the man immediately; it looked like this was going to be a productive interaction.

In the next few weeks, Uri became more and more familiar with the computer searches, as well as the suspect web pages. Lara was patient with him, and soon he was contributing and not just learning. He recognized some of the non-native speech patterns from his interactions with the Arabs, and picked out some conversations on a couple of University-linked web pages. So far, these had turned out to be students cheating on take-home projects and exams.

With Jim joining them in the cafeteria, they would typically break for lunch and discuss the leads they had uncovered. Jim had some good ideas about breaking into the web pages with false information, but both Uri and Lara felt it was a little premature; they didn't want to make any irreversible errors.

In the evening, Uri would retire to his small apartment, watch the news on TV, and let his thoughts wander: the project, Danielle, his life back in Israel. Sometimes he could not avoid the image of Lara; their relationship had remained totally professional, but he couldn't help but think of her in more intimate fantasies. He wondered about her personal life. He knew she was near obsessive about physical conditioning, and it showed. But she never spoke of a boyfriend, certainly not a husband. At these times, he would leave the apartment and have a late dinner at one of the many small restaurants in the area. It was truly amazing how diverse the eating opportunities were, even late at night, within just a few blocks.

Just around the corner there was a Middle-Eastern type deli run by some Kurdish immigrants, from southern Turkey. The counter man, who Uri later learned was named Haran, spit vehemently on the wooden floor when Uri had asked him if he was, in fact, a Turk. "No, we are Kurds," he said, "We hate the Turks." He spit again. Uri was surprised by the intensity of the man's emotion, but did not pursue the issue. It just reminded him of all the intense hatreds that infected the region, hatreds with hundreds of years of history. For all Haran knew, Uri was an American, with little knowledge of Middle Eastern politics. Uri did nothing to change his judgment; he took it as a compliment on his American accent.

Haran served Uri delicious meat rolls on a sort of pita bread, as well as American-style hamburgers. He also enjoyed their hummus dip; it was a slice of home. He listened as Haran spoke of the mistreatment his family had suffered at the hands of the

Turkish authorities. The children were not even allowed to be blessed with ancestral Kurdish names. But it turned out Haran had positive feelings for the Israelis. He spoke with some pride as he told Uri how a Kurd had once been defense minister of Israel. "You know," he confided once," I think the Israelis can help convince the Turks and the Iraqis to let us have a homeland, like they do."

"You mean an official Kurdistan?"

"Yes, you know about that?" Haran replied, evidently impressed.

"Well, you know, here in D.C. you can't help but hear things about the region…How could the Israelis help?"

"Their technology, they could help the Turks produce more, agriculture, whatever, like they do, in the desert."

"But what would the Israelis get, in return?" Uri was intrigued with this logic.

"Stronger relations with a Muslim country. You know they have a lot of common interests." Haran leaned closer to Uri, over the counter. "I have a customer, works in the State Department, says there are talks going on—the U.S., Israel and Turkey, even now."

Uri did actually know about these supposedly secret negotiations that would allow a small part of southern Turkey to be autonomously Kurdish, but did not admit it. He had learned it was best to be a good listener.

"You have these people here, they call themselves 'intellectuals,' like this guy Chomsky. You know of him?"

Uri nodded ruefully. He knew indeed of Noam Chomsky, a writer who, Uri had heard, considered Israel a "terrorist State." He was surprised and impressed with Haran's knowledge on the subject.

"You are surprised, no? That I know of these things."

Uri nodded, smiling.

Haran went on, "I take some classes, at George Washington, in the afternoon, when my brother, Medya, runs the store. It's funny how little these professors know about the real situation. They make us read things, like by this guy Chomsky. We listen to these kind of guys, the Al Qaeda will have us all for lunch." He

66

went back to the grill and flipped Uri's burger, the meat sizzling. Uri remembered how hungry he was.

"During Clinton's time, you know, there was a lot going on that people still don't know about. It's too bad he couldn't be President some more."

"But I thought Chomsky was a promoter of a Kurdistan?" Uri took a chance here; he didn't want to look like he knew too much about the subject. Most Americans, he knew, thought Kurds were something that went with whey.

Haran was the one to be impressed now. "Yes, on the surface. That's what my professor said, too. But, see, when he calls Turkey a 'terrorist State,' he just makes things harder. These things have to be done quietly, you know, without stirring everybody up. Now the Turks have to show everybody how tough they are. No Kurdistan." Haran made a slicing move across his throat with his left thumb. He flipped Uri's burger onto a steaming hot bun, laced it with mustard and ketchup, and laid it on a large plate along with a heaping portion of French fries, fresh from the hot oil. Then he motioned Uri over to a table in the back, where he could watch for customers.

"Look at it like this, Steve," he began. Steve was the name Uri used around the neighborhood; much less ethnic than Uri. "Suppose I have a neighbor who lets his dog onto my property and he's ruining my garden. Now suppose I get mad, go over to his house and yell: 'Keep your goddam dog off my property or I'll kill your wife and rape your daughter." Not a great idea, right?" Uri nodded.

"Now suppose I go over there with a bottle of wine and say: 'I've got a little problem I'd like to talk to you about. Do you think we can come up with a way to keep your dog from ruining my garden?' Which way do you think will work better?"

Uri thought for a moment and replied, "I guess it depends on whether the neighbor is basically a decent person or not."

"Right you are, Steve, but you got to start on the hopes that he is, see what I mean?"

Uri smiled as he gobbled down the delicious hamburger and fries, washed down with a Coke. What a pleasure to be able to go out safely at night and have a late meal like this.

Later, at home, as he prepared for bed, Uri reflected on what Haran had been saying; much of it made sense.

Haran was indeed right. If you were dealing with a decent man. On the other hand, Uri thought as he drifted off to sleep, when you were dealing with men like Mughniyah, Arafat or Nasrallah, you could forget the civil dialogue. That's where Mossad came in.

Chapter 10

Lara picked Uri up at his apartment; actually he waited outside for her, not having the amenities necessary for guests. She was right on time, as he had expected. She was wearing a chic, but modest, brightly colored blouse with a mid-length tight black skirt and heels. She was wearing makeup, he noticed, not excessive, but not her normal workday appearance either. In the car, Uri could see more of her shapely thighs than he was used to. He had on his typical open-neck sport shirt and ready-to-wear trousers. But he did wear his one pair of dress shoes, polished up nicely.

"So, where are we going?" This was more making conversation on his part than anxiety about their destination.

"Don't worry, you'll like it; it's just a little surprise." She sported a little grin. "And it's my treat." Uri had learned in his short time in this country that when a woman offered to pay for dinner, or even split the cost, it was a sign that this was not a "date," in the romantic sense, but rather dinner with a colleague. Not that Uri had anticipated anything more; he was just happy to have an evening out. And he was not totally out of the relationship with Danielle, there was still a slim hope…On the other hand, Lara's appearance and demeanor told him this was at least a social occasion and not just an obligatory welcome dinner. He decided to let the profundities go and just enjoy the company.

Lara drove through some neighborhoods Uri had not seen before, ones with different ethnicities, until she spotted a parking place on a street lined with several Asian restaurants. "My favorite Thai place," she said sprightly. "I love a chance to come here. And I know already you don't 'keep Kosher.'"

"Right you are, and I happen to love Thai, Chinese, Japanese, you name it."

They went in and were seated near the back, at Lara's request. It would have been Uri's choice as well; they both were disciplined to avoid recognition from the street. "Like to start off with a drink?" Lara was unusually animated this evening; or maybe this was her typical evening attitude. At any rate, this was not the Lara from work, and Uri was perking up as well.

"Sure, a beer, Thai beer for me."

"OK, I'll join you. When in Rome…" The waitress came, took their drink orders and detailed the specials for the day.

"I try to stay away from the fish," Lara offered, "But how about sharing some of the other stuff, maybe some curry?"

"You know what, I'm going to let you pick everything," Uri replied. "When in a Thai restaurant…," he began. She laughed brightly. The small Thai waitress brought their beers, along with two very chilled glasses. "At least let me do this," he said as he poured out their Singha beers. They clicked glasses as he toasted, "To a successful partnership."

"Tell me a little about Uri," she said playfully. "How'd you get into this business?"

Uri glanced instinctively around the restaurant. It was a weeknight, and seated at the back of the restaurant as they were, there was no one else around. Not that they were about to discuss classified information; it was just habit that, when job-related conversations were carried out, he was especially careful, as he knew she was. Anyway, the light clatter of the kitchen would have made surveillance all but impossible. "It started with my father… or is that too corny?"

She grinned and shook her head. "This sounds like a good story; tell me everything."

"All right. He was a pilot flying for the British in World War II, in Egypt. He was part of what they called 'The Jewish Brigade.' He was born in Palestine during the British Mandate— you know about that, right?" Lara nodded, her head on her fists as she listened to him intently. "Anyway, they harassed the Germans in North Africa, then flew some other missions later in the war. When the war ended, the Jews in Palestine expected the British to live up to their promise in their 'Balfour Declaration,' that they made to us at the end of the first World War. We were supposed to

70

have a homeland in the Holy Land, even though the exact boundaries weren't set up." He looked at her lovely eyes watching him as he spoke. "You know all this, right?"

"Not the way you're telling it. Gives me a whole new outlook. Keep going, I'm loving it." The waitress silently brought their food and Lara parceled it out as Uri continued.

"Well, as you know, the British also promised some land to the Arabs who were living in Palestine along with the Jews. But the Arabs had sided with the Axis during the war, carrying out espionage and sabotage against the Allies. So we, I mean the Jews living there at the time, my father included, expected at least a fair share of the land. And then there was the problem of the immigrants from Europe…well, you know all about that. Anyway, the British screwed us around pretty good; I suppose they didn't want to antagonize the whole huge Arab population, with all their oil. My father helped sneak in a lot of the immigrants from ships and overland through Turkey right after the war, in 1945 and '46. But it was the U.S. who eventually settled things: your president, Harry Truman, let it be known that we would have our country, and the U.N. went along. It was a pretty exciting moment, according to my folks, when the votes were tallied in 1947. They were all huddled around the radio, listening as all the countries voted…boy, am I getting off the track!"

"Don't stop, but please try the pear salad, it's terrific."

"All right, all us Jews know how to talk with our mouths full. Oh, you're right, it's delicious. So where was I? Right, 1948. Palestine was officially partitioned into a Jewish state and an Arab state. Now, let me go back a bit. Originally, back in the 1920's, after World War I, when the British and French were splitting up what had been the Ottoman empire, they established the boundaries of what would become Lebanon, Syria, Iraq, Saudi Arabia and, most importantly, Jordan. Those countries didn't have recognized borders before then. In fact, Syria still thinks it owns everything from Saudi Arabia to Turkey. The Syrians don't officially recognize Lebanon, Iraq, Jordan, and especially not Israel. Anyway, it was generally believed that the Kingdom of Jordan, which was established in 1920 or thereabouts, would serve as the homeland for the Arabs living in Palestine. The Jordan

River would be its western boundary. But the Arab countries weren't having any of that, so the U.N. divided Palestine into Jewish and Arab sections; most of the Arab section became known as 'The West Bank,' and the rest was the infamous Gaza strip, but don't get me going on that.

"Try the curry, you'll love it, but, anyway, keep going."

"Anyway, the partition was supposed to go into effect on May 14, 1948. But the Arabs weren't having any of it; they wanted the whole thing. In fact, they still do. So the Armies of Egypt, Jordan, Syria, Iraq and even little groups from Saudi Arabia, Lebanon, Libya and Yemen brought all their forces to the borders; I mean we were completely surrounded. And on that day they all attacked; but they were totally disorganized. They had good reason to be optimistic; after all, the Jews had gone like sheep during the Holocaust. Who would come to their aid now?" Uri noticed Lara's eyes getting moist, but, to her credit, she did not wipe them.

"Anyway, getting back to my father, he was one of just a few World War II pilots, some British, some Americans, who made up our little Air Force. But the Arabs didn't know how many there were, they figured they could just fly in and bomb wherever they liked. My dad loved to tell us this part. The little Israeli Air Force consisted of just a few old propeller planes, but the pilots were all seasoned veterans. They were all set to give the invaders everything they had; which was way more than they expected. Anyway, they put their few planes up in the air as soon as the radar showed flights of enemy planes coming from both Syria, to the north, and Egypt, to the south. Radio wasn't all that secure in those days, and our pilots picked up the Arab transmission right away. The Arabs could see the few Israeli planes taking off, and we could see and hear them. So the pilots started transmitting on the Arabs' frequency, like they didn't know the Arabs could hear, 'Squadrons 2 and 3, take off, head south, Egyptian planes over Gaza. Squadrons 4 and 5, take off, head north, Syrian planes over Tiberius,' and all like that. That was all it took. The Arab pilots turned tail and ran back to their bases. It was our first 'intelligence' victory and it set the tone of the whole War of Independence.

The army took heart from the air victories and finished off the job on the ground in a couple of months. There was a lot of crying to the U.N. about how the Jews had attacked the poor unsuspecting Arabs and so on, but, believe me, if the Arabs had won that day, the U.N. wouldn't have done a thing, and there wouldn't be an Israel today. And if the U.S. hadn't stopped us we'd have taken everything from the Suez Canal to the Jordan River."

"But that wouldn't have been good; I mean the rest of the world would have looked on Israel as a real aggressor, right?" Lara was in earnest.

"You'd get arguments from some quarters, but you're essentially right. I mean, look at the press even now. You'd think Israel was the one sending in suicide bombers and killing civilians." He sampled the curry and gave his approval. "Wow, this is tasty!"

"Better take some rice with that or you'll be sorry," she said knowingly.

"Right. Where was I? Oh yeah, the intelligence service. I'm sure you know about the coups Mossad had during the Entebbe thing, the hijacked airplane in Uganda?" Lara nodded as she ate some of the beef salad. "And the wiping out of the Munich assassins, after the Olympics?" She nodded again.

"But I think my favorite story, at least that's public knowledge, comes from the Six-Day War, you know, in 1967? My dad flew in that one, too. The Egyptians and the Syrians had formed an alliance under Nasser, who was sure they could knock out the country this time, with a coordinated attack. Nasser even had King Hussein of Jordan in on it; he was promised a big piece of the pie. The all had large air forces, provided mostly by the Soviets, who looked at the Middle East as a good proving ground for their new MiG's. Our guys were flying French Mirages and American F-15's and 16's. We had totally penetrated their military operations: we even knew when their pilots were going to the bathroom. Had their codes, plans of attack, times of shift changes, everything.

"So, just before the Arabs were going to spring their 'surprise' attack, my dad and his guys took off over Egypt. They knew their pilots were on a break, and our guys came in over the Med, under their radar. The Egyptians had laid out hundreds of decoy aircraft, looked like the real thing but made out of balsa. They were perfect replicas, except for one thing: the real planes had gasoline stains around the filler caps; the wood ones didn't. Our intelligence flights had picked that up. So my dad and his buddies knocked out about 300 Egyptian planes, on the ground, and killed about 100 of their pilots in the air, all in the first few hours. The Egyptians couldn't figure out why all the decoy aircraft were still sitting there unharmed. Totally one-sided; probably saved thousands of lives on both sides.

"Mossad even picked up a phone conversation between Nasser and King Hussein, can you believe it?" Riveted, Lara had quit eating. Nothing got to her like military intelligence. This stuff rivaled William Stephenson's exploits. "So Nasser tells him, and these recordings are public now, even though Nasser knew that his air force was in ruins, that Egyptian planes were over Tel Aviv and his armor was advancing on Israeli positions. Meanwhile, Israel had called Hussein and promised that if Jordan pulled out of the attack, Israel wouldn't invade the West Bank and Jerusalem. But Hussein believed Nasser, disregarded Israel's offer, and invaded Israeli territory. Had Hussein listened to Israel, the West Bank and Jerusalem would still be in Jordanian hands. Instead he sent his troops into the Israeli section of Jerusalem, and, well you know the rest."

"That business with the fake airplanes, that's like Patton on the southeast coast of England before D-day."

"How do you mean?"

Lara was glad she had a story, too. "When Eisenhower was setting up for the invasion of Normandy, he had General Patton pretend to be getting ready to invade Calais, on the French coast, from a spot right across the channel, in England. He had thousands of tents, phantom trucks, jeeps, tanks and planes—all made out of wood and rubber. That, along with fake news reports and radio messages, kept the main German armies away from Normandy until it was too late."

"You're right. I bet that's where Dayan got the idea to look for fake planes on the Egyptian runways."

"Dayan?"

"Moshe Dayan, one of our greatest generals, you know, with the eye patch?"

"Right, of course. We agree, it's the intelligence corps that win the wars. If only the generals would listen." She raised her glass and toasted Uri again.

"Anyway, that's how my father got me into the business. He was a real role model to me, a hero."

"And is he still active, I mean, in the armed forces?"

Uri was silent for a moment, and instinctively, Lara was sorry she had asked that stupid question.

"No, my father was killed on Yom Kippur, 1973, when the Egyptians sneaked across the Suez before dawn. I was just a kid at the time, but I remember how my mother cried until she just ran dry. Nobody could get her to eat, or anything. She just literally faded away." Uri looked at Lara with a glance that said, "It's OK, I've dealt with this already."

Uri took a breath and went on; he had opened the door, so... "My mother had come from Eastern Europe, Poland...the camps...and my father was everything to her. She looked on their marriage as a gift, a second life that she never expected, never deserved, after all the others...well, you know about survivor guilt, I'm sure." His eyes were dry as he told her this; he had long ago buried this memory, let it go.

"Wow," he said, sitting up straight in his chair, "I bet you never expected to hear a soap opera tonight."

"I appreciate your telling me all this, Uri," she said, as she placed one hand over his.

"Next time you tell me all your family secrets," he said with a smile. Lara paid the check and they left the restaurant. The drive to Uri's place was relatively silent, both lost in their own thoughts. Lara pulled up in front of Uri's building, and said to him, "This was really fun, I hope we can do it again."

"Me too," he replied as he shook her hand and headed out the car door. "Only next time, I pay."

"You got it. See you at work." They both waved goodbye.

Chapter 11

Lara waited patiently for Carter Fredericks to arrive at the scheduled meeting. Since his abrupt appearance at her office, she had been silently fuming. They apparently were taking away the main target of her operations, the university web pages. It had taken a long heart-to-heart talk with Trotter to even arrange this meeting with the Homeland Security guy, Fredericks.

The day before, she had scoured the resources of her computer to learn what she could about him. She quickly found that he was a political appointee, with no real field experience. Like many of Homeland Security people, he had been rushed into position by the party in power, to show the country that the new department was staffed and ready to protect the country from all invaders, human or alien. Lara was nothing if not bitter, about the bureaucratic jungle that interfered with the smooth workings of the FBI, her department in particular.

Fredericks, she read in the classified "Federal Employee Resource Guide," had graduated from the University of Pennsylvania with a degree in Political Science, but with no apparent training in intelligence or military affairs. He had, however, worked as a high-level advisor for the junior Senator from Pennsylvania in his successful campaign to dislodge the previous incumbent. That Senator now sat on the powerful Ways and Means committee, a huge plum for such a junior member of the Senate. This appointment was clearly payback for the ousting of the previous incumbent, who had been a thorn in the side of the President on matters concerning the military budget.

That man had been especially vocal in demanding that the administration make public the "sole source" contracts that had gone to the companies from the President's home state. Not only were these contracts "sole source," which meant that no competitive bidding was involved, they were also "cost-plus." This meant the company received remuneration from the government for all its costs in procuring the equipment specified in the contract, in addition to a set fee of anywhere from six to ten percent. Costs due to errors, mishaps, and changes in direction were all covered. The rationale for this type of contract was that the sensitive nature of the military hardware and software precluded making it public information. Also, the elimination of the bidding process allowed the chosen company to avoid the cost and delays involved in preparing a "proposal." The ten percent fee seemed reasonable, to the casual observer, for the supply of such important material to the government.

Lara, and many others who were familiar with this process, felt there were at least two pitfalls in this reasoning. First, the need for the hardware was typically generated by the company in question; that is, the company's executives knew what exotic hardware they were able to supply, and could make a strong case for its need to the congressmen in charge of procurement. The guys, on one side of the aisle at least, all loved to see the fancy new toys that were capable of killing with deadly efficiency.

The second fly in the ointment was related to the calculation of the "cost" part of the equation. In this calculation, the company was allowed to cram in every possible associated item. For example, research and development were considered allowable costs. If the company was supplying a new type air-to-ground missile, the salaries of all personnel working on future weapons of this type were fair game, as were all the associated costs of running the R&D department. So the fee was effectively a great double-dip, guaranteeing the company great quarterly profits and secure positions for all the employees.

If this weren't enough, many of the weapons systems were targeted toward nonexistent threats. Long after the Soviet Union was no longer a threat, the U.S. government continued to purchase and maintain a fleet of missiles capable of destroying the Evil Empire hundreds of times over. It pointed out the prescience of President Eisenhower in his famous farewell speech more than forty years ago, when he warned of the "military-industrial complex," and how the country need be cautious of becoming ensnared in its grasp.

What was particularly galling to Lara, was that it had been evident for some time that the real threat to the country was not from high-tech missiles, but low-tech suicide bombers and saboteurs. All over the world, the religious fanatics were feeding on our treasuring of life, to promote their own hate-filled conquest of it. Our national defense budget was being wasted on high-tech toys when it needed to be spent on vastly improved intelligence networks. This was made all too clear after the attack of September 11, 2001, but should have been obvious at least twenty years earlier, when our foreign bases and diplomatic centers were blasted by Muslim radicals. She had been shocked to find out, when she had joined the Bureau, how few Arab speakers were available in all the intelligence services. They, of course, were crucial to her first efforts at deciphering the electronic transmissions flooding the airwaves. That we did not have many hundreds of Arab-speaking deep-cover agents, both overseas and at home, was more than frightening.

Lara was popped out of her frustrating musings by the appearance of Carter Fredericks. She had almost forgotten what he looked like since his brief appearance in her office when she had been too angry to pay much attention. But now she recognized Fredericks as every bit the Ivy-League Fraternity president she had read about in his resume. Where the FBI agents were physically impressive and well dressed, this man looked like he had stepped out of a Brooks Brothers catalogue. He was tanned, fit and impeccably dressed in finely tailored haberdashery. From hundred-dollar haircut to thousand-dollar shoes, he shouted money and influence. Fredericks could probably charm the pants off wealthy women and the money out of wealthy men's pockets; no wonder he had been a successful campaign manager.

"Well, let's get started, shall we?" A man Lara had barely noticed took his place at the head of the polished, walnut table. Trotter sat at his left, Fredericks at his right. Lara sat two chairs down from her boss. They had driven over together, but arrived in the conference room separately. Across from Lara was a woman who definitely looked like a high-class stenographer, and was not introduced. Each had a fresh pad of paper, three sharpened pencils and a glass of water in front of them. Trotter had told Lara that the Homeland Security deputy chief, Reynolds Macarthur, would be in charge. Funny, she thought briefly, how these Homeland Security guys all seemed to have first names that must have been passed down through their blue-blood family trees. Macarthur was a generation older than Fredericks, but had a similar pedigree. She had checked him out, too.

"No need to go through preliminaries here. We are all familiar with the terrific job agent Edmonds has done with the electronic eavesdropping and the computer programs." Macarthur had no doubt been briefed on Lara's successes; he was going to praise her to the heavens before he took the rug out from under her.

"What I want to do here is to set out our, I mean Homeland Security's, mission and how it dovetails with yours," he continued, nodding at Trotter. When dealing with visiting teams of people, the old, established military canon was to speak only to the person in charge. This was obviously the way it was going to be here, Lara recognized grimly.

"We want to use the tools you've developed and move to another level of attack," he said calmly, looking straight at Trotter. "Basically, we're going to track all the college students who are here on student visas from the target countries." Lara knew which countries he was referring to: the ones that harbored the known terrorists. This included essentially every country from Libya in the west, to Pakistan in the east.

"That includes tens of thousands of students," Trotter said. "Do you have the resources to do that?"

Macarthur smiled indulgently. "We've narrowed it down a bit. Focusing only on the areas of expertise that pose the highest threat: nuclear and chemical engineering." Before Trotter could again interrupt, Macarthur continued, "Furthermore, we've whittled the number of schools down to just the top ten in those fields. The reasoning is this: any terrorist operation that is really a threat is going to have an unlimited budget. This means they can grease the skids, so to speak, at the schools of their choice, with magnificent grants. You'd be surprised how easy it becomes to get a student into, say, an MIT or Stanford, after they receive a million dollar gift."

Trotter was impressed; they had done some homework. "But how are you going to approach these students, and you're still talking in the hundreds, at least?"

Macarthur had anticipated this. "We're not. We talk to the professors; see whom they've spotted as potential targets. But not quite that directly; instead we approach them as though we're quietly looking for recruits. Then we watch those individuals for tell-tale signs of Jihadist influence. Like attendance at suspect mosques."

Lara immediately spotted some obvious dangers in the plan. First of all, some of the professors would not feel kindly to this kind of interference. Many were even sympathetic to the "cause," this included the large number of engineering faculty who were immigrants from the very countries Macarthur was suspicious of. Then there was the clear probability of leaks. It would just take one suspicious professor or student to spread the word like wildfire that the feds were tracking them. Any cell that was operational would quickly go deep underground, making their detection much more difficult.

Trotter sensed Lara's uneasiness, and perhaps felt the same himself. He glanced over at her briefly, but she was too depressed by this foolhardy plan to make any comment; it probably would make things worse. Macarthur spotted the displeasure and no doubt had planned for it.

"We have a very skilled team of investigators on the job. Fredericks here handpicked them. They go through the files secretly, pick out the most likely from schools that have recently received large unrestricted grants from the suspect countries. These are the kinds of funds universities love; they can do anything with them. Go after big names in the field, for instance. Then they spot recent graduate enrollees from these countries, see what subjects they're studying."

"You mean they actually enroll in bomb making and the like?" Trotter was clearly agitated. He didn't want all the progress Lara had made in infiltrating the electronic network to go down the tubes because of the meddling of these amateurs.

"No, of course not," Macarthur said, somewhat condescendingly. "I think Carter can explain better than I." He turned his head ever so slightly to his junior officer.

"What my folks are trained to do is to engage professors who have federal or industrial funding in fields like explosives manufacture; that's a subject some chemical engineers deal with. Then they make a formal appointment to talk to them about some large imaginary project the government has in mind, and how they might be just the man to be the technical advisor. Of course, my man would be fully briefed on the professor's publications and awards—all these guys have lots of both. And once you flatter him by mentioning the fact that you're familiar with his work and his prizes, he opens up like a cupcake. He'll do anything and tell you anything you want to know. After that, my man can find out anything about the new graduate students he wants. Then we take it from there."

Fredericks paused, crossed his legs, and took a drink of water from the spotless glass in front of him. He was quite pleased with himself, she noticed. She also noticed that he referred to all the faculty and students in the masculine gender. In fact, a large number were now women. Well, that was the least of her problems. She had to admit, they had thought this thing out a bit. She did know they were right about the flattery angle; the professors would tumble for that approach. But the danger was still there: one suspicious student, and the whole plan was down the drain. And all her hard work as well.

Trotter gave her a little look that implied she better take this opportunity to speak her piece, or forget it. She took it. "This sounds like a good plan, except…" As she paused both Fredericks and Macarthur looked at her menacingly. "If even one of the graduate students gets suspicious it might jeopardize our whole operation," she continued. All she got in return were icy stares. She decided to tune it down a bit, give them some room. "What I'm suggesting, is that we keep up the electronic surveillance on our end, and keep in communication, should anything come up. You know, we've been pretty successful at identifying foreign-sounding emails." They looked unconvinced, but at least were letting her continue. She played her hole card: "You know, Trotter

81

has brought in this Israeli specialist, a guy who knows Arabic, and he's actually found some Hezbollah literature that may lead us to some active cells." She didn't go into detail, but she did notice that the credit she gave to Trotter for Uri's cooperation evoked just a hint of a smile. Yesterday she had been pretty upset at the idea.

Fredericks turned to his boss to see if there was any reaction. Macarthur tapped one of his pencils on the table a moment, presumably deep in thought. Lara figured he had no room to object; they weren't actually proposing to cut in on the Homeland Security turf by keeping up the email spotting. And she definitely wasn't going into detail about the Hezbollah find. She reasoned, and correctly as it turned out, that these guys wouldn't want to appear interested; that would give her too much credit in their eyes.

Finally, Macarthur said grudgingly, "Well, I don't see as it hurts anything to keep up surveillance. As long as you keep Homeland in the loop, Deke." He still wasn't going to acknowledge Lara.

Trotter glanced at Lara, saw that she was satisfied with this compromise, and got up from the table. "All right, sounds like a plan." They shook hands all round, and the two FBI agents left the room. Lara started to say something to her boss, but he motioned her to keep still until they got outside. There was no telling what kind of internal spying went on at Homeland. As arranged, they took separate paths downstairs and out to their FBI "greyback" sedan.

As soon as they departed the parking lot, Lara pointed out what she had been trying to tell Trotter. "They're focusing on just the top tier of engineering schools. What if Hezbollah is one step ahead of them?"

"What do you mean?"

"If they're worried about surveillance, and I think they would be, they might avoid the good colleges, and send their guys to the mediocre ones."

"Sounds like a long shot, if they really wanted to learn the technology."

"All right, say they send some of their guys to MIT, Stanford and so on, as a smokescreen, then put some of their more mature folks into the lesser known schools, ones that are sure to take the money."

"I think what you're telling me," Trotter said, grinning as he drove, "is that your network can keep tabs on all of them, and then if those Homeland goofballs screw up at MIT, the other dudes will think they're home free."

"Right, and they might even give something away along the line. We might see a warning over the web if one of the profs get suspicious."

"But don't you think that will just put another layer of cover on their transmissions?" Trotter was playing Devil's advocate.

"I think it's worth the risk. Especially since Fredericks doesn't see the angle we're playing. He may just bring the fish to the surface."

"I guess we'll see, won't we?" Trotter ended the conversation just as they arrived back home.

Chapter 12

It was a pleasantly cool summer evening as Lara left her place, on her way to pick up Uri for dinner. She found herself really looking forward to another evening out with him. Here was a man who was self-confident without being aggressive. Someone she felt as an intellectual equal, but one who had much she could learn. The sun was still above the horizon as she got into her car. Vivid streams of red and gold streaked across the western sky. The breeze off the river had tousled her hair, and she self-consciously checked herself in the driver's mirror, something she rarely did. The traffic was light, as it was well past rush hour, and she made it to Uri's apartment building well ahead of the agreed-upon time. Uri, however, was waiting for her, patiently, by the curbside. His shoulders were relaxed, his hands in his pockets, and he had a slight smile on his face as he watched the children playing ball on the sidewalk. She liked it that he was not checking his watch and searching for her up and down the street. He turned as she pulled up to the curb, his smile broadening as he saw her.

"So where to?" Lara was her charming, after-work self as Uri climbed into her car.

"I have it on good authority that this Japanese place is the top of the line." He handed her a card with the name and address and she nodded. "And tonight it's my treat," he added.

"I hope you brought along some bucks, or did you get a credit card? This place is expensive; I've heard mention about it around the office. I think Trotter's even taken some foreign bigwigs there."

Uri just smiled. "I've got it under control," he said enigmatically. As they passed through the now familiar area of D.C. near the river, Uri commented on the number of visitors, and how many appeared foreign. "This must be the biggest draw in the country for visitors," he said.

"You may be right, but I bet Disneyland is close behind," she replied.

"Have you ever been there?" Uri was honestly curious, not just making conversation.

"No, my family used to take us to the National Parks on our vacations when we were kids. My dad loves the outdoors."

"And 'we' would be…?"

"Oh, my brother Bob and I. I actually wanted to see the Smithsonian, but I figured I could do that on my own later. And sure enough, I did." They approached the area of the restaurant and Lara hunted around for a parking place. "It's lucky you like to go out to eat during the week; on weekends we'd be out of luck." They parked, and on the short walk to the restaurant, Uri could smell, or at least sense, the nearness of the Potomac.

"This is what I find so different from home, I mean Israel. Unless you're right on the Med, you don't feel that sense of water, like you do here. I mean, it rains here all the time, it seems. I hear people complain about it, but at home any time it rains it's like a blessing."

Lara nodded. "At home, I mean my folks' home in Ohio, it's either not enough rain or too much. The farmers seem to always complain. But we live in a small town, and without the farms, the town would disappear, so we grew up liking to see it rain, just not too much at one time. But I've read that in Israel it's a whole different story, isn't it?"

Uri nodded as they reached the restaurant, "Yes, from day one the pioneers, the kibbutzniks figured out how to make the most out of what little water there was. Then later on the scientists invented all sorts of schemes, like 'drip irrigation.' To be continued," he said, as the hostess brought them to their little table.

The restaurant was gloriously appointed in silver, white, and gold. But the main theme was a polished ebony look. Long white Japanese paintings hung from the ceilings throughout. The low, black tables were immaculately outfitted in crisp linen, with bamboo place mats. On the mats were polished dark red chopsticks, not the kind found in paper packages. The hostess handed them huge black menus as she politely pointed out where their shoes were to go. As they eased into place beneath the low table, their legs brushed together briefly, and Uri felt his stomach tense. There was no doubt that he was attracted to her. Tonight she had worn a simple white blouse and tight fitting, but pleated skirt that showed off her well-tuned midsection. He was getting familiar with her body a little bit at a time.

"Well, Mr. International Gourmet, you've impressed me already. Not a place like this in Baxter."

"Ohio?"

"Right. I think I'll let you do the ordering tonight. But no raw fish for this girl."

"Where's your spirit of adventure?"

"OK, you order it, I'll taste it. But get some cooked stuff, too."

"Eel?"

"Yuck, you've got to be kidding."

A waitress appeared and took their drink orders; they both opted for beer, Japanese beer. Then Uri ordered them some *edamame*, tuna roll, one helping of *sashimi* and some beef and chicken teriyaki.

"Alright, now you promised to continue that story about the irrigation."

"Wow," Uri said, "I completely forgot. OK, well we grow lots of what are called 'high value-added' crops like banana, avocado, kiwi, mango, and assorted vegetables. These are crops totally unsuited to desert surroundings, mainly due to their need for water. But back in the 1930's, a settler noticed a tree growing without any apparent water source. He found there was a water pipe nearby that had a tiny leak, and that's all the tree needed. Over the years, when plastic film became available, the Israelis developed this process where a polyethylene film is laid down about fifty centimeters below the surface, and plastic pipes with holes in them are set down above it. And they called it 'drip irrigation.' Works great where you can't afford to be spraying water into the air and losing ninety percent to evaporation."

"But where do you get the water from? Are there lakes, like our Great Lakes?"

"No, not really, other than the Sea of Galilee up north. So, a lot of water is reclaimed from sewage..." Uri saw Lara wrinkle her nose. "...and then there's desalinated sea water. But the main thing we do is to conserve. It's a whole different life style from here. No long showers and mighty flush toilets that could sink a battleship. I have to admit it's a real luxury here, I'm ashamed to admit, but I'll have to get over it when I go back..."

There seemed to be a subtle change in Lara's posture when Uri said these last few words. Or maybe he was imagining things. Anyway, the food came, and he showed her the multiple flavors of the Japanese cuisine, along with a stern warning about the *wasabe*, a most potent horseradish.

"OK, now you promised to tell me about your family, remember?"

"Sure, but it's a lot less exciting than yours. My dad runs a small auto and farm implement repair service. I've got a brother who's mostly into sports, and then there's me, the only one in town who went to college—at least from my high school class. My uncle and my dad's uncles were my inspiration: they were all in the service, and I grew up really proud of them. I used to read about all the exploits of our OSS, which became the CIA, and how much difference they made in the War. So I wanted to be someone special, a woman who did something special for her country." She paused for a second. "Boy, that sounds sappy, doesn't it?"

"Not at all. But I have this image of American kids being totally anti-war; I guess that's the Vietnam War picture we see, with the demonstrations and things in the '70's—before your time."

"No, it's still pretty much like that, especially at college. There's a strong feeling that our government lied to the people pretty badly about Vietnam, and then again about Iraq, so they're suspicious of politicians who come on strong about patriotism and fighting for your country, no matter what. Most of the kids now want a better reason to go get killed than blind patriotism, that might just mean a way to line the pockets of some rich guys."

"You don't sound like the typical FBI agent," Uri said smiling.

"I guess I've been telling you just one side. There's the other side, the foreign agents and cells that are using our way of life to destroy us." He knew she was referring to the relative freedom Americans had, to read, travel and communicate. They both looked around to make sure no one was listening. In any case, the discussion wouldn't go further on down this path, they both knew.

"How is it in Israel?" Lara wondered what it must be like to live in a land surrounded by people who wanted to kill you.

"As you can imagine, not quite as carefree as you have it here. And for good reason, despite what you might hear from the more naïve idealists. You just have to see the aftermath of one café bombing to have that bubble popped, real quick. Believe me, the Arabs who live in Israel, even those who visit, have a lot more freedom than they do in the Arab countries. Not to mention what a Jew would find in an Arab country."

"You mean there were Jews living in the Arab countries, I mean before..."

"Millions, at one time or another. But right after the War of Independence, the Arab governments clamped down on them, and nearly a million immigrated to Israel. There are even a hundred thousand or so black Jews from Ethiopia who were allowed to immigrate, actually secretly flown out."

"I remember that, the Falasha."

"Yes, only we don't use that term, it means 'strangers,' Instead they're known as 'Chabashim.' A tribe of Hebrews cut off from the rest of us a long time ago, and now reunited."

"Why did it have to be a secret, their return?"

"The Muslim governments didn't like the idea of having a group of their citizens prefer to live in a Jewish state. Sort of like the way the Soviet Union couldn't abide anyone choosing to live in the capitalist West."

"I know this sounds like a dumb question, but when do you suppose the Muslims will stop their 'Jihad' against Westerners?"

"Our former prime minister Golda Meir, said it best: 'We will have peace with the Arabs when they love their children more than they hate ours.'"

"That's a good one. Did you know she grew up in Milwaukee?" Uri nodded. "She was another role model for me," Lara added. "I love it when women are heads of state. Like Margaret Thatcher." Uri nodded again, and there was a pause as they nibbled on the remaining food.

"So tell me," she said dramatically, "about women. The story in the office is that you're secretly married."

"Not so secret, I'm afraid. We're separated." Lara waited for more, hoping he felt at ease enough to continue. "Danielle, the love of my life. We grew up together, in a kibbutz near the Lebanese border. In the peaceful times we even had Arab friends. That changed later on. But we were always together, Danielle and I. But she ended up hating the violence, and I, well you know how I feel. That we'll only end it when, well like Golda says. In the meantime we have to keep the pressure on."

"You're getting off the subject, mister."

"OK," he laughed. "She left after…well, a little while back." He looked knowingly at Lara, who nodded. She knew he was referring to the deadly raid into Lebanon a short time ago. "I keep hoping she'll change her mind, but…" He stared off into space as if to say it was a lost cause.

"Children?" Lara hoped she was not prying too much.

"No, we agreed way back that we were too busy. In the kibbutz children aren't a problem, but when we decided to be urban dwellers, that pretty much settled it."

"No regrets?"

"Not yet, anyway. Now wait a minute; let's hear your story, at least a little."

"Wait 'til we get out into the air," she said laughing. She was having a good time.

"All right, I'll get the check. By the way, how'd you like the eel?"

"You didn't…"

"No, just kidding." He waved at the waitress, who arrived promptly with the check. Uri peeled off a few twenties and left them on the table. "Don't forget your shoes."

"As you were saying," Uri teased playfully, when they were outside.

"Well, as I said, I was the only one in my high school class who went to college."

"So where did you go?"

"A place called Ohio Wesleyan. It's a liberal arts college in the middle of Ohio, near Columbus."

"Oh, that's where Ohio State is, isn't it?"

"Oh, shit, don't start that!" She caught herself immediately. "Oh, my God, I am so sorry." If she was blushing, he couldn't tell in the night air, but she definitely sounded like she was. "See, that's like a huge deal around Columbus. Ohio State is this enormous university with about a hundred thousand students and this football team that is the pride of the state. You would think that's all college was about, football.' And OWU, that's what we call Wesleyan, is all about learning, with small classes and professors who know everybody's name. I feel like I got a real education, and not just four years of parties. And I didn't miss the football!"

"Wow, I think I hit a nerve," Uri said laughing.

"Yeah, I guess so. I get tired of explaining it all the time. But you're excused; you probably don't even know where Ohio is. So how come you know about OSU, anyway?"

"The football team. We had a guy from the States visiting, and all he could talk about was Ohio State and how terrific their football team was. We got a big kick out of it, since big time sports in Israel isn't anything the Universities get worked up about. But if one of our faculty wins a Nobel Prize, or something like that, well I guess it's like when an American University wins the Rose Bowl. Different priorities, I guess."

"But you get off on the Olympics, right? I mean there's lots of national pride involved, isn't there?"

"You bet. Jewish athletes are like, what's your term for it, 'oxymorons?' We Jews aren't generally known for prowess on the soccer field, or wherever, but we're talking about you. What did you study at 'OWU?' "

Lara smiled inwardly; he really was interested. "Political science; we have a well-known faculty, and I think I really learned a lot about it. But then I found out there's not much you can do with a degree in political science except teach, and you need a doctorate to even have a chance."

"And you didn't want to go that route, right?"

"Right. I wanted to do something. So one day I saw a notice that the FBI was going to have a recruiter on campus, and I jumped at the chance. After all, that was a way to serve my country, like my family has always done."

"Being a woman wasn't a handicap?"

"Just the opposite. The government loves having more qualified women on the rolls. The recruiter, who was a man by the way, was extremely courteous and encouraging. When he found out I had an 'A' average in Poly Sci he got me an invitation to Washington and directly to the Hoover building to meet with some big shots in suits. I got to stay in a nice hotel, and even had a day off to visit the Smithsonian. I was hooked."

"What was it that they liked about you?"

"They liked the facts that I could handle firearms, run a mile in five minutes and had a family with a military background. And of course my grade point at a tough school like Wesleyan didn't hurt. But before I got an offer, they interviewed everybody I ever knew, back in Baxter, and at OWU. Took about six weeks; people called and told me about it."

"What kinds of things did they ask, how you voted, information like that?"

"No, not at all. They wanted to know if I had a lot of friends, if I drank or smoked dope, that kind of thing. They're afraid of loners and druggies."

"And so then you got in and then what?"

"We had comprehensive training at Quantico; I can't even tell *you* about it. But we had physical training, too, and I qualified for field agent."

She was proud of that, he could tell. He glanced quickly at her trim form, revealed somewhat by her dress; it was clear she was in good physical condition. But that glance also stirred feelings deep in his gut; she definitely aroused him. He had no idea if anything mutual was going on with her, and he was determined not to do or say anything that might be considered as "coming on" to her; however, she had promised to tell him more about her private life, so he decided to probe just a little.

"Now, you know all about Danielle, so what about you, have you been married?"

"No. I've had some boyfriends, nothing serious. Guys around my home town like to think of a wife as just someone to take care of the kids and the house. I wanted to do something more with my life."

"And now...?" The two bottles of beer with dinner had loosened up the path between his groin and his head.

"Now I don't have time for any social life," she laughed. They reached her car and drove to his place.

"That was fun," he said, taking her hand. But he did not try to draw her near as he desperately wanted to. He got out of the car, waved goodbye, and climbed the stairs to his empty flat.

Chapter 13

Washington "Wash" Neil headed out of the meeting at Langley with a sour look on his face. He had just heard about the strategic decision to put Trotter at FBI, in charge of the latest counter-terrorism effort. He knew it was because of Lara Edmond, who supposedly was a computer genius. She had dazzled everyone at Homeland Security with her consolidation of the programs written by all the computer geeks in the various alphabet soups of agencies. He knew that now all the electronic transmissions being intercepted, billions of items, were being filtered using her giant, interlocking programs. These programs, if the rumors could be believed, could identify messages being sent in English, but originating from Arab-speakers. It was hard to believe, but apparently, several high quality plots had been foiled already, though it wasn't public information. No one wanted to deal with the public outcry that would arise if the country knew that every single email and web page was being scrutinized by the FBI.

Another troubling item had come to his attention. One of Israel's master spies, going by the name of Uri Levin, had joined her in her newly-formed campaign. Neil was wary of any Israeli connection, for two reasons: First, he didn't want foreign agents from any country accessing America's secret files and techniques. Second, and perhaps more important, he had lately been attending services at a local mosque, hopefully not under the scrutiny of the Bureau. The FBI didn't trust the CIA on matters of internal security; the competitive nature of the agencies was legendary and had been for decades. The establishment of the Homeland Security Department, in his view, simply diluted resources best used by the Agency. He had been careful not to call attention to himself at the Masjid-el Allah mosque, at the Friday services. He dressed just like many of the other hundred or so black men in the neighborhood, in the traditional Pakistani *salwar kameez*, as instructed in the *hadith,* consisting of baggy trousers with a long, loose, long-sleeved top. A colorful turban topped off the attire, giving him even more anonymity.

Wash had been reading many of the pamphlets that lay on the tables in the entry of the mosque; he liked much of what he had read, though he was not yet ready to formally convert. The literature stressed the similarity between the black man's struggle in the West and the Arabs' in the Middle East. Both cultures had been oppressed by the marauding, white, colonial occupiers for centuries. Only now, in the last forty years or so, had the true nature of their mutual heritage come to the fore. As the black men in America could now hold their heads up high, so too could the Arabs, as they slowly but inexorably, gained back their rightful birthright.

The literature stressed that the struggle must be peaceful, as stated in the Holy Quran. But in smaller group meetings he had attended, some other passages had been revealed to him, ones that made quite clear that force was sometimes necessary, and that innocents may have to die in the battle for the greater good of Islam. "Innocence?" he had asked naively, when he first heard this phrase.

The Imam had chuckled, "No, my son, innocent people, people like the prophet himself who suffered at the hands of the infidels." Wash was unsure about this philosophy, as it certainly clashed sharply with his strict Christian upbringing. But then he had thought of the wars in Iraq and Afghanistan, and how thousands of those people had died, innocent victims of the American bombardment. When the *mujahadim* in Afghanistan were fighting against the Russians in the 80's, America was solidly behind them, giving weapons and other assistance to them. But in 2001, they were the "Taliban," and became evil personified. *One man's terrorist is another man's freedom fighter*, he thought. The hijacking of the airplanes into the World Trade Center on 9/11 had struck him deeply, like all Americans. Sure this was the act of some lunatics. But as the Imam had pointed out, would this have occurred if America had not been giving aid and encouragement to the occupiers of Palestine, the country known as "Israel?"

All this had been stewing around in his mind for some months, and now when he heard of this Israeli being allowed access to our greatest intelligence treasures, he was ambivalent, to say the least. He stopped outside his car and called his old colleague, Phil Jordan, over at CIA training. Jordan, he knew, had instructed this Uri Levin some years ago in some of the basic Agency techniques used in "terror abatement."

"Jordan, you old dog, how you doin', my man?" He remembered Jordan liked the ghetto talk even though he was as white bread as they come.

"Couldn't be finer, and how you, my main man?"

"Just cruisin' by the place," Wash said, referring to Langley. "Thought we might share a cup."

"Know just the spot, up on three. When you be there?"

Wash was quickly tiring of the bro' talk, but he replied, "See you in twenty." He didn't want Jordan to know that he had just been in the building they were referring to; keep it casual. After a few minutes perusing the bulletin board on the first floor, Wash took the elevator up to the third floor and headed for the intimate little coffee shop. It was smaller than the cafeteria, without the clatter of trays and silverware. He never could get over the thriftiness shown by the government when it came to creature comforts, even in a multi-billion dollar a year agency. He supposed it had to do with congressional oversight; never give those bastards a chance to publicly humiliate you over a nice wooden desk or tablecloths in the employee cafeteria.

He went in, got a cup of coffee, sat down and waited for Jordan. As expected, Jordan kept him waiting, but after a few minutes, he saw the familiar white hair. Jordan was grinning as he came around the corner, quickly got a cup and came over to Wash, hand outstretched. "Good to see you, been too long."

The two men could not have been more different in their appearance. Neil, the tall, broad, muscular black man could have passed for an NFL defensive back. He was dressed impressively in a dark gray, double-breasted, tailored suit. On the street, he might be a high class businessman or a black ward politician. Jordan, on the other hand was an older white man with thinning gray hair, noticeably mussed.

"It sure has, I've missed our little sessions." Wash noticed Jordan had gotten older, more sedentary. He still had the bulk he had in his field days, but now some of it had turned soft. Still, he would be a formidable adversary, with a world of tricks.

"So, to what do I owe this honor; I assume you've got some trouble brewing, as usual?"

"You're part right, buddy. It's not trouble, at least not yet. I was wondering if you remember a guy you trained in Israel some years ago, Uri Levin."

Jordan sipped his coffee thoughtfully. "Sure, I remember him; one damn terrific field agent. Best I've seen in hand-to-hand—outside of you, of course. How come you're asking?"

"I don't know if you've heard, he's over here working with Trotter, international terror."

"Sure I've heard; in fact, I recommended him. Like I said, damn fine field agent, speaks great Arabic, and knows lots of those bad guys. Why, what's worrying you, Wash?"

"I don't know, Jordan," Wash lied, "I just have a funny feeling about having non-citizens in on Agency business, especially with national security at stake."

"Wash, you were fine when we had that Brit working with us after the subway, excuse me, 'Underground' bombs a while back. This wouldn't have anything to do with the fact that this foreigner happens to be an Israeli, would it?"

Wash wondered how Jordan had put that together. He didn't know about Wash's leanings toward Islam—or did he? "All right, that's part of it. It seems like we give them an awful lot of access to our latest stuff, hardware and intelligence, both."

"Right you are," Jordan replied immediately, "But you may not know how much we get back from them."

"Like what?"

"Like the last raid we made in New York on that Al Qaeda cell. That was all set up by Israeli agents working deep cover in Afghanistan."

"Afghanistan?" Wash was surprised that they had agents there.

"Right. They speak the language and look the part, at least some of them do. They've given us a lot of leads. Why, what's really bothering you?"

Wash was ready for that; he had done some studying since the meetings at the mosque had stirred up his curiosity. "Are you sure of their motives, I mean how far they'll go if they get the chance?"

"Oh, you mean like that Iraqi nuclear reactor they took out in the early '80s? They checked that out with us first; but you're too young to remember that, aren't you?"

"You're right, that was before my Agency days, but I can read, you know."

"Hey, don't get defensive on me, we're old buddies." Jordan clapped his hand over Wash's in a gesture of friendship.

"No, it goes back farther than that. I guess it's the 'Liberty' business that worries me." Wash was referring to the Israeli attack on the U.S. warship during the 1967 war, the so-called "Six-Day War."

"That attack caused us a lot of grief, I can tell you. I was working communications in our Beirut office then; but you probably know that." Wash nodded. He was interested in what Jordan had to say. The newspaper reports from the time that he had looked up on the web were equivocal on the matter. One thing was certain: Israeli warplanes had attacked the Liberty, a U.S. warship off the coast of Israel, near the Egyptian border, during the hectic days of that brief, conclusive victory of Israel over the Arabs. The Liberty was flying a U.S. flag and offered no resistance, at least at first. The Israeli attack was responsible for the deaths of 34 U.S. sailors, an event that many in the Navy still remembered resentfully.

"I know that they killed a lot of our sailors in an unprovoked attack," Wash stated flatly.

"I'm with you. Believe me, I was mad as hell when we heard about it. Then, slowly, the facts started coming in; it took months, maybe even years, to sort it all out." Wash sat up straight, his attention full on Jordan, a man he trusted completely. "It seems we, the Americans, had told the Israeli Foreign office that we didn't have any ships in or near Israeli waters. Then, southern

Israel began getting shelled from what they thought was offshore. You know, forty years ago they didn't have the satellite tracking available now. Anyway, they see this ship off their coast that looks a lot like an Egyptian warship. In the heat of battle, you make mistakes; even we do it." He looked Wash right in the eyes; he didn't have to be explicit when referring to the "friendly fire" incidents during the Iraq and Afghanistan campaigns. The U.S. had lost more troops to accidental fire from their own guns and planes than to enemy fire; a tragic but true fact that they were all too aware of.

Wash carefully considered what his old friend was telling him. While it didn't exactly conflict with what he was learning in the mosque, it did throw a different light on the relationship of the U.S. with Israel. "So you think it's okay, this Israeli guy, Uri, getting into our game?"

"Well, that's a big jump from the Liberty affair, but yes, I trust Uri. He's solid, and would never do anything to hurt U.S. interests."

"Even if it meant going against Israel's interests?" Wash persisted.

"I get the feeling there's something else going on here, Wash. What is it?"

"Well, I've been doing a little research, you might call it. It doesn't look like Israel is all that sweet and innocent. I mean, when you look at all the aid we give them every year and all the arms and intel, while the Arabs are starving in those camps…"

"Wash, I read the same crap all the time, about how the Arabs are suffering, while the Israelis are persecuting them. I've been there, seen how things are. Most of the Israelis *want* the Palestinians to have their own country, the 'Two-State' solution they call it. It's the Arabs who don't want that; they want Israel gone, as in g-o-n-e. The Israelis vote in their Peace party, and the Palestinians vote in Hamas, who vow never to recognize Israel as a State. So who's keeping the war going? It's pretty clear when you know all the facts."

"And what about all the PAC money the Israeli lobby throws at the members of congress to make them vote Israel's way on every bill that comes up?"

"You know how much money the American-Israeli lobby gives to congressmen?" Jordan asked. Wash shook his head. "About two million dollars a year, all above the table. I mean it's all accounted for. But do you have any idea how much oil money comes in from the Arab States, especially the Saudis?" Wash shook his head again. Jordan smiled, "Neither does anybody else. But I guarantee you it's hundreds of times what the AIPAC gives, and it's all pretty much uncontrolled."

"There are laws against that."

"Money talks; and we're talking big money here, not to mention the fact that we're totally dependent on Arab oil to keep this country running."

Wash was thoughtful, but not convinced. Still, the Black Muslim argument was not one he could discuss with Jordan; his friend, but not a black man. He needed to do a lot more research on his own. "Thanks, pal, I appreciate the lesson. Next one's on me." He got up to leave, giving his friend a hearty handshake and a slap on the shoulder. "I got to get back. The bad guys never take time off." He grinned at Jordan as he walked briskly away.

Outside the weather was turning ugly. A storm was brewing, and there were whitecaps on the Potomac. He hustled to his car as he considered what his old friend had said.

Chapter 14

Summer was making its slow, inexorable way into autumn, and the days were growing noticeably shorter. Uri had gotten into the swing of things at his shared office with Lara. They spent most of the day going over the hundreds of suspect web pages identified by the sophisticated programs Lara had put in place. They received input from all the various agencies that had been part of the process. Occasional exciting moments were overshadowed by the hours of grinding work common to intelligence activities.

So it was that the daily regimen had taken hold of Uri. But it wasn't all work; Lara had taken him around and shown him the recreational activities that he was now free to use. The FBI valued physical fitness to a high degree. In the large, well-equipped gym, open to employees around the clock, Lara, Uri noticed, never worked out in the brief, skin-tight costumes he had seen in the public gyms. She, instead, opted for modest sweat suits, albeit with the FBI logo. Uri was amused by this logo, which many of the employees wore, since no one but FBI types had access to the gym at any time.

It was another day at the office when a registered letter appeared for Uri. He had to sign for it at the mail clerk's office. He immediately recognized the country of origin from the distinctive postal stamp, and he had a sinking feeling about what he would find inside. As soon as he tore open the envelope his fears were confirmed: He found the seal of the Israel Family Court. This court had jurisdiction over divorce actions not hindered by religious law, and where no children were involved. He quickly scanned the document, which was a form letter written in Hebrew, and found that Danielle was not requesting any sort of financial reparation, known in Israel as "spousal maintenance;" however,

100

the man still had to formally request the finality of the decree. This placed a heavy hand on Uri's heart; he was the one who must divorce her, not the other way around. He knew that he could never violate Danielle's wishes; if she wanted out, then so be it. It would take some time for him to absorb the blow and sign the form that lay there waiting for him.

Uri returned to the office with a grim look on his face; Lara saw it immediately. "Bad news from home?" she asked quietly. Uri just nodded and sat forlornly at his desk. "Is it Danielle; something wrong?"

"She wants a divorce," he said flatly. "I have to sign the papers and send them back, and then that's it." He sat for a few minutes, silent. Lara did not know anything to say to him so she just sat there as well. Finally, Uri rose and said, "I think I'll call it a day and head home, I need some time to think." But he knew, that he would follow through according to Danielle's wishes.

He went back to his flat and sat glumly, watching the early news on his rented TV. At about five o'clock, the phone rang, a rare occurrence in his sparsely populated life. "Uri?" It was Lara. Somewhere, deep down, he must have been expecting her to call. He hated sympathy; but, on the other hand, he really did not want to be alone tonight. "I just wondered if you have dinner plans."

"No, I'm just going to head to the deli down the street."

"Listen," she said, "I have some pasta I was planning to make, and I have more than I can possibly eat myself. How about helping me out?"

Uri was silent for a moment as he considered this offer. His immediate reaction was to refuse, but then his loneliness overcame his reluctance. "Sounds great, can I bring a bottle of Chianti?"

"That's a deal, how about 7:30?"

"Perfect."

"See you, then," she said cheerfully, and hung up.

As Uri cleaned up and changed into his casual attire of jeans and sweatshirt, he considered her invitation. He figured it was one of two things,: either his pending divorce made him a free man and she was setting up a romantic evening, or she was just being a good friend at a sensitive moment. It didn't take him long to realize it was the latter. He knew her well enough by now, and silently castigated himself for even thinking about… Well, he'd better go get the wine and figure out how to navigate to her house.

At 7:30, he rang her bell. She buzzed him up to her flat on the second floor, and was waiting for him at her open door with a big smile. "Hi," she said, and gave him a sisterly hug. "I'm really glad you could come over."

Lara held out her hands to take the bottle of wine and his windbreaker. She had dressed as he had, in sweatshirt and jeans, but she looked a whole lot better. He had never seen her in jeans, and these fit so snugly it sent his heart racing. Her shape from the waist down was perfect, and perfectly outlined by the well-worn jeans. A lump formed in his stomach that almost matched the one trying to form lower down. If she noticed his discomfiture, she didn't react, which relieved him greatly. To take his mind off her form, he glanced around the small, but well-furnished apartment. She had simple furniture, but, unlike his, it all matched. The pastel shades of the upholstery were set off against the bright Chinese rugs on the polished wood floors. It all described her as a bright, cheerful person with excellent taste, something he already knew.

"Sit down, over on the couch is good. I've got some martinis made; do you like them?"

"Sure, sounds great, and I'm not driving."

"Here you go," she said as she poured the martinis out of a stainless steel shaker. They clinked glasses and just for a second looked deep into each other's eyes, as she said, "To a great success."

Uri's mind raced as he thought about what she might have meant, but quickly realized she was talking about Hezbollah. "L'Chaim," he added, to bring in a little international flavor.

"Hey, I know what that means, I saw 'Fiddler on the Roof.'"

"You're not going to believe this," he said, laughing, "but half the non-Jews who visit Israel expect to see people like Tevye and his family all over the place."

"And you wouldn't believe how many people coming to the States for the first time expect to see either Indians or gun fights in the streets," she added.

"I guess television and movies are the thing everywhere."

"You got it. Hey, let me throw the pasta in. I hope you like it 'al dente.'"

"Hey, if we can eat raw fish, why not?"

She laughed, and jumped easily off the couch and went behind the small bar that divided the kitchen from the dining area. He couldn't stop himself from getting another look at her from behind in those tight jeans. He took a deep breath to stop the palpitations. His heart was racing, against his will.

A pot of water was already boiling lightly on the gas stove. Lara took a heaping handful of what appeared to be freshly prepared angel hair pasta into the boiling water. "Fresh from the Farmer's Market," she said over her shoulder. "Have a seat at the table; we want to eat this while it's hot." She took two plates that had been heated in her microwave, and ladled the steaming pasta onto both. Then she took a warmed dish of green pesto sauce and poured it generously over the pasta. The smell of the freshly made pesto added perfectly to the fresh angel hair. To complete the picture, she pulled a fresh loaf of French bread from the oven. It had already been basted with garlic butter, making Uri's appetite overwhelm his procreation urge. She handed Uri a corkscrew and the Chianti bottle. She had somehow managed to produce two Chianti glasses during all this, and they were ready for him to pour out the wine.

"This looks and smells fantastic; do you do this all the time?"

"Only for visiting spies." She was laughing again.

He was in such a good mood, he had nearly forgotten about Danielle and the many wonderful dinners they had enjoyed together. For some reason, maybe not so obscure, they had become part of the past, now that she had actually presented him with the legal papers. Or was it the fact that he was in another country, with a beautiful, talented woman who appeared to enjoy his company. Could he really switch his feelings on and off that easily? The wine was helping.

"How often do you cook?" He quickly realized the question might sound like: "How often do you have men over?" He quickly added, "I mean do you do it for yourself, or do you eat out most of the time, like me?"

She smiled, recognizing his slight embarrassment, and said, "Only on special occasions, like on Farmer's Market day."

They ate leisurely, Uri commenting on her skill in the kitchen; Lara accepting the compliments gracefully. Uri had to restrain himself from eating like a released prisoner, the meal was so tasty. Lara was clearly pleased at his healthy appetite. When Uri finally had his fill and noticed that Lara had long since finished, he made a gallant attempt to clear the table.

"Come on back over to the couch, and don't you dare try to clean off the table! The dishes can wait 'til later."

"Yes, ma'am," he said with a grin. "I'm not much for housework, anyway."

They sat easily on the couch for a while, totally comfortable in each other's presence. The sexual tension that, at least Uri had felt, had now abated. Lara had magically made the dishes disappear and had produced a bottle of brandy. She poured them each a generous portion of the amber fluid. She had told him about life in the small Ohio town, the routine and the gossip, the almost incestuous nature of the dating and marriage cycles.

"So going out into the world of the FBI was a huge change, right?"

"Even going away to college was a huge change, meeting people who didn't know all about me and my family. It's quite a shock."

They sat in silence for a while, listening to the soft jazz she had put on the radio. "You like this?" she asked.

"How did you know? I like all the old 'West Coast' guys. There are a couple of clubs in Tel Aviv where we go and listen to them improve a bit on Tuesday nights..." He stopped himself, and Lara caught on immediately.

"You mean, with Danielle?"

He recognized the subject had been cracked open, and by him, at that. "Yes, I guess I should use the past tense."

"Then you're going to sign the papers and end it?"

"It's already ended; I just never let myself..."

He looked so forlorn, Lara came over next to him and hugged him gently, then kissed him lightly on the cheek.

"Pretty pitiful, huh," he said, trying to smile.

"No, not all. Listen, Uri, why don't you stay here tonight, you've had a lot to drink...on the couch, I mean." She blushed charmingly.

"It's OK, I'm not driving, and I know the Metro well by now, even drunk, or at least semi-drunk."

"I'll compromise with you; I'll call you a cab."

"OK, I'm a cab," he said, repeating the old joke, laughing at himself.

"God, you know that one, even in Israel?"

"All the old Jewish comedians are very popular, especially the Marx Brothers."

"I bet you could have been a comic, if you weren't so good at catching bad guys."

"All Jewish guys think they're comics. Just go into any restaurant in Tel Aviv; all the waiters think they're Jackie Mason."

They both laughed as she helped him into his jacket, then called a taxi service. "I hope the driver is Iranian; it'll serve you right for turning down my couch offer."

"I promise not to dispose of him, even if he looks suspicious."

She walked him downstairs, and they waited for the cab together silently, each considering what might have happened if he had stayed. They stood silently, next to each other, like two lovers separated by miles, but bound together in their thoughts. The late autumn mist blew through their hair, and blurred the streetlights into giant halos. That, combined with the reflection of the lights off the wet pavement, and the effects of the night's drinking, gave Uri a surreal feeling, which he attempted to recreate later, as he tried to fall asleep. When he did finally drift off, his mind was a confused jumble of feelings, partly due to the assignment, partly his memory of Lara, that evening, her smile, her scent...

Chapter 15

Uri was the first to spot the warnings coming over an MIT web page. In a page entitled: "Engineering Communications 145" there was a note from the supposed teaching assistant to all students in the class to *"disuse all direction to homeworks now due."* A quick check of the course catalogue showed no such class; furthermore, the erroneous syntax indicated a non-native English speaker under some stress to get a message out quickly. Lara then picked up similar directives from other East Coast schools, all emanating on the same day. Something clearly was up.

When Trotter heard about the apparent leak, his face turned a mild shade of scarlet. He was on the secure phone to Reynolds Macarthur at Homeland Security at once; not bothering to check with Fredericks first. "We have a problem, Reynolds," he said.

"What's up, Deke?"

"We've come up with something that looks serious. We need to meet right away; with Fredericks, too."

"Can you come over here, say in an hour?"

"You got it," Trotter replied. Lara was surprised at this behavior from her boss. He was always cognizant of the formalities of rank, and the head of Homeland Security clearly outranked Trotter. Macarthur must have been too alarmed to take umbrage at Trotter's insubordination. "Get everything together; we need to be one hundred percent on this. There's no chance of a mistake here; you're both sure?"

"The odds are a million to one that these messages could all be random events. They're on to us; or I should say, to Fredericks and his boys."

"All right, let's motor." Uri and Lara pulled together all the documentation they had shown to Trotter, in addition to some other web pages from the same apparent locations in the past weeks. By infiltrating Opera they had a pretty good idea of the broad location of the sources. Many of the web sites originated around Boston, where there were a number of highly rated engineering schools.

As soon as they entered the windowless, but elegantly furnished conference room in Homeland Security's Washington office building, they could sense the tension; it was almost palpable. Reynolds Macarthur sat at the head of the table, grim faced, with a sharpened pencil and fresh pad of paper, nothing else. At his right hand Carter Fredericks sat stone faced. The two appeared like judges about to order an execution. Trotter led the FBI delegation to the other side of the table. Lara held the briefcase containing the damning evidence; Trotter sat to her right, Uri to her left. As usual, Macarthur spoke directly to Trotter, and him only.

"All right, Deke, what's this all about?"

"Lara can show you the bad news best herself, Reynolds," Trotter said calmly. He knew who had the cards here.

"OK, Ms. Edmonds, let's see what you've got," Macarthur began tersely.

"I'm afraid it's what we were worried about at the start of the penetration mission, sir, We've intercepted some web communications from four universities in the Boston area. Our preliminary spotters picked up on the strange syntax, and the false class listings."

"You mean to tell us that a few web messages from some ragheads have got you all worked up?" Carter couldn't contain himself, and in return, received a sharp glance from his boss. The term "raghead" was on the official list of pejoratives not to be used within the walls of the U.S. government buildings. But the Department of Homeland Security was notably devoid of Arab-speakers, and so few of its employees felt obliged to adhere to the rules. It was much like being in a men's club in the Old South, and being expected not to use the old terms for people of color.

Lara had expected resistance to their evidence and was ready for combat. She did not want to see all their efforts at cracking the Hezbollah networks go down because of some bumbling amateurs. Fredericks, on the other hand, saw this as a turf battle only, with his manhood at stake.

"We've been monitoring these particular sources for several months; ever since we picked up on the Opera connection. There's never been as dramatic evidence of simultaneous warnings before. And they're clearly linked to the 'visits' by your agents to the schools. When exactly did they go to these universities?" She turned the list of schools she had prepared so that it faced Fredericks as well as Macarthur.

Fredericks colored noticeably as he carefully read the damning list. His boss looked straight at him. "What do you think, Carter?"

There was a noticeable pause as Fredericks adjusted his perfectly formed tie. "It's possible, but it might also be coincidence."

There are no coincidences, not in this business, Lara thought to herself, as she bit her tongue to keep it still.

"All right, Deke, I think it's best we shut down the university visits, for now. Let's keep an eye on the electronic traffic, see if it cools off." Macarthur nodded cursorily at Fredericks, who sat without moving a muscle. Macarthur was only mildly apologetic; he knew he had lost some points, but he also knew what was best for the Department. He'd rather have a pissed-off employee than an internal departmental review, sometimes known as being dragged onto the carpet. "Keep in touch, OK? And keep up the great work." This last he said to Lara, as he shook hands with all three of the FBI team.

The three headed back home, all without saying a word, but secretly enjoying the victory. After they had entered the building and were in the secure zone, Trotter finally said to them, "Well, we won that battle, now let's make it pay off. Let's see if maybe there's a way to pinpoint these sources, see if they're really dangerous, any of them…"

Chapter 16

December 2013

Walid drove the forty-five minute trek down the 405 freeway to the Marina freeway, followed it to its western terminal, and made his way to the designated parking lot and slip. It was easy enough to get in through the gate; a credit card pushed open the simple lock. As he gazed over the vast array of million dollar yachts along the slipway, all over forty feet in length, he was once again reminded of the vulgar wealth that these people had accumulated, and the utter disregard they had for the hundreds of millions of starving Muslims. The view bolstered his courage anew to the task at hand. Still, he hesitated for another moment at the gate, before going down to the yacht he knew was waiting.

His mind flashed to Sarah and her father, as it had frequently these past few weeks. He had been warned that this might happen as the moment of victory approached. Allah himself was watching him at this very instant, he had been told over and over again at the madrassah. The latest web messages had also reminded him of the glory coming with his martyrdom. Surely none since the blessed 9/11 bombers had been so graced for their courageous acts. They were certainly looking down upon him now, giving him strength, Allah be praised. Still he did not take those last few steps down to the boat that would bring him everlasting fame and glory.

Walid had not slept well these past few weeks; that was unlike him. He usually made love to Sarah, then turned over and yielded to blissful slumber. But lately he had been troubled with strange dreams. In the one he feared most, he found himself in a car, headed downhill on a rain-swept highway, like the Coast highway he and Sarah sometimes drove north on toward San Francisco. But in the dream he was alone, headed down the treacherous cliff side road, unable to slow the car down. He would press as hard as he could on the brakes, to little effect. He tried dragging the right side of the car along the side of the road, but still it kept gaining speed, heading toward the sharp curves ahead, with the steep cliff to his left and the Pacific waiting for him beyond. Then, just as the car was about to leave the road, he would wake in a cold sweat, his right foot pressing helplessly against the foot of the bed. Fortunately, Sarah slept soundly, oblivious to his terror. A variation on this dream was one where he was on an escalator, like the one in the Nieman Marcus department store where Sarah loved to shop. The escalator kept going down, but there was nowhere to exit from it. He would try to go up the moving staircase, but he only exhausted himself with the effort. Finally, gratefully, he would awaken, not so much with the fear that accompanied the racing car, but with a depressing sense of foreboding.

He looked on the internet to see if he could gather some free, anonymous explanation for these dreams; all he found was some Jungian baloney about fear of radical changes in life. There were some radical changes coming, all right, and he was about to go down in history as the one who made them! He would wash his face in cold water, and read some special sections in the Holy Quran to regain himself.

Walid must trust in what has been planned, and carry out Allah's wishes. He would then be fine for the rest of the day, but often found himself dreading the night.

A blast from an air horn on a boat in the channel brought him back to the task at hand. He took a deep breath and headed to slip L26. There was quite a bit of activity on the pier; many boat owners and crews were refurbishing and making repairs after the long race to Ensenada and back. The *Fairy Princess* sat calmly in her slip as the mostly Mexican crew brought neatly tied garbage bags up from below deck, remnants of the long but apparently uneventful trip back to Marina del Rey. Only one of them, a man whose name Walid just knew as "Juan," gave him more than a casual glance. Walid skipped the formal "permission to come aboard?" and stepped lightly onto the fiberglass deck. Juan nodded slightly, and led him to the ladder leading below. All this had been choreographed, via the internet. Juan led him down another flight of steps, into the bilge, where a rattan mat covered teak planking hiding access to the keel. Twelve bronze machine screws were all that separated them from the greatest revenge ever imagined for the latest "crusade" that the Jews and Christians had brought against Allah and his true followers.

Walid's breath was shallow, and he could feel his heart pounding wildly against his chest. As Juan unscrewed the planking, Walid felt strangely giddy, and grabbed hold of a brass rail for support. Juan, watching intently, gazed at him with what could only be described as misgiving. To mollify the Mexican, Walid pulled a large manila envelope stuffed with bills from under his jacket. Juan could see the corners of the one hundred dollar bills clearly; there were a thousand of them. To Juan and his crew, this was a windfall. For all they knew, the package under the lead cover inside the keel was heroine of the highest purity, destined for the streets of South Central LA. Walid placed the envelope on the steel table, bolted to the floor of the bilge, above the pumps. When he did so, Juan handed him a small electronic device that looked like an Ipod. There were five lights blinking on the display, three green and two red. Walid nodded and Juan left him to himself with his precious cargo.

He could hardly control his bladder as he gently lifted the wood planking, revealing a lead cover the length of the keel. It took all his strength to lift the lead aside, revealing the beautiful device itself. The normal lead keel had been removed and the nuclear device placed in the recess. Walid knew, mostly from Hossein, that the enriched uranium fuel emitted only a weak radiation signal, one that could not even penetrate the thin piece of lead covering it. Even if the U.S. authorities had been scanning the boats entering the marina with the new radiation monitors "Homeland Security" had been bragging about, a small likelihood, no telltale emission would penetrate either the lead or the seawater surrounding the keel.

Suddenly he could wait no longer and made tracks for the marine head. Gratefully relieving his bladder, he gained back some of his composure.

What am I doing? he suddenly thought. Needles of fear pierced his heart. He had left the keel compartment open for any of the crew to see! He raced back down, and with relief flooding his every pore, saw that everything was as he had left it. *Damn it*, he was going to have to be more careful. He went back and looked at the device again. Sure enough, the same lights were blinking on the display as on his remote. He went over the plan as he had thousands of times in the past five months. Those blinking red lights on the device told him it was armed, but was not set to explode until he gave it the coded signal on his remote. Even then, he could disable the device from the remote with another coded transmission. This was a safety feature that Hossein had insisted on, in case of some unforeseen occurrence. Walid would then have to rearm the device with his remote, from no further than fifty feet, the limit of the Radio Shack garage-door opener IR transmitter they had installed. Thanks be to Allah for the consumer electronics available in America! Walid was grateful for this failsafe feature; it showed the faith Hossein had in him to trigger the device and fly to martyrdom.

Walid went back on deck. The crew had vanished, well on their way back to Tijuana with their hard-earned cash. He knew the trip back from Ensenada had been long and tiresome, motoring all the way, but they had made more money than they would have in a year of labor. Retracing his steps back to the "keel," Walid took a deep breath and tapped in the safety-off code on his remote. Both the remote and the bomb reacted immediately: one of the blinking red lights went to a steady green. There would now be a thirty minute window during which he must place the "fire!" order. He input the safety code so that he could rethink his final moves. He wanted to be absolutely sure he went to martyrdom in peace with himself. He casually looked down at the remote, expecting to see the red light blinking again, but it was still a steady green! And so was the display on the bomb! He had been tricked; they didn't have confidence he could go through with it!

Thirty minutes, that's all he had. Suddenly the dreams all made sense. He was being dragged to a fate he didn't want, and bringing with him thousands of innocents, and not just Sarah. He raced to his car and fled the marina. He had to warn everyone, but how? If it were only like television, Kiefer Sutherland could be here, disarm the bomb, and everything would be fine. But this wasn't a television show with omnipotent heroes; this was a real, desperate situation, one that was all his doing. He wasn't headed to heaven; he was going to be despised as no one since Hitler. He grabbed his cell phone, no sense worrying about his identity; they would know soon enough who was responsible. He dialed 911 (that was funny, wasn't it?) as he raced east on the Marina freeway.

"Nine-one-one emergency, what is the nature of your call?' came the even, female voice on the phone.

"A bomb is set to go off in the marina, a nuclear bomb!" he cried into the tiny phone.

"Who is this, please? This is a serious matter, making false threats is a federal offense."

"What's the difference who it is, there's a bomb going to go off in less than twenty minutes—Marina del Rey!"

"Hold sir, I'm connecting with the shift officer, it will only be a moment."

Walid flung the phone out the window onto the freeway and headed straight for the apartment where he knew Sarah would be waiting, expecting a nice dinner. He had just reached the Sunset Boulevard exit from the 405 when the sky lit up like a thousand suns.

Chapter 17

December 2013

Uri and Lara sat across the table from each other in the small lunchroom. They had grown into a certain easiness with each other, but there had been no romance; it had remained all business. Lara noted with a slight smile that Uri had given up his Mossad-style short-sleeve, open-neck shirt for the more FBI-style pale blue long-sleeve version, complete with muted tie, and had even added the dark blue jacket. At least he didn't stand out like Lawrence of Arabia, or the Israeli version of him.

The break about the web pages had set them out with a jolt of excitement; all of the teams had been shunted off the email circuits and onto academic-looking web pages. Unfortunately, there were literally millions of them, all in their own format. Usually in a criminal investigation, the agents had at least one crime to use as a paradigm. Here they had nothing but a threat, and a veiled one at that. Some of the web pages were legitimate exercises or assignments, distributed by professors all across the country. The addresses were usually unhelpful; sometimes they identified the college of origin, mostly they were anonymous. The identifiers were distributed in class, to avoid computer vandalism. But, in addition to that, some students wrote their own web pages, with amateur criticisms, jokes and ribaldry posing as academic information. The volume was staggering, and growing daily. Fortunately, the agents were used to lengthy, boring tasks; it was part of being an FBI agent. They all hated to think it, let alone say it, but if they only had an incident, however small, that they could work backward from...

Uri was drinking his usual black tea, Lara her lightened coffee, when the omnipresent CNN program on the television set over the microwave ovens suddenly went into its "Breaking News" mode. Just about everyone stopped and watched, at first with only mild interest; probably just another Anna Nicole type thing...

The voice of the blond newswoman was shaking as she read the paper in front of her. In the split-screen, a huge outdoor fire could be seen blazing away. This video feed brought everyone in the lunchroom to full attention. "We have just been informed that a blast, presumably a bomb, has felled a number of buildings in the fashionable Marina del Rey district on the west side of Los Angeles. There are casualties, but it is not yet known the extent of the deaths, injuries or damage to the city. As of now, and this is very preliminary, the damage appears to be limited to the pleasure-boat harbor called "Marina del Rey...," She paused at this obvious redundancy, then regained her composure. "...and about ten surrounding blocks. Eyewitnesses report seeing a 'mushroom cloud' over the area, giving rise to speculation of a nuclear device, but the chief of police has assured us that there is no evidence of such a device, and that it is most likely that a warehouse containing paint and solvents, common in this area, was the source of the explosion. Investigators, as well as emergency medical teams are already on the scene, and the police assures us there will be further announcements as they become available."

"Jesus Christ," someone in the lunchroom muttered quietly. Cell phones were out and buzzing all over the room. Chairs scraped the floor and fell over as agents hurried to their offices. Lara and Uri just looked at each other. Each knew what the other was thinking: you wanted an incident, you got one. They shot up to their office to check the official wire. They immediately switched on their office TV, also tuned to CNN.

The emergency FBI internal news wire was displayed on a closed circuit television set mounted into the wall opposite the windows. This monitor was always on, but the sound could be muted, if desired. The bottom half of the screen was devoted to emergency orders to various arms of the government agencies: FBI, CIA, Homeland Security, and the Secret Service. Orders were displayed as a constantly moving list of coded entries, much like the monitors at airports showing flight departures and arrivals.

This was a redundant feature, of course. All federal agents were required to have their beepers and cell phones on at all times. The top half of the screen was showing the same feed as CNN, which had been patched in from one of the local Los Angeles networks. Lara was nervously switching the sound between the official and the CNN broadcasts.

Outside, in the hall, there was a feeling of muted bedlam, as agents responded to their beepers and carried on hushed conversations on their phones. All of this while they raced around the hallway in panic mode. A few agents crowded into the office with Uri and Lara. They eventually focused on the slightly more intelligible CNN report. Then, the official set on the other wall gave three warning blasts: an important announcement was imminent. Lara turned off the sound on the CNN channel and turned up the official set.

The live feed, now filled the entire screen, preempting the digital order display. On it, a tanned, fit-looking man in a blue suit talked into a hand-held microphone as he stood outside the Los Angeles Federal Building. The blaze was clearly visible in the background. "This is Special Agent Farley, FBI. We have confirmed an explosive device was responsible for today's incident.

"Damage is limited to a ten square block area adjacent to the Marina, as well, of course, as the Marina itself. It is completely destroyed. The blast is certain to have originated in the Marina. Casualties have been estimated, and this is only an estimate at this point, at seven thousand dead and twenty thousand injured. Local hospitals, fortunately, have been able to respond to the scene, and triage has been set up on Lincoln Boulevard." Lincoln Boulevard, Lara knew, ran parallel to the ocean a few blocks inland from the Marina.

Agent Farley paused to listen to his headset. "Yes, all plane, road and harbor traffic is halted. Only emergency personnel are permitted access." He listened again. "There is speculation, and only speculation, at this point, that a nuclear device was responsible." He again paused and listened to his earpiece. "The radiation detectors are going nuts, that's how!" His eyes shifted from side to side in embarrassment at this unprofessional exclamation. Someone, it appeared, had recruited this guy from a Journalism school somewhere. He regained his waxy composure and continued, "Sorry, the huge response from the radiation detectors leave little doubt that it was a nuclear device of some sort." Back to the earpiece. "No, we are not publishing this information to the public as yet. We don't want any more panic than we've already got."

Listening again, Agent Farley's brow furrowed. "The Hazmat guys are reasonably certain it was not a 'dirty' bomb. The signature looks more like... Wait a minute, I got something else coming in from Hazmat." Silence again.

"They've got some pieces, small pieces of..." Then the screen went blank.

Chapter 18

Walid waited as the freeway came almost to a standstill, while drivers and stopped to gaze in horror at the mushroom cloud in the west. Then emergency vehicles started pouring down the southbound 405, headed toward the Marina. Walid wound his way slowly to his apartment, his head in turmoil. His immediate feeling of accomplishment was tempered by the realization that he had been duped by those he had trusted. For some reason now he had to know that Sarah was all right. What was happening to him? He had never had any conscious feeling of regret for what he was about to do. Sarah, her family, their friends, and all the others who had died at his hand this morning, were all part of the Zionist conspiracy to take the world away from the true believers. The words from the Holy Quran, (Al-Anfal 8: 6), that were drummed into his head so often in his training, repeated themselves in his head:

"Make ready for them all thou canst of armed force, that thereby ye may dismay the enemy of Allah and your enemy, and others beside them whom ye know not. Allah knoweth them. Whatsoever ye spend in the way of Allah it will be repaid to you in full, and ye will not be wronged"
"...and others beside them whom ye know not..."

He considered again those astonishing words. So what if he had killed, or more accurately, helped kill tens of thousands of innocent people. In Allah's eyes they were not innocent! He had carried out the will of Allah, and he would reap the benefits when he passed on to Paradise:
"...eighty thousand servants, seventy-two virgin wives..."

118

These words also rang in his brain as he tried helplessly to reconcile his tremendous feelings of guilt with his knowledge of Islam and the teachings of the Holy Prophet. His hands were shaking as he finally arrived home. Inside he found the television on full blast, and Sarah shrieking in horror.

"Oh, Walid, I'm so glad you're all right! Oh my God, do you know what's happened? They blew up the whole Marina, all those people down there, they're all dead! My God, who would do this kind of thing? Here, in the United States?" She was shrieking and wailing, crying in utter despair, as she clutched desperately at him. "My parents, Walid, they were at the Ritz Carlton in the Marina for some kind of party, I can't get hold of them! What are we going to do?"

"Just a minute, Sarah, OK, calm down, I'm sure they're all right," he said as he pried loose from her desperate grasp and headed briskly for the bathroom. He realized suddenly that his bowels had released. Now his humiliation was truly complete. He jumped into the shower, clothes and all, trying in vain to cleanse both his body and his conscience. Finally, having done the best he could, he pulled off his wet, filthy clothing and threw them in the hamper. Then he emerged to the bedroom to find something to put on.

Sarah did not even notice him; she was still in a state of total horror. "Walid, where were you? Did you see it? Oh, my God, what are we going to do?"

He was finally able to decipher some of what the blond newswoman on CNN was saying: "The authorities aren't certain yet if the blast was nuclear in origin. No word on anyone or group taking responsibility. Everyone is urged to stay off the roads, and to stay away from the Westside at all costs. Emergency vehicles are on their way, and the injured are being evacuated as rapidly as possible. The local hospitals are overwhelmed; blood donors are urgently needed..."

Sarah clung to him again, still crying, "Oh, Walid, you're all I have left. Thank God you're alive!" She rocked back and forth, pulling him with her, overcome with grief. He felt exactly like the waste he had just washed down the shower drain. "What are we going to do?"

Just then the phone rang; it was their friend Josh Green. "Sarah, are you OK? What about your family?"

"I'm OK, Josh, but I don't know about my parents; they were in the Marina. Oh my God..." The tears started flowing again.

"Listen, Sarah," Josh said, "There's an emergency meeting down at the Veteran's Center, starting in a few minutes. All the latest word on the missing people is supposed to be available there. Come on down. Is Walid there?"

Sarah looked over at Walid, who could hear both ends of the conversation through the speaker-phone. He nodded approval of the idea; anything to get her to stop wailing, and give him some time to think. "Yes, let's go, maybe we'll hear something. Come on, we can take your car, I'll drive." He was afraid of what he might have left in his car. In any case he didn't want to be in it, and certainly not have Sarah in it.

She continued to cry and shake as they drove north on 405 to the Veteran's Center in Woodland Hills, for decades a bedroom community with a large Jewish population. Police were everywhere, directing traffic, indicating parking areas, and moving the dazed crowd into the building. As Sarah and Walid headed for the door, they saw Josh Green and David Grossman waiting for them. "Those sons of bitches," David was muttering over and over again, shaking his head.

"Come on," Josh said, "Nobody even knows who did it yet!"

"Yeah, right," said an older man who overheard their conversation, "It's probably the Serbs getting revenge for Kosovo. Who would it be but the Arabs?"

"Come on, Mike, don't start up out here," a woman in her 60's, clearly his wife, chided him, as she pulled him by the arm.

Inside the large hall, people were milling around, some crying, some shrieking. Against one wall an elderly man stood, garbed in traditional Jewish prayer attire, rocking back and forth, as indecipherable words trickled from his mouth.

"Will everyone please try to find a seat?" A large man in military uniform was trying to control the disorganized crowd. "We have all the latest information for you. There's a board at the back of the hall where we have a preliminary list of the ... casualties... that we've identified so far. There's also a roster where you can register the names of your family and loved ones, and we'll try to get a match with the unidentified survivors."

"Who did this, that's what we want to know?" A large, middle-aged man with a full black beard screamed at the man on the podium, while shaking his fist in anger.

"And what are we doing about it?" A woman in front was yelling and crying simultaneously.

The military man spoke over the noisy crowd, using the powerful public address system: "We don't know for sure yet who's responsible, but we have a pretty good idea of the origin of the...bomb."

"It was a bomb!?" Someone in the front row hollered loud enough for the military man to hear.

"Yes, unfortunately, we know that it was a fission device, a nuclear bomb."

The huge crowd went wild in anger, sorrow and disbelief. Weeping was the overwhelming sound, echoing in the large space.

"But, wait, everyone, please wait," the man on the podium tried anxiously to soothe the angry crowd. "We have every reason to believe the damage was contained to the immediate area around the marina, and the wind is pushing the radiation offshore. Communication systems are in working order all over the city, except for the area west of Lincoln. Even the airport, miraculously, is pretty much intact, though all flights have been suspended."

"How many people...?" A tremulous voice came from somewhere in the crowd.

"We're not sure yet, but it looks like a few thousand, probably like 9/11. It could have been much worse..."

"Who did this, like we don't know already?" The bearded man was in full fury.

"As I said, we don't have a credible communication of responsibility at this point, but all indications point to a Middle-Eastern source..."

Walid sat transfixed; he somehow had divorced himself, at least for the time being, from his responsibility. While he knew he should now be feeling the euphoria of triumph, he was overcome by the grief that was all around him. When he had been in the *madrassah*, planning the attack, it had all been so surreal. The only thing that mattered was the furthering of the Jihad, returning the world to the true faith of Islam. Destruction of the decadent West was an abstract goal; certainly people had to die, but they were infidels, nonbelievers, and their elimination was an unpleasant but necessary part of the overall plan. It was like brushing unwanted ants off the picnic table. But now, these were real people he had killed, people who had befriended him, loved him even. At the same time the people he had trusted these past years, whose bidding he had faithfully carried out, had not trusted him.

He said to Sarah, "I have to go outside for a minute, I think I'm going to be sick." He stumbled out of the meeting hall and walked around the block, his whole being in turmoil. For about fifteen minutes Walid considered his alternatives: Sheikh Nasrallah, Hossein and the rest of the network would think he had been obliterated in the Marina. If he didn't make contact, they would have no reason to suspect he was still alive. Likewise, he had left no trail to connect him with the blast. In his imagination, he had envisioned his name being associated with the strike; yet, in the end he had not taken public credit. True, in the days and weeks to come, the truth might well surface, either from his side or theirs. He knew Hezbollah would take credit, and make the demands concerning U.S. support for Israel; that had been the plan all along. Whether they would name him as the main perpetrator was doubtful; why should they make the FBI's job any easier? They certainly didn't want to open any trail to the other operatives and the potential coming strikes. No, he decided, this was not the time for him to do anything rash, and bring down the wrath of either side upon him. He returned to the meeting hall, still lost in fear and despair.

Chapter 19

December 2013

Deke Trotter replaced the phone and sat, ashen faced. Lara and Uri had rushed up there in response to both their beepers. In the years Lara had worked under his command, she had never seen him in such a state of grim disbelief. Even during 9/11, when the events were unfolding on news television in front of everyone in the Bureau, there had been no sense of imminent doom. Early on in those attacks, it had been clear to the Bureau who was involved, and they knew at once that quick retribution would result. It was true that some in the Bureau were faulted for not having stopped the perps as soon as they had requested flight instruction. But their excuse was immediate: how were they to act under the constant threat of "violation" of civil rights, even of these Muslim visa-holders. They were in the country legally, with no restriction on their right to attend flight school.

Today's blast in Los Angeles, even though less catastrophic than first feared, must have some consequences not yet disclosed. Lara could plainly see that something much more threatening than 9/11 was occurring now. It had been barely an hour since the first reports. She didn't have to wait long for the answer. Trotter handed her a one-page white paper, fresh off the Bureau's "eyes-only" printer. The borders of the page were painted with bright red diagonal slashes, indicating it must not leave the room. She read it quickly, with a mixture of fear and anxiety:

"To the infamous leaders of the villainous State of the United States of America:

Today you have seen a demonstration of the power of the Islamic Revolution. Through the hands of the Hizbollah, and its blessed leader, the most glorious and revered Sheikh Sayyed Hassan Nasrallah, the wrath of the blessed Prophet has rained down destruction upon the Zionist center known as Los Angeles. This ruinous event is only a precursor to the destruction that will befall your infidel State if you do not accede to the demands of the Islamic Revolution, as defined in this letter.

The illegitimate Zionist State known in radical Western world as "Israel," but which in historical fact is the country of Palestine, must cease to exist. The Zionist State exists only at the pleasure of the United States, who continues to provide it with military and financial aid. This aid serves to prolong the existence of this illegal State, and continue the enslavery of the true residents of Palestine. To end this slavery and illegal occupation of Palestine, the United States must end its aid to the Zionists.

An Act of the United States Congress must be passed within thirty days of the receipt of this pronouncement. This Act will end immediately all U.S. aid, both military and financial to the illegal Zionist State. Furthermore, all private financial aid to the Zionists will be deemed illegal under the terms of aid to 'terrorist organizations,' which include the 'Israel Defense Forces,' 'Hadassah,' and any other organization that provides money and comfort to the illegal State. Finally, aid to the true citizens of the State of Palestine, under the names of Hizbollah, Hamas, and Islamic Jihad, which heretofore have illegitimately been deemed illegal, shall now be permitted, and given tax-exempt status, so that the true citizens of Palestine will be able to rebuild their country.

The current occupiers of Palestine, who in actuality are Europeans, will be allowed to emigrate, so long as they leave all property to the true citizens, the Palestinians. Hizbollah will assume control of the land from the Jordan river to the Mediterranean Sea, from the boundary with Lebanon in the north to the State of Egypt in the South. Practice of religions other than Islam will be forbidden. The city of Jerusalem will become the holy shrine of the Dome of the Rock, and all infidel structures will be removed.

If these terms are not met, the following will occur: nuclear devices similar to the one today in Los Angeles will be detonated

in other major U.S. cities at the rate of one per week. They will be much more powerful than the sample of today. Losses of persons and property will be extensive. This plan is already in motion. We cannot and will not be stopped. Act now to save your country.
Allah be praised!"

"Are they for real?" Lara asked.

"It looks like it," Trotter replied. "This just came from Al Jazeera. They're holding off on publication for five days, for us to come up with a response."

"Wow," she muttered, "that's something for Al Jazeera."

"Yeah, even they don't want to be accused of starting a World War based on a phony claim."

"What makes you think they're for real?" she repeated.

"The Hazmat teams in LA have come up with some preliminary analysis. Fortunately, the office out there cut that moron Farley off the air, even the closed-circuit, before he could let out any more information. Hazmat sent some drones up to sample the air for radiation, and there's plenty. As you know, we lucked out. The Santa Anas were blowing, and pushed the main plume out over the ocean, rather than into the city. The radiation east of the Marina area is relatively low, thank God. The wind is blowing pretty heavy. That's probably saved a few hundred thousand lives. But we don't know yet whether it was a real nuke or a conventional bomb covered with radioactive material, a 'dirty bomb.'"

"When will they know?" Uri asked.

"The official word, for now, is that it had to be a small dirty bomb, and there is limited danger to the public. All roads and airports are shut down to all but military traffic. I'm hoping by midnight, we'll have more definite information. What we need to know immediately, is who was responsible. So far, all we have is this letter."

Uri finally entered the conversation, "It's Hezbollah, like the letter says. It's the gang I've been following; the ones who've been shooting rockets at us for years. Nasrallah is their leader."

"Probably, "but we're not sure. It could just as easily be Hamas, using the Hezbollah name to throw us off." Trotter turned

125

to Lara. "That's where you come in. We want you to go through the emails and find the links to the agents in the U.S."

"If they're Hezbollah, Uri is the best source we've got. He's been on their trail for twenty years, and has plenty of scalps."

Trotter nodded. "The President and State want to keep the threat out of the press as long as possible. Of course, that limits us to the five days Al Jazeera has given us,…and we've already started counting." Come up with whatever you can. Nobody goes home tonight."

Chapter 20

December 2013

U.S Ambassador to Israel, William Paxton Doring, hurriedly dressed as he recalled the events of the last half hour. He had been watching the news on CNN, when the story broke about the Los Angeles blast. He immediately got a call from the U.S. State Department on the secure satellite line, and then a fax with the terrorist demand letter. A short coded message was also sent to the Israeli Prime Minister, with a note saying that Doring would be bringing the full threat to the PM's office in Jerusalem, immediately.

According to Al Jazeera, the source who delivered the message was a Hezbollah insider; he had the creds to prove it. In any case, no other terrorist group had claimed responsibility. Doring was also to personally deliver the U.S. assurances on the matter, in the form of an official faxed letter.

He looked himself over in the full-length hall mirror. This was not the time to look sloppy or ill-prepared, despite the late hour. The posting was a major step upward for Doring. He had been ambassador in Ghana, Ireland and Peru. When the old ambassador in Israel retired, he was asked to consider the posting. It didn't take him long to accept. At age 55, he was getting worried about the end of his career. He spoke no Hebrew, but that was not considered a liability. All the Israelis spoke English, and if they wanted to speak privately, while in his presence, they had only to switch to Hebrew.

It was 11 P.M. in Israel. He had alerted his driver and security guard; they were ready within minutes. The young black driver and the lean, blond muscular lieutenant were both ready and waiting; they were U.S. Marines and supremely confident. Doring

127

entered the black Lincoln Town Car, as he had so many other times, the lieutenant holding the rear door; Doring just muttered "Jerusalem."

Despite an act of the U.S. Congress, authorizing the movement of the U.S. Embassy from Tel Aviv to Jerusalem, the President had so far failed to do so. He feared fierce retaliation from the oil-rich Arab States if the U.S. officially recognized Jerusalem as the capital of Israel.

It took less than an hour for them to travel the 60 km or so to the capital. As they traveled the winding, pitted road, storm clouds rolled down from the Judean hills, pelting the car with angry sheets of rain. *This road is dangerous enough in daylight*, Doring thought. *I would hate to die ingloriously in a collision with a donkey cart.*

As they slowly rose into the hills leading to Jerusalem, the rain changed to snow, the landscape an eerie white in the moonlight. Just after midnight, the black Town Car with the diplomatic plates arrived at the gates of the Israeli capitol building. It flew no flag; there was no need to alert any terrorists on the route. The guards at the gate recognized the car immediately, but went ahead with the check of identification.

The car was stopped at the concrete barriers outside the entrance to the underground parking garage. All official guests were allowed to park here alongside the prime minister and other government officials. Other, unofficial guests, visitors and household staff parked in the large, fenced-in outdoor parking area. The car was searched, inside and out, and the three men checked for identification and for weapons. Finally, after manipulating the three sharp U-turns, meant to stop any unwanted vehicles from making it into the building, the Town Car came to rest at one of the two spots reserved for the U.S. Embassy. Here they were met by a young Israeli army sergeant, who escorted Doring up to the conference room, while his driver and guard were taken to a waiting area, known locally as "the Green Room."

The emergency meeting was already in progress, as Doring had expected. He waited patiently for the sergeant at arms to admit him. Inside, the Israeli cabinet was in disarray, dismayed by the lack of public and private support for their tiny country. They had already been informed, albeit unofficially, of the terrorist demands and the U.S. position. Public polls in the U.S. had already been taken and were not assuring. Could it be that the world had gone so mad that it could not see the fate that awaited it?

"So what do we do now?" the diminutive Israeli foreign minister asked. Reis Har-Even was the son of Holocaust survivors, and was the physical opposite of his name, which was Hebrew for "giant." He was, however, a brilliant diplomat who could negotiate with anyone. He spoke eight languages, some, including English, without an accent. Har-Even had primary responsibility for keeping the American diplomats, both Republican and Democrat, firmly in Israel's camp.

"We wait," the PM said with finality. "We all know what happens if the Americans comply." This was an unsaid reference to the deadly response that would be unleashed if the U.S. were to accede to the Hezbollah demands. He then motioned for the sergeant at arms to admit the ambassador.

The cabinet here in Israel, as Doring had quickly learned prior to his posting, was far different from the U.S. or other cabinets he had been privy to. These men, and they were all men at the time, represented the whole spectrum of political philosophy. It was not uncommon to hear them all shouting at each other across the mahogany conference table. However, when Doring was admitted they became respectfully quiet, and the PM welcomed him in English. He stood and briefly acknowledged Doring to the cabinet, all of whom he knew well.

They shook hands warmly. Despite his calm exterior, however, the prime minister was uneasy. Doring could see his hands trembling ever so slightly. Doring, every bit the career diplomat, impeccably dressed, a full head of white hair, straight of stature, did not reveal his recognition of the PM's discomfort. Doring's job was simple: to carry out the orders sent him by the State Department. His instructions had been firm: we do not negotiate with terrorists, period. Doring handed the prime minister the terrorist demands and the official letter of response from the State Department. The PM quickly read them and passed them around the table. There was nothing unexpected in its contents. In the past two hours, everyone here had witnessed the Los Angeles tragedy and heard the contents of the Hezbollah threat.

Doring knew, despite the strongly worded message in his diplomatic pouch, what was not specifically stated. The official position of the U.S. government, of course, was to never negotiate with terrorists. But everything was fluid, especially when national security was threatened. Save your own skin first.

The prime minister was somewhat the antithesis of Ambassador Doring. While Doring was dressed in a blue pinstripe suit and red tie, the PM was attired in his usual short-sleeve sport shirt and casual slacks. He was from the "old school," one of the few remaining pioneers who helped mold the State right after World War II. He was short, nearly bald, with just a few white strands of hair carelessly strewn across his large head. He wore reading glasses that looked as if they came from a drug store counter. He had survived all the crises that had tormented the young State in the past sixty or so years. But this one was different, it seemed to him.

After greeting the ambassador, the PM stroked the few remaining strands of hair on his head. The "ultimatum," to be broadcast on Al Jazeera in five days time, would be met with a mixed response from the American public, both he and Doring were sure. Although the terrorist letter had not yet been made public, the American people were pretty sure, after the disaster of 9/11, that Muslim radicals were responsible. Even before they knew the exact source of the terror, there was a huge polarization of opinion. If the instant polls taken right after the blast could be believed, forty percent or more wanted the government to quickly accede to any terrorist demands. Another twenty were ready for a full-scale attack on any country involved. The remainder either didn't have an opinion or were willing to leave it up to Homeland Security.

"How is it that forty percent of Americans think that giving in to the Arabs will give them any security against more attacks?" the deputy PM asked.

The PM just looked at Ari ben Nathan, sighed, and told him, it seemed for the tenth time: "First of all the U.S. public doesn't know yet who it is that's responsible. But they can guess. The U.S.

citizenry is bombarded by Arab propaganda, through all their media. There are newspapers, magazines, and websites that carry anti-Semitic and anti-Zionist messages constantly. There is no censorship of any of it, no matter how blatantly false."

The PM had actually directed part of this speech to Doring, though he knew full well Doring was aware of the situation, and partly to Har-Even. It was something of a reprimand for the foreign minister's lack of success in countering the pro-Arab press. He now excused himself from the cabinet, turning his attention totally to Doring, as the two of them headed for the PM's private office.

The prime minister's office, on the same floor as the conference room was in sharp contrast to the "Oval Office" in the White House. Doring had been there on only two occasions, but its opulence was engraved in his memory. In the prime minister's office a large but unadorned wooden desk held forth at the one large window, overlooking the circular drive and the armed guard who patrolled constantly. The carpet, plain, austere dark blue and the State flag, a large blue Star of David on a white background, hung on a wooden staff to the right. Somewhat surprisingly, to one who hadn't been there before, was the smaller American flag that was planted to the left. Three comfortable leather chairs were placed around the desk, in addition to the large, high-backed chair the PM used. It was well known that he had chronic back problems and the chair had some sort of therapeutic devices.

Pictures of ex-prime ministers and other noteworthy Israelis hung on the walls. Directly behind the prime minister's desk, on either side of the window, were large photos of Chaim Weizmann and David Ben-Gurion. Pictures of the other prime ministers and famous Zionists graced the other walls of the room. The favorite of all was the one of General Moshe Dayan that hung on the wall opposite the PM's desk. It was the classic picture of the famous hero of the Six-Day War, the war that had changed forever the international status of the young democracy.

The PM placed himself gingerly into his chair, sighed slightly, and motioned Doring into the chair at his right. "What are our options?" The PM lit a cigarette, his hand still shaking; he did not even try to hide it. At 70, he was old, even by Israeli political standards.

This was arguably the worst situation the tiny nation had to deal with since its birth sixty years ago. The United States had always been there to give a helping hand, even as a last resort, should it ever come to that.

But now, today, this threat to peace came at a time when most Americans were tired of being involved in armed strife in the Middle East. The terrible mistake of the Iraq invasion was now seen as aiding the terrorists responsible for the 9/11 attack, rather than quelling them. There was strong sentiment for appeasement, rather than confrontation, especially if it meant avoiding loss of American lives. Of course, there was the element that would see the nuclear attack on an American city as a call to arms; but again the bitter experience in Iraq was too fresh. If it came to a political judgment, there was no clear outcome at hand. It would be far better if the problem could be snuffed out without arousing the populace.

Doring knew that the President's instructions were valid only for the time being; if the terrorists could not be caught in the next five days, there might be a ground swell of public support for capitulation to almost any demands. To many in the U.S., Israel was of little use; its annihilation could ease the situation in the Middle East by giving the Arabs dominion over the entire area. Then they could fight it out with each other, as they had done for ages. Fewer and fewer remembered the disaster at Munich in 1938, when Britain had yielded to the demands of the Nazis, and brought on the slaughter of tens of millions worldwide in World War II.

"We figure we only have the five days, maybe a couple more. If we can stop them from their next demonstration, their next nuclear bomb, in other words, the pacifists won't have too much momentum. We're hoping our field team can bring these guys in; it looks like it's just a small splinter group of Hezbollah, not a whole government, like Iran or Syria."

"You mean we have confirmation from their embassies?" the PM asked eagerly?

"Unfortunately, not yet," replied Doring. "But we do have feelers out. It looks like nobody wants to take sides here until the smoke clears." He immediately regretted the metaphor. "Meanwhile, this team we have working is our best hope."

"What team is this?"

"A few months ago, one of your Mossad agents found an important document on an excursion into Lebanon." Doring looked at the PM for confirmation. That it was unacceptable under the terms of the ongoing peace negotiations was clear. By the look on the PM's face, it was clear that he knew of the raid, and that it would have to be "acceptable" under these new circumstances.

"That agent, Uri Levin, was transferred to FBI headquarters shortly after that, you know."

The PM just shrugged. Of course he knew.

"He has been working with our top internet cryptologist, who also happens to be a terrific field agent. They've been sent out to L.A. to pick up the trail..."

"Two people against a dedicated bunch of suicidal lunatics with nuclear bombs?" The PM came out of his chair, the pain in his back notwithstanding.

"Don't forget they have the resources of the FBI, CIA and Mossad behind them. They've already made some remarkable progress. We think we have Hezbollah's communications network compromised."

"And if another bomb goes off in the U.S., is there a chance the government would negotiate with these thugs?" The PM did not seem to be optimistic about the chances of these two agents bringing down the Hezbollah network in the U.S.

Doring paused, seemed to think carefully about what he was going to say. "How much say do you have in the matter? I mean, will the cabinet go along with your action or lack thereof?"

"Well, of course they know the terms; they saw the letter. If and when the demands are made public, it's a whole different story. The country will come to a standstill; but after all, it's happened before—I mean a nuclear threat. But never to our strongest ally. The fear will be that the U.S. might even consider these demands. But for now, the cabinet, at least, will stand behind me, and you, with whatever the U.S. decides to do. What else can we do?"

Doring paused again. Then he said tersely, "We're laying it all on the line with these two agents. Frankly, there wasn't enough time to assemble a whole team at this late date..."

"You mean you have people to handle this kind of thing, but they need more lead time? How can that be? These terrorist attacks always come without warning, don't they?"

"Not really. We've stopped a number of attacks in the making, as you know. Airports, the Port Authorities, a couple of nuclear power plants. We let Homeland Security take credit when we can, to show the world we're on top of the matter, and of course, justify the budget. But these guys caught us by surprise. The problem was that there's so few of them, nobody to rat them out to our field agents. The only crack in their dike was this computer network break we got, and the papers your man picked up in that raid in Lebanon. Without that information to go on, we'd really be up shit's creek.

"Sorry, Doring said. "I forget sometimes you're not familiar with all our little sayings. The whole thing goes 'Up shit's creek without a paddle.' You get the idea."

"I get it. You're telling me that our whole future is riding on one of our field agents who happens to know Arabic, and one of your desk agents who knows a lot about computers."

"She's actually a terrific field agent, too. She also consolidated all our electronic intercept programs into one all-inclusive routine that has them pretty well pegged. We think we can spot their next move." This last claim was a little ad lib on Doring's part, but he wanted to give the PM as much confidence as possible. A rogue effort set out by Mossad now could jeopardize the whole case. "And they've been working together for months now, strictly on this case. The fact that this little gang is the one with the bombs is actually a break for us. We don't want to tip them off by starting a major campaign, and scare them off to a point where we have no trace on them at all. The fact that it's a small group means we may be able to stamp out all of them, and maybe get a lead on their handlers back in Syria, Iran, or wherever."

"So what you're telling me is that we're gambling on two people to save our whole country from international blackmail. Is there a backup plan, just in case…?"

Doring said nothing. He had gone out on the limb far enough as it was. "I've told you everything I know, that's the honest truth." The two men looked each other straight in the eye, but said nothing. All the words had been spoken.

"I appreciate your candor, I really do," the PM said flatly as he took the other man's hand in both his own, and gave him a firm handshake. "We'll count on your success; just keep us in the loop,"

"I will."

As Doring strode out the door, the PM grabbed his red phone and got the chief of the IDF, the Israeli Defense Forces.

"Izzy, it's bad," he said grimly on the ultra-secure line. "Get ready for 'Ekdikeo,' we've got about five days, max."

On the other end of the line General Yitzhak Weiss sat speechless for a few seconds, then asked for confirmation: "Is this red or yellow?"

"It's the yellow bird right now, Izzy, get ready to fly."

"I'll get things rolling, give me notice with the go code."

"You got it, hope for the best."

Weiss sat motionless in his chair for nearly a minute before picking up his interoffice phone. "Ekdikeo" was the ancient biblical word for the vengeance of the Lord, and, if carried out as planned, it might seem to the world as if it were. The plan was the drastic measure that would be adopted if the nation found itself with its back against the wall. It was an attack against its most antagonistic neighbors that was so severe it would strain relations with Israel's most friendly allies. Its existence was well known among all the Arab nations, and of course Iran as well. It was meant to be. The hope was that it would never have to be used.

Israel's entire military would be involved: Army, Navy and Air Force. In his head, Weiss saw the various weapons and their delivery apparatus. They were formidable indeed. The first assault would be from both sea and land. Warships just off the Lebanese coast carried Harpoon missile launchers. These missiles, with their range of 130km., could easily reach all major Syrian cities and military targets,

Simultaneous with the attack from the sea would be surface-to-surface attacks from hidden bases inside Israel; with their Jericho long-range rocket systems, whose capability was awesome. With a conventional payload, it could knock out several city blocks; with a nuclear payload... He shuddered as he imagined the worldwide reaction to the damage inflicted by these blasts.

Then there would be air assaults from the fleet of F16's, F-4's, and F-15's, unleashing multiple warhead rockets to take out airfields, anti aircraft installations and other military targets. Closer in, the "SPICE" system would allow the attacking aircraft to destroy the target without getting into the enemy's threat zone. Since it's not dependent on coordinates fed to it by satellite, the Israeli-made missile can't be jammed. Nor can it be fooled by false coordinates sent by the enemy.

Finally, to protect the homeland against an air-based counter-attack, there is the LAR-160 "Arrow" Light Artillery Rocket System, a multiple rocket launcher mounted on a mobile platform. Its clustered warheads have ranges up to 45 km, far more advanced than the system successfully used against the Scud missile attacks vainly launched by the Iraqis in 1991.

The Arab countries knew *about* these systems, but not their specifics. The threat of their use would severely curtail any ambitions of a preemptive attack on Israel, but now the PM must have something else on his mind: a threat must already exist. Weiss sighed deeply, then started the calls to his officers he had hoped never to have to make. His one shard of optimism, though dim at this point, was that the signal to unleash these deadly forces had not yet been made; it was still code "yellow." This meant there was some diplomatic or other effort ongoing.

Reluctantly, Weiss called each of the eight men who would be responsible for setting loose the horrors of Ekdikeo. Then, he sat back in his chair and lit a cigar. He turned and looked out the window at his beloved country, took a long, deep puff, and hoped with all his heart that he would soon get the call to stand down. He did not want to hear the dreaded word "red."

Chapter 21

They were desperate for any sort of lead they might garner from the web pages they had identified. They scrolled through tens of sites, those that contained suspect transmissions. It was past ten P.M. when a startled Lara cried out to Uri, "Look at this!" Instead of pasting her screen onto his, he jumped up and looked over her shoulder. On one of the pages identified by Opera, and targeted by irregular syntax, was the title: "Architectural Design 258." Underneath the title was the statement: "Next homework due by Thursday may to include bridge for Tampa-St.Petersburgh."

"Man," Uri exclaimed, "They didn't even spell the name of the city right. This has to be something. Do we have any schools with 'Architectural Design' classes?"

Lara skipped over to a list of colleges and universities with Architecture programs and quickly scanned for "Architectural Design 258." As she suspected, none existed.

"Let's check all the sites," Lara said.

A few minutes later Uri jumped up. "Look at this one!"

Lara patched in Uri's screen and saw another suspect site with an entry that read: "Construction Techniques 107A." A quick check of schools offering Civil Engineering classes dealing with construction showed no such animal. The page went on to inform the "students" that their projects dealing with a tunnel under Galveston Bay near Houston was to be moved up by a week, and they should be ready to "present to their results" by Thursday.

On they went with this apparently fruitful search. The suspect pages they were finding stood out markedly from the authentic ones. They exhausted their stock of sites in a little over an hour; four cities were potential targets: Tampa, San Francisco, Houston and Chicago. Now they had to come up with a strategy.

Uri sat at his desk considering the information they now had. Unless they could pin down the specific site, their chances for intercepting the terrorists were miniscule. They had less than five days to find the correct city, and the specific location in that city; let alone prevent the attack and apprehend the plotters. Suddenly he sat up and said, "Wait a minute!"

"What!" Lara said, startled. "What is it?!"

"Remember that story you told me when I first got here, about the fresh-water plant on Midway, in World War II? Well, maybe we could do the same thing here. Set out some false information that our boys might get worked up about, something specific for each of the target cities, and see what comes through on the web."

"Uri, you're a genius," she replied. "Let's give it a try. I think we have some pull with the newspapers, or at least our local agents should have. We'll have to keep it pretty innocuous, something that won't disrupt the local citizenry too much."

"Or the local cops. We're going to need them on our side when push comes to shove." He loved to show off his knowledge of American slang. "We need something that relates to traffic in the downtown areas, something that might get them thinking about how it will affect their getting in and out."

Lara agreed. "It has to be different for each city, but we have to try to get them all going at the same time, we can't wait for each one. I hope our local guys can handle it. Let's think up some stuff, and we'll take it to Trotter."

"Tampa-St. Petersburg and San Francisco both have major bridges; if there were going to be some repairs, closing some lanes, that ought to make them re-think things." Uri said, as he chewed on a pencil.

"Good idea. Now what about the other two?"

"Doesn't Houston have a ship channel that runs right up to the downtown from the Gulf of Mexico? That might be just the place they have in mind; so if there were going to be a lot of Coast Guard activity, say because of drug smuggling…"

"Right again," she said. "You know more about American cities than you let on."

"It's part of our training, along with learning the language. You'd be surprised how many of the terrorists we catch have gone to school here." He thought about that a moment, then said, "Well, maybe you wouldn't, after all."

She smiled at him; no, she wouldn't be surprised to find that all of them were getting their technical training in the U.S. "All right, that just leaves Chicago; any ideas on that one?"

"Major freeways, airports?"

"I don't know, that might be going a little too far," she said. "But maybe, if we kept the caution to *possible* delays..."

"Right, let's give it a shot. We have to keep the wording different, and make sure the individual perps don't know there's more than just their own city involved."

They sat down and quickly wrote out stories for publication in the local newspapers about emergency bridge work in Tampa and San Francisco, Coast Guard surveillance in Houston, and airport slowdown in Chicago.

"You know," Lara said, "These little items are bound to catch everybody's attention, now that the date's been set by the terrorists."

"That's right. So the gang has got to get their people alerted."

It took them just thirty minutes to write up the brief notices. Then Lara called Trotter and told him they needed to see him right away.

They hurried up to his office, which looked like it had been hit by a tornado. Stacks of papers and news releases lay everywhere. Several of his phone lines were blinking on hold. Assistants ran in and out, tacking status reports on a large map hanging on one wall. All four target cities, as well as Los Angeles and D.C., had several notes pinned, each with date and time. As new reports came in, the old ones were discarded. These notes reflected the status of the various tips that were flooding into the offices of the CIA, FBI and Homeland Security. Thousands of these tips came in every day; most were delegated to the "crazy bin," to which were relegated the most far-fetched and useless— like the visions of Saladin's armies landing in force on the beaches of Florida. Other, more credible reports were handed down to the local authorities for action. Only the most urgent made it to the "Big Board."

Lara briefly filled him in on their plans. He quickly agreed to have his minions contact the local field offices and get them to reach the newspapers. For now, no one at the newspapers could know the origin or the purpose of the false alerts; it would have to be just a personal favor, in the name of national security. It was inconceivable that any editor would want to be responsible for denying a mild hoax that might end up saving their city.

As they waited for further instructions, Lara mused on the false messages they were sending. "What if the Hezbollah troops catch on to our little scheme, and actually figure out that we have broken their webpage-Opera network."

Uri picked up on her thinking, "If they're smart enough to know the history of unencrypted messages, they'll know it's been done before and might become suspicious."

Lara nodded. "Especially since Fredericks and company have planted their big, flat feet right in the middle of the nest up there in Boston. No telling how many hornets they've stirred up."

"We just have to hope they think those clumsy Homeland boys are all they have to deal with."

"Let's make sure Fredericks and company don't find out about this until it's too late for them to screw it up. And hope the bad guys read the papers."

Chapter 22

December 2013

Hossein got word from CNN, just like the rest of the world. The blast had been nuclear, thanks be to Allah! But why the low body count? Sheikh Nasrallah would not be pleased; however, they had achieved their main objective, had they not? Their capacity for destruction in the "Homeland" had been proven! Their demands must be met now, he was sure of it.

The path had not been simple. The first part, by boat to the coast of Mexico had gone just as planned. He had received the innocuous-looking text message in just four days: *fish are biting, landed a big one.* Of course, the crew had been hand-selected and were well paid, commensurate with a shipment of high-quality cocaine, which is what they thought they were transporting.

But the second leg had not gone so well; the truck had broken down after just fifty miles. Fortunately, one of the crew was able to hitchhike to the next village, where he found a mechanic. After a jury-rigged repair, they had been able to limp over to Monterrey, where they had purchased a newer model. Within the next three days they had reached the west coast of the mainland at Mazatlan, and again found transport around the Baja to Ensenada, this time using a relatively new Chris Craft. Once again the experienced Mexican crew had known who to bribe to get their cargo on board and be on their way.

Then came the storm-filled voyage around the Baja. Hossein could hardly sleep as he awaited the message that they had reached Ensenada. The trip had taken nearly two weeks, with a stop at La Paz for supplies. They had to find an appropriate-looking sailboat for the trip up the coast to Los Angeles. Luck again was with them; they found a forty-five foot sloop for sale in

141

a shipyard. Again with enough dollars, a crew of locals loaded the "drugs" into the keel while minor repairs and re-supply were ongoing. The timing was perfect; they would be able to sail back to Marina del Rey along with the pack of returning yachts. The crew leader, Ramos, found an internet café and used one of the assigned web pages to post the message: *Problem 3-1 is solved with the triangle rule.* Hossein had slept well for the first time in a month; he knew the others would see the same message, and they would be pleased.

The last message was almost an afterthought. It had taken only three days, without incident, to sail into the Marina. The sail number had been recorded leaving weeks before, if anyone had actually been checking, and they slid easily into a temporary slip arranged by Walid. Walid had posted the message on the web: *The last problem uses the rule of Riemann.* That was it; the bomb was set for the next day. The message would be delivered to Al Jazeera as soon as CNN reported it.

The first news had set off jubilant displays all over the Muslim world. Cheering crowds were seen from the West Bank to Indonesia. Hossein had been ecstatic. But then came the later news of the low number of fatalities. What had gone wrong? Even if the blast had only been of the kiloton range, the prevailing onshore winds would have blown the radioactive debris right over the densely-populated, and mostly Jewish, areas of Santa Monica and Hollywood. Then he caught the latest CNN report: the winds had uncharacteristically been off-shore rather than on-shore—"Santa Anas," as they were called locally.

An East Wind, he thought bitterly, a *khamsīn*, the dreaded hot, dry wind of the desert, traditionally bringing misery and despair. After all the carefully crafted plans, a *khamsīn* had minimized the damage. Still, he told himself again, the main message had been delivered. Their capability had been demonstrated. If they could do it in Los Angeles, they could do it anywhere, and the next ones could only be more devastating. The factor of fear had been implanted; the Americans would panic and give in to any demands that would save their precious "way of life." *To hell with Israel*, they would say, *what have they done for us? Give the Arabs what they want.*

Hossein knew that the letter of demand would have been delivered by Al Jazeera by now, with the five day delay before it was made public. That gave the U.S. government time to deliberate their response before the people knew the details, but it also gave Hossein time to get his next bomb into place before there was widespread public surveillance. He knew the government would be hustling to protect all the airports and major highways, but a lone individual could still infiltrate the large cities.

He was still troubled by the lack of devastation in Los Angeles. The news had correctly identified the blast as nuclear, but he had anticipated far more destruction. The material had gone critical; he knew that. The only missing factor was the *total time* at critical. That had to be it. If he could only be sure of what the government knew...

He hadn't checked the web pages since the news hit. Quickly logging in to the "bulletin board," a page dedicated to informing all operatives of the status of events, he found a message of congratulations to himself and Walid. Using the coding provided by Opera, he immediately responded, giving all credit to Allah. He looked in the blogs for an entry from Walid, but found none. That could be due to many reasons, but not likely that he had been killed in the blast. Walid had been instructed to martyr himself, but Nasrallah had been sure he would survive. Walid was one who wanted to see the fruits of his labor before martyrdom. As soon as Walid could reach a computer he would receive his instructions.

He went back to the web bulletin board and asked Nasrallah, or, more exactly, his minions, for help in the next stage. Surely Khallad could send him one or two aides, perhaps even he would be assigned to carry out the next attack. It was unlikely that the Americans would cave in after this one, rather pitiful, assault on Los Angeles. He still had enough uranium fuel for two more devices, but one more successful explosion should bring the U.S. government to its senses.

From details he had gleaned from news reports, toxic waste teams had recovered material that proved conclusively that a uranium device had successfully been triggered; a nuclear bomb had been exploded on American soil! That meant he had brought critical mass together, at least for a split second. He needed more information before he could finish putting together the next device; for example, what exactly did the waste teams find? If he knew that he might be able to engineer the bomb to really cause some devastation. Sheikh Nasrallah must be asked for some intelligence help as well. Hossein knew that Hezbollah had a source, or sources, inside the U.S. government; exactly where, he didn't know. He was told that these sources could only be called upon for the gravest of matters; well, this certainly fit the bill. He got back on the internet.

Chapter 23

"Come on, Chief," she pleaded, using a title she almost never used for him. "There's no way our troops can find and disable these bombs, and catch all the bad guys, in three days!"

Lara and Uri had been called up again to Trotter's office a little after midnight. No one in the building had left since the blast that afternoon. They had already been told of some important findings made in the past six hours. The Hazmat team in LA had come up with some pretty damning information. It almost had to be a fission device, an atomic bomb, a small one, but still…

"How could they know that, so soon?" Lara was astonished.

"The air samples clearly showed the presence of fission products. So it was a nuclear device. Low yield, again lucky for us, but a nuclear bomb. They had enough fuel to reach what they call 'critical mass,' but the device was so poorly made it didn't stay critical very long. That's why it was 'only' about a kiloton; it could have been more than ten times worse if they really knew what they were doing."

"Any idea who it was?" she asked.

"Hazmat sent out some robots to collect the hottest fragments around the Marina. Right now they're still analyzing them…"

"At least we have a good idea who made the fuel. It's from Russia, they're pretty sure, but don't ask me how. Apparently they can tell from the crap they found."

"You mean we're sure it was the Russians who pulled this off?" she asked. "Then how come it was so crude? Wouldn't they have been smart enough to…"

Trotter cut her off. "The Russians say it could be their fuel but it wasn't their bomb. Looks like some rogue engineer stole the fuel elements and sold them to some bad guys. They claim they don't know any details yet. Conversation is ongoing."

"Then we've got to find these guys and stop them. I mean if they have any more fuel…"

"I agree with you, of course, but the Boss doesn't want to send the country into panic mode, at least not yet, by mobilizing the whole National Guard and going door-to-door. And I agree with him. Our best shot is to send out a small hit team, find out if they really have more bombs, and stop as many of these guys as possible. That way, when the story breaks, the president can assure the people we're well on the way toward neutralizing them." He paused and looked directly at both of them. "A hit team of two, to be specific."

"So how did we get picked for this suicide mission?" she asked.

"The President, joint chiefs, and the cabinet met an hour ago. After a lot of squawking, mainly from Homeland Security, the President and Secretary of State agreed the Bureau ought to give it their best shot. That way, the least suspicion will be raised by the news hounds. If they do get too curious, the cover will be that we got wind of a big drug shipment, and we're going after a major sting." The normally reserved bureaucrat felt the agents' skills were wasted hunting down dealers of "recreational" drugs. With as much sarcasm as he was capable of showing, he added, "The press knows the Bureau is totally focused on coke and meth."

But the strategy he outlined made a lot of sense. A small team, equipped with all the resources of the FBI, CIA, NSA and Homeland Security, had the best shot at a quick success without arousing undue alarm. Uri was a field agent who spoke fluent Arabic; Lara, an analyst with ties to the entire computer network. If they could make a strike within the next few days, identify and capture two or three terrorists and locate the next bomb, the country could be alerted to the threat knowing their leaders had already begun to round up the gang. It was a big "if."

Before Lara had even digested the orders they had just received, Trotter stood and sent them on their way. "We've got you on a plane at Andrews. Don't even think about going home first; we'll get anything you need and take care of any loose ends for you."

"Where are we going?" she asked.

"Where do you think? Los Angeles."

Chapter 24

Jim got to Trotter's office just after 7:30 A.M.; the others were already there. He recognized Washington "Wash" Neil, the well-dressed, broad-shouldered, black man from CIA, Bruce Baxter, the "bearded wonder" from Homeland Security, and Jonah Greenberg, the lawyer who served as liaison between Trotter's office here at FBI and the White House.

"I guess everybody knows each other," Trotter began. Then without any small talk, he said, "Now, what have we got so far?" He was looking right at Baxter. Baxter was not a favorite of the others in the room, including Trotter. They had all come up through the ranks; Baxter had been handed his position when the Office of Homeland Security had been hastily established following the 9/11 attack. He didn't have any of the field training required of the CIA and FBI agents, for example, and his bulk revealed an apparent lack of physical fitness. Baxter was heavy, but not in a muscular way. The folds of his neck drooped slightly over his starched white shirt, which looked at least half a size too small, as if he had bought it sometime before his last weight gain. His beard was black, probably dyed, unkempt and curly; he might have been an opera tenor showing the signs of age and disuse. He was, in their eyes, simply a bureaucrat looking for something to do.

"Well, Chief," he began, to everyone's annoyance, "You probably know as much as we do at this point. The Hazmat guys tell us the samples they picked up in the air and on the ground all point to a uranium fission device. We did get late word that there was some beryllium stuck to some of the unexploded pieces of fuel. They consider that real strange; it means they didn't keep the thing together very long, like milliseconds, or there wouldn't be any unexploded fuel left. So that means it wasn't a bomb made by any of the major sources, you know, Russian, Chinese, or anybody like that. That rules out a rogue-crazy inside the major powers; instead it points to stolen fuel elements assembled by some group who doesn't know a whole lot about what they're doing."

"Except they got the damn thing to blow up," Wash Neil interrupted, "I guess they know something about it." He gave Baxter a disdainful look. Neil was the opposite of Baxter in almost every way. Clean-shaven, he looked sharp and fit in his three-piece suit.

"They got it to blow up, but that's about all; they didn't maintain critical mass for any length of time."

"How do you know that," Neil asked?

"The pieces of unexploded fuel we found in the street..."

"What are you talking about?" Neil rose to his feet. "Unexploded fuel?"

"Right. It was a poor attempt at a bomb. Didn't even use all the fuel. But we did find beryllium with the unused uranium..."

"Meaning what?" an exasperated Neil was growing quickly impatient.

"Meaning these dudes knew how to put on a neutron reflector, but they didn't know how to hold it all together."

The room grew completely silent as the men tried to absorb what they were being told. Trotter finally assumed command: "Tell us what that means. Do they know more about building a bomb than we've given them credit for?"

"I'm afraid so, Chief," Baxter replied. "Beryllium metal used as a neutron reflector has been kept pretty well out of the public media. Luckily they didn't know how to contain the explosion long enough to get the whole bang."

"Do we know who these guys are yet, I mean for sure?" Jim asked.

"You saw the demand letter, I'm sure. We don't know if it's legit yet, but chances are that it is. So it's probably Hezbollah, but it still could be Hamas or Al Qaeda, especially considering they got the note to Al Jazeera. We want to make sure the information about the beryllium and the uranium stays absolutely secret."

"Why is that?" asked Greenberg, the lawyer. "The public already knows it was a nuke." Greenberg was the corporate lawyer

149

from heat to toe. His tailored suit was perfectly fitted, but not flashy. He wore a pale blue shirt, with a gold tie that was tied in a tight Windsor knot with a centered dimple. His French cuffs, which he shot at regular intervals simultaneously with crossing and uncrossing his legs, were clipped with plain, square gold links that flashed in the stark room lights.

"But the bad guys don't know why the explosion was so puny. Any leads they get will help them build the next one better."

"You really think they have another one?" asked Greenberg, sitting up in his chair, clearly more concerned than before.

"Well, we can't be sure, but the fact is that it's stolen Russian fuel, so there could be more. We've asked the Russians to see if they can get a better handle on that, but so far, no luck."

"All right, about all we can do now is wait and see what we can find out from our field sources, and wait for the next message from the bad guys." Trotter was grim-faced as he ended the meeting. "Oh, Jim," he said as Turner was leaving, "Can you get hold of Lara and see how they're doing out there? We've only got five days or so before that demand letter hits the streets."

Jim headed to his office. He'd have to wait awhile before he called Lara, because it was just about 5 A.M. out in Los Angeles. Before he called he'd do some literature searching; to learn what he could about nuclear bombs and beryllium. He used some of the browsers available to the general public, as well as those specific to the Bureau, but the information he found was so full of scientific jargon he could make little sense of it. He knew little about physics and less about bomb making, so he flipped on the news to see if Al Jazeera had reneged on their promise to withhold the demand note until Friday.

So far, it seemed like nothing more had come out of the Arab press. The news networks were full of reports, some conflicting, about the source of the Los Angeles blast, the size and who was responsible. The government was staying pretty tight-lipped, it appeared, just urging public caution. He wondered how long this hiatus would continue.

Chapter 25

The big man stayed in the shadows outside the restaurant. The rain, as it did this time of year in D.C., misted down continuously on him. It gave him a good excuse to pull his hat down even further over his eyes, as he scanned the street in both directions. He had switched Metro lines three times, as per his instructions, on his way here. Then, leaving the Metro at the Smithsonian stop, he circled back to the restaurant, checking all the pedestrians and auto traffic. There was no tail. These were much more cautious instructions than usual; something must be up. He headed on foot to the Wall, just a few blocks away. His contact would have noted his brief stop outside the restaurant as a guarantee of a "clean" meet. The Vietnam memorial was a good place to meet; they had used it many times without a problem. Here perfect strangers would often stop, stroll along quietly and sometimes exchange a few words; Vietnam vets and their families, mainly.

Here he stood in front of the Wall near the 1969 entries, his rolled up newspaper in his right hand, the final guarantee of security. Ten minutes went by, as he casually glanced at the names on the rain-wet granite. Finally the familiar figure of his contact showed up, also carrying a rolled up newspaper. He wore a casual tan raincoat in deference to the light rain.

The contact, known to the large man simply as Ali, was of Middle Eastern or Mediterranean origin, with swarthy complexion and dark, deep-set eyes. In order to minimize his ethnicity, even in this city of multiple ethnic groups, Ali Muhammed el-Fahid was clean-shaven, in violation of common Islamic cultural rules. He was of average height and build, further blending him into the urban mix. In his dark blue suit, he could easily have been a Greek businessman or an Italian importer. In actuality, he was born to an affluent Egyptian family; but after being educated in a radical Islamic school, he joined a cell dedicated to the overthrow of the secular state. It wasn't long before he had graduated to the more lofty goals of world domination, and fell under the spell of the Most Blessed Sheikh Imad Fa'iz Mughniyah. Mughniyah, who with his slight build and calm demeanor, outwardly displayed nothing of his deep inner hatred of all things Western. He had, Ali knew, been a co-leader of the infamous bombing of the Khobar Towers apartment building in Saudi Arabia, killing 19 American soldiers.

Ali, and many of his friends, teenagers at the time, reveled in the successes of Sheikh Mughniyah. Perhaps no event was more relished than the 1983 car bombing that killed 241 U.S. servicemen in Beirut, most of them the haughty "Marines," and demolished the embassy building in the process. The joy they felt when they learned of the carnage was multiplied when the vaunted President Ronald Reagan, who thought of himself as the personification of the "cowboy" hero he played in the movies, pulled all U.S. forces out of Lebanon. Reagan had, in one stroke, handed Lebanon over to the forces of Hezbollah and her accomplices in Syria and Iran. Ali still felt a surge of pride and satisfaction at the futility the Israelis must have suffered. They had realized their northern border was once again a killing zone for Hezbollah's martyrs.

"We have a need," Ali said simply, as he subtly scanned the area for listeners. But the inclement weather had limited the visitors to just a few, and they were not of any apparent threat.

"You've got to be kidding," responded the big man. "As you can imagine, the place is pretty tight."

Ali enjoyed his hold over this man immensely. It was, he felt, a reflection of the power the Arabs held over the Americans. No matter the military victories the Americans may have enjoyed in Afghanistan and Iraq. All they had accomplished was to give birth to millions upon millions of Jihadists throughout the world. They may have killed a few bees, but they had awakened a countless multitude of angry hornets, ready to do the bidding of the Jihadist leaders.

"The letter goes public in a few days, no matter what," Ali said grimly. "After that, the plan goes as scheduled. We just need a little information about the post-blast analysis, the chemical tests; things like that. We know the government hasn't told the public everything."

The big man thought about this for a few seconds, then replied, "You mean so the next one can be even worse?"

"No, of course not, we just want to know all the cards they're holding before we start negotiating, that's all."

"Why should I believe you; you told me the warning would come before the first one went off?" The big man looked around carefully to see if any curious eyes had appeared. He was in a box, a terrible box of his own creation. He could see no way out for himself, not at this juncture; he just needed some more time to plan a course of action that would stop this madness.

"These things are beyond my control, my friend," the Arab replied. He calmly pulled an American cigarette from his raincoat pocket, shielding it from the rain as he lit it with a stainless-steel Zippo lighter. As he did so, Ali also checked the area again for strangers. "Besides, you really have no choice in the matter."

The big man thought about this for a few seconds, silently, then told Ali: "I need until tomorrow noon, at the earliest."

"Same place, and you'd better have something for us. He didn't need to add the "or else." It was quite clear.

To maintain the appearance of a casual meeting, the two men strolled along together, occasionally glancing at the Wall, pointing at a name or two. Then as the path split, the two walked in different directions, not looking back at each other. Ali, however, stopped after a block or so, crushed out his cigarette, and made a careful check of the area. There was no evidence of a tail on either man, as far as he could see. He walked casually toward the nearest Metro station.

Chapter 26

Just minutes before noon, the big man appeared again at the Vietnam Veterans Memorial Wall. As he had the day before, he carried a rolled up newspaper to signify "all clear." He had taken an even more complicated path today; the weather was clear and cold and he could be seen for some distance. As he had exited the Orange Line at Metro Center to catch the Blue Line for the Smithsonian station, he turned quickly around, and saw a man in a topcoat bend over to tie his shoe. Fearing a tail by someone from Trotter's office, he had gone up the escalator, then watched in a glass-covered station map to see if the topcoat had followed. Sure enough, the man exited the escalator about thirty seconds later. The big man waited until the Red train departed, then before another train came, went back down to the lower lever. The man in the topcoat had not boarded the Red Line train. The big man boarded the first Blue Line train that arrived, which was headed toward National Airport, then checked the platform. Mr. Topcoat was not to be seen. The big man had stayed on the train to Rosslyn, a transfer station, then headed back on an eastbound train toward Smithsonian. When the train had reached Metro Center, he scanned the platform: no topcoat. Feeling only slightly relieved, the big man had exited at Smithsonian and taken the same circuitous route as the previous day, past the restaurant to the Wall.

It was now a few minutes past noon, and the big man nervously lit a cigarette as he tried to appear a casual visitor. Seemingly from nowhere, Ali appeared, carrying his newspaper in his right hand. "Right on time," he said with a mirthless smile. "It's cold today, don't you think?"

The big man tried to think of what possible code this remark might refer to, but could not come up with anything. After all, it was he who had been summoned. He finally left it as just an annoying Arab attempt at familiarity. "I'm afraid I don't have much."

"You are too humble," Ali replied with a slight bow and conspiratorial grin. "Tell me what happened."

The big man hoped no one was watching this charade; he quickly glanced around, expecting to see Mr. Topcoat standing a few feet away with a camcorder. But the area was reasonably clear of visitors today. A couple of middle-aged men were watching as a teen-aged boy traced a copy of one of the names, rubbing a pencil on paper over the engraving. He imagined the boy taking the tracing back home and placing it on a mantel covered with medals next to the picture of a man in uniform, no doubt his father. It was a ceremony he'd seen all too often, and one he hoped would not have to be repeated after another foreign war.

"What do you mean?" the big man replied.

"Don't be cute, we know about the meeting this morning."

The big man slumped slightly; there were others at the Bureau who knew, he now realized in dismay. He had been hoping that somehow he could extricate himself before more damage was done, but that looked less and less likely. "Actually, we don't know much more than what's been on TV, believe it or not."

"Not," said the Arab, showing a little more knowledge of idiomatic American-English than the big man had been aware. *One of the unrecognized benefits of American TV and movies*, he thought.

"Hazmat has confirmed the U-235 fission. The only thing is, there were some unexploded pieces of fuel found in the streets around Marina del Rey, and they've traced the material to the Russians."

"You mean they think it was a Russian attack?"

"No, they've been in touch with the Kremlin; the Russians don't want anything like this going on. They see this now as looking like their fault; not great for their image in Europe, not to mention their own country and their satellites."

"But it doesn't hurt their status with us," Ali reminded him. "Especially if it looks like they just happened to let some bombs get loose on the Americans." He paused for a second, savoring this morsel of international propaganda.

"You really think Uzbekistan, Turkistan and all the other 'Stans' are going to be thrilled to think the Russkies are into nuking their enemies? Just imagine the reaction in Chechnya, for example."

Ali pondered that for a moment, considered the fact that these matters didn't really concern him anyway, then asked, "So then, anything else? Body count, suspects, witnesses..."

The big man thought back on the brief meeting; he wanted to give the Arab something, anything, to at least make him think he had been of use. "Oh yes, there was some talk of a trace component they found that they didn't expect from the fission. Something called 'beryllium.' I didn't write it down, of course, but it seemed to them to be something amateurs wouldn't be expected to use in a crude bomb. It raised some eyebrows." He was pretty sure this information was inconsequential, but it had been withheld from the media, so it should be good for a few points.

"I'll pass it on." Ali said. "Meet me again on Friday after the announcement goes public, say 6 P.M." Ali left the big man standing alone, and afraid. It was at times like these that he found himself balancing the weight of the pictures they had of him, the damage they could do to him, against the damage he was doing to his country.

He had always rationalized his actions by considering the value of the information he had been giving to them. It had started out with insignificant details, things that were barely classified: names of ships under construction, their design tonnage and speed; things that "Jane's Fighting Ships" would have published in the public domain in a few years anyway. Then the requests had become dicier: location and composition of the various Fleets, especially those in and near the Persian Gulf. He had balked only when they asked for names of agents working undercover in the area. Maybe these requests were tests to see just how far he would go, at least until they really needed something. Then, he realized, feeling slightly nauseous, the noose would tighten, and decision time would be at hand

Ali went back to his hotel room in the outskirts of Washington, and thought about the information he had just received. Could it be this was something urgent? It seemed trivial to him, but of course he was not trained in nuclear physics. He had felt uneasy in this assignment. He was pleased to have an important position in the organization, but he was more at ease with matters dealing with personnel, not technical issues. He had a keen eye, he felt, for how much pressure he could apply to their agents.

The big man was easy; he had spotted him in one of Washington's famous bathhouses, cruising for young men, boys really. Ali and his partner knew the man worked for, or at least had business with, the FBI. They had seen and photographed him entering and leaving headquarters. Their initial assignment, two years ago, was to observe middle-aged men with connections with the FBI. There were certain signs they could spot with their targets: the looks they gave to young attractive men on the steps of the building, for example. Then, after office hours, the bathhouses were watched, to see if any of the targets turned up. Ali had spotted the big man after about six months, then tailed him on the Metro back to a fashionable suburb, and a four bedroom home. A family man for sure.

The big man was clumsy about approaching his targets, a sure sign he was a novice at this sexual adventure. It had been easy to tempt a handsome young male prostitute into an encounter with the big man: a hundred dollar bribe, and a room at one of the cheap downtown hotels near the bathhouse. Ali and his partner had set up the cameras; another couple of hundred dollars for the clerk to make sure of the room assignment each time.

The trickiest part of the whole operation was the initial contact with the big man, and the revealing of the pictures. Ali had done it about a month into the sting. He approached the big man as they waited for a Metro train one afternoon. Ali had pasted one of his surreptitious photos onto the front page of the Washington Post. As they sat on the bench waiting for the train, Ali, dressed in his best D.C. attire, a blue pinstriped suit with highly polished shoes, handed the big man the paper, saying politely, "Have you seen this latest Russian Mafia guy?" The big man just gave him a

157

cursory glance, and went back to his own newspaper. "I think you might recognize the guy," Ali said, handing the paper over again. This time the big man looked first at Ali, questioningly, then at the front page with his photo on it. He was good, Ali thought, not even a sharp intake of breath as he had expected. There was only a slight slump of the shoulders, a moment's pause, and an almost inaudible response.

"Who are you, what do you want?" The big man did not turn in Ali's direction, but rather glanced up and down the platform with no obvious alarm.

"Take another look, my friend," Ali replied. He had taped a time and place just below the photo. The big man said nothing; He rolled up the newspaper, placed it under his arm and walked down the platform, ready for the approaching train. Ali was pleased; the hook was set.

Their first meeting had been perfunctory. Against the grim background of the Vietnam Veteran's Memorial Wall, Ali had assured the big man of the innocuous nature of his requests. The incriminating pictures would never see the light of day, in return for his help with some commercial ventures; no matters of national security were involved.

"Who do you think I am?" The big man knew he was in a precarious situation, but there might be a way out of this, if he could convince this Middle-Easterner that he was dealing with nothing more than a low-level government clerk.

"We know who you are, my friend. You are FBI. And we know where you live." He handed the big man a note containing his name and address. That part had been easy, using a reverse phone directory. Ali was bluffing, of course; the man might be nothing but a mailing-room helper. But his dress and manner suggested otherwise. Besides, Ali had little to lose. "Oh, and we have lots more pictures, very interesting for your wife and boss."

The big man just stood there; the fact that he had even shown up at this clandestine meeting had proven his vulnerability. Still, he might be able to play this to his advantage, or at least limit the damage. "What is it you think I can give you?" His manner was conversational and confident; he did not appear in the least intimidated.

Good, Ali, thought, this man was somehow involved in covert operations, he was sure of it. Anyone else would be shaking in his boots by now. "My firm is in the international trading business. We know the FBI has a list of organizations they think are connected to what they call 'terrorists.' I just want to make sure that the firms we are doing business with aren't on that list. You know, to keep our own nose clean, as you say. Contact me here, this same time, the same way when you have something." The big man just looked at him briefly, then turned away. They were in business.

Chapter 27

Ali considered what the big man had told him. If this information were "Code 1" stuff, the kind that could mean the difference between success and failure, he would need to check in with Nasrallah immediately, through one of their highest security links. Unknown as yet to the U.S. government, a Washington-based cell of Hezbollah agents, trained in communications at one of America's premier universities, had developed a "virtual private network (VPN)" system based on the one used by the highest levels of the NSA.

Like many universities, this one had contracts with the Department of Defense to develop "foolproof" communication networks, ones that incorporated self-contained encryption-decryption programs. The concept was similar to that developed by the Nazis before World War II, based on the famous "Enigma" machine. But the enormous strides made in computer technology had brought the art to magnificent levels of sophistication. The U.S. government, to enhance their recruiting capabilities at the best technical universities, had established multi-million dollar programs that employed some of the top professors, and their graduate students, to develop multiple, redundant, secure communications systems. Of course, all the professors and students had to be vetted by the FBI. But with the dearth of native-born students willing to devote their careers to this kind of dreary work, foreign nationals had come into the program. Their vetting proved more difficult, and, naturally, to get the work accomplished, a few corners were cut. So it was that Middle-Eastern students leaning to the cause of Islamist terror had penetrated the system.

Because the transmissions operated on the very frequencies used by the CIA and other intelligence branches of the NSA, the feeling was that intercepted signals would be considered as communication between branches of the various autonomous arms of the agencies, and thus not be analyzed.

Nasrallah had insisted on saving the use of this VPN for the highest level emergencies, when the normal web pages would be insufficient, in either time or detail. This information, it seemed to Ali, fit these criteria. He pulled out the innocuous-looking "FM radio" and started the transmission in motion.

Khallad reacted with alarm at this new information. By itself, it was not all that threatening. Hossein could be contacted and his device altered, if necessary. Even if the second blast were only as potent as the first, their mission would be a success. Still, Khallad wanted to be known as the man responsible for the killing of hundreds of thousands of Americans, many of them Jews.

What disturbed Khallad more was the news he had received from the cell in Boston. Over the "school" website, he had learned that certain people, definitely untrained in engineering, had been in contact with faculty members at MIT and other well-known and respected universities in the area, inquiring about government-sponsored research programs in explosives and nuclear power plant safety. The guarded messages on the web pages had been vague as to detail, but one of the professors happened to be descended from Iraqi roots, and was not at all happy with the apparent intrusion into his research. He had mentioned it to his graduate students, almost all of them Middle-Eastern, and word had spread.

It wasn't long before one of Nasrallah's operatives had reported that no fewer than four research groups had been questioned by these clumsy federal agents. Two things had to be done: First, the students not in on the plot must be reassured that this security check did not affect them or their status in their school. Second, and more important, word must be gotten to Khallad and Hossein that the FBI had become suspicious, and that all future communication should be kept to essential items only.

Sheikh Nasrallah's decision to send Hossein to a second-tier nuclear engineering school showed its genius now: the Americans apparently were limiting their search to the top-ranked schools only. The plan was still secure. But it meant the U.S. government was at least alert to the fact that their universities might well be the breeding ground for the next attack on their corrupt society. The fools let their campuses open to all kinds of anti-U.S. activity, and this type of ridiculous permissiveness would lead to their downfall.

Khallad thought again about his homeland, how the campuses were patrolled for any seditious activity. The Holy Quran was the only real reading material students needed, all else was silly fluff. If technical information was needed, the West was a wide open resource. It truly was as if the U.S. and their lackeys were the slave states to the burgeoning Islamic empire, they just didn't realize it yet. He smiled to himself as he once again recognized how wise the Blessed Ayatollah Ali Khamenei truly was. Keep the children in fear and the women in submission; that was the path to greatness. He retired from his reverie, back to the necessities of the here and now. Hossein must finish his deadly mission without delay. Khallad would give him all the help he needed.

Chapter 28

December 2013

Lara and Uri sat on opposite sides of the rear seat in the unmarked limo taking them to Andrews Air Force Base. The limo, equipped with wailing sirens and flashing lights, maneuvered through the streets of southeast D.C. with amazing speed, reaching the Air Force base in less than twenty minutes.

Domestic air service had been curtailed, of course, in the wake of the attack, but Trotter had been able to squeeze them onto a military plane. This, despite the fact that military transports had been overwhelmed with troops armed with sophisticated radiation detectors. They were headed for the major metropolitan areas, aimed at controlling traffic in and out. The problem was enormous. Discretion was necessary to avoid panic and a catastrophic flight of civilians from all the large cities.

Their instructions were vague at this point: they were to meet with the Hazmat and other civil defense teams in Los Angeles and pick up whatever they could in terms of clues as to the manufacture of the bomb and possible witnesses in the area of the blast, Marina del Rey. The official reports up until now had been disappointingly lacking; and witnesses were a total zero. No one had come forward with anything at all unusual, and the owners of the rental slips in the various harbors had also been unhelpful. With the Ensenada sailboat race just concluding, there had been a huge number of temporary slip rentals, and no ID's were required, just a deposit and payment. A team from the LAPD had been assigned the enormous task of checking the credit card receipts for the past month, mainly to see if any of the cardholders were of Arab origin.

Meanwhile, Lara's teams of web page hawks in Washington were on the job round the clock checking the suspect sites. The traffic had been light since the blast; the terrorists may have suspected the sites had been compromised or, more ominously, all future plans were in place.

The limo dropped them off on the tarmac where an Air Force 747 sat waiting. They had only carry-on bags with them and boarded after a careful check by an Air Force captain stationed at the entry ramp. Their Federal ID's showing yellow "Top-Secret" clearances helped get them through with a minimum of grief. Uri's was a unique forgery constructed in the FBI lab; if the bad guys can do it, so can we, was the quick rationalization. They were traveling as man and wife; Trotter wanted to keep their profile as low as possible. Neither carried weapons; both were uneasy about this, especially Uri, who felt like his testicles had been temporarily removed. They were assured that weapons of their choice would be available in Los Angeles.

The flight to LAX was uneventful, each lost in private thought, each overwhelmed with the gravity of the situation and the weight of their assignment. They had been warned to limit their conversation to trivial matters, with absolutely no mention of the matters burning in their consciousness. Lara took the time to review the suspect web pages, to see if she had missed some clue or other. Only in the hotel room, with the TV blaring, could they discuss their mission. Lara had found this security a bit much, since they were apparently dealing with a small bunch of loonies, and not a sophisticated foreign power. But much of the caution was to prevent scaring the public more than it already was, and that included the military personnel on the plane.

Uri and Lara were aware of the meetings between Ambassador Doring and the PM of Israel. They knew they had a maximum of only a few days to break up the conspiracy and bring in the leaders. It wasn't the same as with bin Laden, hiding in the mountains of a remote country. These guys were in our country, like rats in the attic.

On the ground in Los Angeles, they took a cab to their hotel, The Beverly Wilshire. Ordinarily, this sort of hotel would be beyond the price range of government employees. This, however, was no ordinary situation, and they had opted for a secure hotel not too far from the Los Angeles FBI headquarters.

Though the flight had taken over six hours, it was only ten P.M. in L.A. Both of them were exhausted by the day's events. Now they were escorted to their suite on the seventh floor by a bellman who showed no curiosity at the couple. Of course, Uri realized, they looked no different from any other checking into a hotel room; it's just that at this time of national emergency, no couple could possibly look normal.

Only when they were deposited in the suite did the situation totally reveal itself. They hadn't had a choice of rooms; the hotels were in a sort of holding pattern following the blast, and Uri and Lara had to take what was available. Now they saw the "suite" was actually just a bedroom with two double beds, a bathroom, and a small entryway that posed as a living or meeting room. Both of them realized for the first time the embarrassingly close quarters they were supposed to cohabit.

While they had been working together in Washington for these few months, there had been no talk of a personal relationship. After the day that Uri had gotten his divorce papers and she had invited him to stay over on the couch, their relationship had subtly changed. But Lara recognized that Uri was still officially married; anyway, she was still maintaining her vigorous daily schedule and had no time or thoughts of "dating." But she couldn't avoid noticing his raw masculine attractiveness. The knowledge that he had been a vicious, efficient commando, killing an unknown number of the enemy had secretly thrilled her, even though she did not like to admit it, even to herself. The fact that he was so self-assured and unassuming added to his appeal; she despised the macho image so many of her colleagues affected. But his vulnerability, especially when talking about Danielle struck the deepest chord in her psyche. There was no question but that she was on the verge of an emotional attachment to this man. The only real question was whether he felt the same. She had seen his face brighten when he saw her, and recognized the sexual attraction he felt; that part was obvious.

Uri, for his part, had thought less and less of Danielle these past weeks. He had not heard from her, even though he had tried various means of communication. She clearly was not available, and he understood now more than ever the reasons for her withdrawal. On the other hand, being so close to Lara had made some impact, at least subconsciously. He found, at night, as he had tried to fall asleep in his small rental apartment, that her image played across his thoughts. Little things, like the way she would push her hair back, the blueness of her eyes, the tightness of her skirt across her thighs, all were part of a nightly rehashing of each days events.

Now, as the door closed after the bellman, they realized they were going to have to come to grips with the situation. "There's an old Clark Gable movie like this," she said lightly, "where he gets stuck in a hotel room with a strange woman right after World War II; they hang a sheet in the middle of the room."

"I think I saw that one," he replied with a poor attempt at a laugh.

"Look, we're adults," she said, "We'll be fine. Do you shower at night or in the morning?"

"Actually, in the field, we're lucky to have enough water to drink, let alone bathe," he laughed, "so you can take your pick. But I'll take the bed by the window."

"You got it. I'm going to take a shower and then hit it; I'm beat," she said. She opened her bag, pulled out a vanity case and disappeared into the bathroom. Uri opened his bag on the bed and pulled out the shaving kit Trotter had gotten for him. Then he walked over to the mini-bar and studied the contents, noting the unbelievable prices. These Americans have a different style of travel, he decided. He grabbed a bottle of red wine and poured two glasses; he could at least be civil. Then he impatiently waited for her to finish in the bathroom.

Lara emerged wearing a hotel bathrobe from which her long legs emerged as she walked to her bed. Uri was instantly aroused by the sight, but kept in control. "I poured you a glass of red, just in case you'd like to wind down," he said as he entered the well-appointed bathroom. He saw another bathrobe hanging on the back of the door.

"Thanks, that sounds great," she said sitting on the edge of the bed, brushing her thick, blond hair. Another jolt hit Uri in the gut. He showered quickly and emerged in his bathrobe, heading for the far bed. He noticed Lara had turned on the radio that sat on the table between the beds. He remembered their instructions about blocking any bugs, as unlikely as it was that there were any. He quickly polished off his wine, noting that her glass was empty. He saw her bathrobe lying on the foot of her bed. Another jolt. He turned off the main light and hustled into the other bed, removing his bathrobe as he slid under the cover. Now there was just the light seeping in from the incompletely curtained window.

Several minutes passed, the only sound being the "sixties" music from the radio. "Uri, is it true, what they say about your Branch of Mossad, that you have license to kill anyone, at any time?" There was a long pause as Uri considered her question. He was going into what might be a fatal encounter, for both of them. He decided she should know the truth.

"No, that's not exactly true. But you're right, I am part of a special unit. It's called Kidon, even though no one in government will admit to our existence. We do have the right to kill, or more exactly, to execute, but only persons known to have vengefully killed Israeli citizens."

There was another pause as Lara considered what he had just told her. She realized he had taken her into a very special confidence, one that could cost him his position, or even his life. She longed at that moment to be able to touch him, feel his heart beat. "Have you, I mean you personally, ever had to…?"

There were only a very few people he had ever told the answer to her unfinished question—his bosses at Mossad, of course, and Danielle… "Yes, I have. Most recently in Lebanon, when we found those papers." He wasn't sure if he was specifically mentioning this attack because she already knew about it, or because it so clearly showed the need for the action: the acquisition of the Opera documents.

"What's it like," she finally asked, "taking a life with your hands?"

There were a few moments silence before Uri replied. "The first few times it's terrible, no matter how bad the guy is. I'll never forget the first one; he was just a teenager, but with pockets full of grenades. They fill them with hate, you know, from the day they're born. Still, it stays with you. Then, after a while, it becomes a job. You couldn't survive otherwise. Deep in my heart I know I'm doing the right thing, I'm saving my country, my people. What pains me most, now, is losing any of my men to them. It happens, you know, even though the press doesn't know about it, but we lose some real young guys all the time. And when I'm in charge, it's my fault, every one of them. That doesn't go away...and you, have you had any hand-to-hand encounters, outside of training?"

"Just the usual fending off guys who think a 'date' is a promise of a bedmate."

Uri laughed, but realized this was nearly the first mention she had made of her personal life in the nearly six months they had known each other. This was quickly becoming a very tricky situation. "So I guess that means you're single, so to speak." What a place for this conversation, he thought, in bed, naked, a foot away from a beautiful woman who might be having the same idea.

"Yeah, too busy, I guess, for anything else right now. And your wife, Danielle, back in Israel...?" So she was throwing the ball back to him, he thought.

"We're still separated, divorce pending, you know," he said simply, recalling their recent conversation in her apartment. "The job doesn't appeal to a lot of women, at least for a husband."

"Uri," she said after a moment, "What happens if we don't catch these guys? I mean I have a pretty good idea of what will happen here in the U.S., but what happens to Israel if we're forced to do what the terrorists want? Can your country survive without our help? With all those hostile countries just waiting for a chance like this, not to mention the outlaw bands like Al Qaeda and Hezbollah."

"It's pretty certain we'd be dead meat without U.S. support, I know that. So we've got a plan that even I don't know the particulars of, only the name. But even the name is top secret." Lara nodded that she understood. "It's called 'Ekdikeo,' and sounds like something out of 'Dr. Strangelove,' but not quite as drastic. The word means 'vengeance' in the old language. From what little I do know 'Ekdikeo' involves a wholesale nuclear attack on the main hostile capitals. And, believe me, those leaders know about it. Basically, as I understand it, if the threat of assault is judged as reality by the Israeli government, those hostile capitals will be given notice that Ekdikeo will go into force unless Israel is granted the right to verify all military installations in those countries. That means nuclear as well as conventional facilities and troop locations. By verification, I mean fly-overs in addition to on-site inspections. It's pretty close to an ultimatum of Armageddon. The Arabs will never agree to anything that humiliating."

There was no reply for a while, just the noise from the radio. Then a rustling as Uri realized she was changing position in her bed. "Uri," she said, "You've been on enough of these jobs to have a feeling for what's coming, don't you?"

There was silence again as he processed the question, the vulnerability in it. It reflected an obvious change in her attitude towards him, and a certain crossroad. "Sometimes, but right now all I feel is a lot of uncertainty. How about you?"

"I guess I feel nothing *but* uncertainty; actually, I'm scared to death."

There was a long pause as the radio blared away in its own world. Then he made up his mind it was now-or-forget-it time. He rose quietly from his bed and sat on hers. "Maybe we just need to be close right now," he said, "Is it alright?"

She didn't reply, but didn't react in refusal either. He slid under the cover next to her, just inches away, her wonderful smell reaching him first. He reached for her hand, but accidentally brushed across her breast, the nipple erect. Things happened fast after that. She pulled his head to her, kissing him while their bodies touched: feet, legs, torsos…everywhere. She slid beneath him and guided him into her. It was the first time in months for Uri, and he gasped with pleasure as little explosions rocked his every sense. There was a moment of silence; then he said with a smile that she could feel, if not see, "So much for safe sex."

She laughed with the immediate change in the relationship. "Looks like it's been a while since you've had *any* sex."

He laughed with her, "You're right, it's been a while. But it won't be now." He let that promise hang in the air as they both breathed in each other's fragrance. For what seemed like hours they got to know each other's bodies, caressing and gently kissing. She felt some scars, but didn't ask about them. He felt only soft, silky woman. Finally, she pushed him onto his back and straddled him gently, easing them again into oneness. In near silence, they moved to a rhythm born ages past, blissfully unaware of the incongruous music coming from the radio. At last, he felt her tense slightly, emit a light moan, and then relax, dropping against his side. He tenderly put his arm around her, and they both dropped off to dreamless sleep.

Chapter 29

They awoke even before the call from the desk at 6 A.M., after less than three hours sleep. Their relationship had altered, but not the plan. There was a 7:30 meeting scheduled at the Federal Building on Wilshire, which had luckily been spared from the blast. Breakfast was brought up to their room by a staff member who was clearly drafted for the task. The normal shift changes were not occurring since travel around the city was obviously hampered. The mainly Hispanic dining room and cleaning crews were mostly unable to get to work from their homes in East and South-Central Los Angeles. Whatever housekeeping and kitchen staff who were still available, were augmented with office personnel, unable to get home.

So it was an amused, if somewhat sleepy, hotel management agent who brought their breakfast of eggs, orange juice, cold cereal and coffee. He had forgotten the toast, but that could be forgiven, considering the circumstances. He was still dressed in his business suit and had trouble figuring out how to maneuver the breakfast cart over the threshold. It was clear he knew the circumstances of the sleeping arrangement; this supposedly married, but clearly unattached couple had been forced into using a single room. The happenings of the ensuing night were clear from the disarray of the linens.

Uri signed the tab, which would go on his federal American Express card, then handed the guy a twenty dollar bill, saying, "Thanks for your trouble, Peterson." The middle-manager, probably not used to dealing with guests directly, had forgotten the name tag on his suit jacket. But his grin faded as he took the tip, realizing he had just been formally demoted to a room service flunky.

They checked out by 7 A.M. A long, black federal limo picked them up at the curb and got them to the meeting in fifteen minutes. The streets were strangely quiet, for Los Angeles. There was still a sense of shock, somewhat like in New York after the attack of 9/11. But there was no feeling of fear; it was more the despair after the sudden loss of a loved one. The people who were out on the streets moved like automatons; it reminded Uri of the scenes in London after a devastating air raid, as captured on film in World War II.

The Federal Building was surrounded by armed military, all grim-faced young men. Lara and Uri showed their identification cards three times before they were finally allowed entry into the building. There, in the spacious atrium, they were inspected carefully with X-ray and bomb-sniffing machines. Then they were sent on up, with an escort, to the seventh floor, where the L.A. team was already waiting in a hermetically sealed conference room.

Uri mentally compared the relative sumptuousness compared to the similar rooms Mossad used in Tel Aviv. The room was large, but windowless, painted in a drab, nondescript green. The plush beige carpet that muffled all sound. Along the walls stood well-cushioned "captain's chairs" suitable for important spectators.

A polished walnut table dominated the room. In the center of the table there was large tray with an assortment of rolls, fruit, cream cheese and assorted sliced meats. A separate table to one side held a gleaming urn of coffee, and another of decaf, identified by red and green labels discreetly placed near the spigots. Another urn contained hot water, a basket containing packets of tea, both real and herbal, lay beside it. Another basket contained various sweeteners and cream substitutes. Even in the most stressful times, Uri thought, these Americans maintain their civility, much like the British.

The chairs, similar to those around the walls, were spaced perfectly around the table. Discreetly standing in the corner of the room nearest the door was an armed guard, complete with holstered, military-issue Colt .45 on his belt. As required by military regulations, he wore his "cover," an olive drab service cap with the distinctive "globe and anchor" of the Marine Corps. As soon as the late entries were seated, the escort nodded to the guard, and he made curt about-face as they left the room. The door closed with the audible smack of a bank vault.

Introductions were brief and to the point; the locals had been here waiting for the newcomers and were ready for business. "I'm Mark Higgins," barked a red-faced, heavy man in a blue suit about two sizes too small: "LAPD Counter Terrorism and Criminal Intelligence Bureau." He didn't have to add that, in his mind, at least, he was in charge. He had already taken his place at the head of the table, directly under a framed, glass-covered picture of the current head of the FBI.

"This here is Chuck McElroy from the Hazmat office, Mary Robley from the Bureau, Mike Berry, LAPD, and that's Steve Lawson." He pointed, in turn, to a gray-haired, bespectacled, quiet-looking man in his fifties; a slim woman in a blue business suit, probably late forties; and a guy in cop attire complete with cop suit, cop shoes and cop haircut and with a small cop mustache. The last man, Lawson, who apparently was not attached to any of the offices, Lara picked out as Homeland Security. He was slim, well put together and calm in his thousand-dollar suit; he stood out against the others like an anchorman in a blue-collar bar. She didn't expect to hear from him right away.

"Have a seat, get some coffee if you like." Uri and Lara had been assigned seats toward the end of the walnut table. Uri noticed how carefully the places had been arranged and outfitted. Each had a thick beveled glass, not plastic, "place mat" in front of it, on a green felt pad to protect the walnut. A fresh yellow pad lay in front of each chair, on the glass, with a single sheet torn off and placed directly in front of the chair. Three sharpened pencils lay neatly to the left of the pad. Each of the early arrivers had already started writing on their single, glass-protected paper. There would be no impressions on the pads for someone to collect after the meeting.

"I'm Lara Edmonds and this is Uri Levin; we're from FBI Counterterrorism Division, D.C." Not much reaction followed her words. The group clearly had been briefed about the newcomers.

173

"We put this meeting together at Mary's request, to fill you guys in so that we can get back to it." Mark Higgins was not happy. "We need to keep this short and to the point. We've got guys out all over the streets and in the labs. Information is coming in non-stop."

"Okay, Mark," Lara broke in, "we don't want to cause any delays, we're here to help. We may be able to aid with identifying the perps. You see, we've been tracking some peculiar web pages and…"

"No offense, ma'am," Higgins broke in, "but we got more leads than we can handle right now. Everybody and his brother have seen more guilty-looking Arabs in the neighborhood than we could arrest even if we wanted to. Mike here has already tracked down the ones we've had an eye on since 9/11 and we're picking them up as fast as we can."

"No offense to you either, Mark," Lara countered, "but we have hard leads on these guys, a running start. And they may not be locals. Now what has Hazmat got for us so far?"

"Look, lady," Higgins said, trying to keep himself in control, his face reddening even more," We'll keep you advised of our progress with daily briefings, but we can't have every fed in the country out here getting in the way. This is an LAPD counter terrorism issue from the word go."

Mary Robley, from FBI West, couldn't let this go by. She had obviously crossed paths with Higgins before, and didn't go for his alpha male attitude. "Mark, Lara has infiltrated their network; she has them tracked. We need all the help we can get if we're going to beat the deadline." She had clearly been in contact with Trotter.

"That's the gun I'm under," Higgins replied, his voice rising, "Beat the deadline. And we can't do it with a hundred cooks in the kitchen!"

Steve Lawson calmly ended the brawl: "Actually, Mark, as you know, this became our problem as soon as we found out it was a nuke. Now, we want everyone to cooperate here. The Bureau has had these folks working on this gang for months; we want to know what they know." He sat down, apparently clearing the way for Lara.

"Thanks, Steve," she said, "I'll fill you in on what we know from the emails, but let us get caught up from Hazmat. What do we know about the bomb?"

McElroy was pleased to show his stuff to the Bureau people from Washington. "Well, we know for sure it was a nuke, and we also know it was a uranium device, enriched 235. We've had people scavenging the area around ground zero, and planes getting airborne samples. We picked up all the expected fission products for a U-235 device, especially xenon, samarium and cesium."

"Go a little slower for us non-physicists," Lara said with a smile.

"Sure, sorry," McElroy replied easily. "A nuclear bomb requires a certain minimum amount of plutonium or uranium, but the uranium has to be enriched in the fissionable isotope—that's the 235, so…"

"Sorry, that's still too fast, I'm afraid," Lara interjected. Uri noticed that the rest of the crew around the conference table were listening carefully; it appeared they didn't know this stuff either.

"OK, there are two fuels for a nuke: plutonium or U-235. Plutonium is made in a special reactor from natural uranium, which is mostly the isotope that weighs 238 on the atomic scale. That isotope is stable against fission; but if you bombard it correctly with subatomic particles, it gains weight and becomes plutonium, which is fissionable. U-235 exists naturally along with the U-238, but at less than 1 percent, so it has to be separated from the U-238; that's called enrichment. To make a device, like a bomb, you need at least 80 percent U-235. The enrichment processes are very complicated and take a lot of large expensive equipment…"

"Not exactly easy for a bunch of Islamic terrorists to do, right?" Lara interjected.

"Right. And the fuel leaves a signature just like a conventional weapon as to its manufacture. The fission products tell us that this was a U-235 bomb."

"How exactly could you know that?" Uri was intellectually curious.

"When uranium or plutonium fissions," McElroy continued, "You get a binary distribution of elements, each averaging in molecular weight about half that of the raw fuel."

"Binary distribution…?"

"It's like splitting a rock in two; each new piece will have roughly the same weight as half the original, but not exactly. The difference between the total weight before and after the splitting is converted to energy; a lot of energy. You know the old $E = m\,c^2$ business? When you split a bunch of rocks, they don't all break into the exact same products; there's a distribution of weights that kind of looks like a two-humped camel, with the weights at the high points of the curve adding up to just short of 235. Some of the products disappear real fast, mainly by radioactive decay, in milliseconds. So you look for key tracer elements that have relatively long lifetimes and are easy to detect."

"And what they found today, is a lot of xenon-135 and samarium-149 in the cloud over the blast site. That's a dead giveaway that uranium-235 was the fuel. You just don't find that stuff in the atmosphere otherwise." He looked into Lara's uncomprehending face, as she nodded lamely, trying to keep up. Uri sat there, thoughtfully, as he tried to take in the full impact of what he was hearing.

"And here's the kicker—we found some unexploded uranium that we linked to the Russians."

"Wait a minute," Lara said, "how can there be unexploded fuel?"

"The bomb was made by amateurs, that's for sure. They didn't keep the mass critical long enough for…"

"Critical?"

"Yes. A U-235 atom fissions when it gets hit with a neutron. Then it gives off more neutrons and a lot of energy—bang! That's what's called a chain reaction. But you only get an explosion if there are enough U-235 atoms close enough together for the neutrons produced to hit other U-235 atoms. That's called 'critical mass.' The exact amount depends on the level of enrichment and the configuration. These guys had enough fuel to trigger a chain reaction, but they couldn't hold it together long enough to get it all used. If they had, we calculate the explosion could have been more than twenty times as big as it was."

"And where does that first neutron come from, the one that starts it all?" Lara asked.

McElroy looked at Higgins for permission to reveal this bit of information. "We think they used a tiny bit of 'polonium' stuck into the center, an effective but dangerous neutron source. We don't use it anymore."

"Polonium! Isn't that the stuff the Russians poisoned their ex-spy in London with a couple of years ago?"

"Right. It's nasty stuff. But it's easy enough to get hold of. You can legally buy it online, believe it or not. If they got the U-235, the polonium would be easy."

"Wow," she said, clearly impressed.

"And we also have a good idea who made the fuel. It's over 90 percent enriched, and also, has the signature of the stuff out of Irkutsk, that the Russkies pulled out of their ICBM's..."

"Whoa, wait a minute," Lara sputtered, "What do you mean 'enriched,' and 'signature'?" She figured this matter was all but settled, but she needed to catch up.

McElroy began again. "When uranium is mined it's in the form of an oxide, like iron or other metals. It's easy enough to reduce, or purify, the oxide to the elemental metal, but it's still totally inert, in terms of explosive capability. That's because most of the uranium is the 238 isotope, which is stable. Less than one percent is the unstable 235 isotope, the one you need for a bomb, like the one used on Hiroshima."

"So you have to separate the 235 from the 238, right?"

"Exactly, and that's the hard part, the enrichment. That's what kept the Nazis and the Japanese from creating a weapon in World War II. They couldn't figure out how to separate, or enrich, the 235. That was the main problem the U.S. worked out during the Manhattan Project, in the '40s. Giant machines called gas centrifuges or other monsters called gas diffusion columns are able to make the separation. Long story short, a lot of man hours and energy are used up just to make a few kilograms of the final product that goes into a bomb. It's not something that you can do in a garage or basement; it takes a major investment of time, money and real estate. That's how we're keeping track of the Iranian effort right now…"

"Don't get off the track, here, please," Lara said in her most pleasant manner, smiling at the bespectacled scientist.

"OK," he agreed, returning the charming smile, "When the enrichment is carried out, with centrifuges or gas diffusion, to separate the U-235 from the far more abundant U-238, some other elements in the raw material stay with the final product. Our guys have known since the '70s what the elemental distribution is like in the Russian bombs, as well as the French and Chinese and everyone else in the club, except the Israelis. Somehow those guys have been able to hide their testing."

"And the 'signature?'…" Lara was getting restless.

"The other elements in the fuel," he replied immediately. "The enrichment procedure leaves a 'fingerprint' in the fuel as to exactly where it came from."

"You mean we're sure it was the Russians who pulled this off?" she asked, trying to keep them on track. "Then how come it was so crude? Wouldn't they have been smart enough to…"

Higgins cut her off. "The brass has already been on the horn to the Russkies. They've acknowledged the fuel source is theirs, but they claim it wasn't their bomb. Hell, what would they possibly gain? We'd wipe them out. Mutually assured destruction, remember? No, they know who got to the fuel, and they've got him in their sights already: a guy named Viktorovich. They don't know yet exactly who he gave it to, but we have a good idea, and it's not pretty." He paused for effect, looked around the room, then continued. "We figure it has to be Hamas. They have the ties to Al Qaeda, and the money from the Saudis, so they're our best guess."

Uri broke in at last. "It's Hezbollah. From all we've been able to intercept and the threat they sent…"

"Goddamn it," Higgins was in a lather. "How the hell do you know about that? That letter is 'eyes only' material."

"Well, Mark," Lara said quietly, "We're part of the eyes. And from everything we've seen, this is Nasrallah's doing."

There was a noticeable silence in the room; then Higgins excused himself and strode into his inner office. He was gone only a few minutes. "All right," he said in a soft, controlled voice, his face bright red, "We're going ahead, for the time being, with the strategy of snagging a small group of Hezbollah terrorists in the next few days. But the Boss doesn't want to create panic mode by anything as noticeable as mobilizing the National Guard and I agree with him," he said reluctantly. "Our best shot is to send out a small hit team, find out if they really have more bombs, and stop as many of these guys as possible. That way, when the story breaks, the president can assure the people we're well on the way toward neutralizing them." He said all this as though he had worked this out by himself and had just gotten confirmation from Washington. Lara and Uri glanced briefly at each other, but did not dare smile.

"So they got the uranium from the Russians, but they made the bomb themselves somehow. Is that even possible, I mean even a lousy bomb like this one?" Mike Berry, from LAPD, was incredulous.

McElroy answered him, "A lot of people didn't think so before now, but a lot of minds have been changed. We've already talked to some people at the 'Nuclear Regulatory Commission.' There's a 'select' committee of scientists, professors and technicians who've had the job of staying one step ahead of any potential amateur bomb-makers. They have been telling us for some years now, that it was just too difficult for a bunch of guys in a garage to put something like that together. But, first of all, we were counting on them not getting hold of any enriched uranium..." Uri, Lara and some others around the table nodded gravely; they got it.

"Even if some hot shots did get hold of some fuel, again highly unlikely, we thought, they couldn't possibly put a gadget together that would hold the fuel critical long enough...as we discussed earlier."

"Well, what's so hard about that?" barked Higgins. "It looks like they did it."

McElroy started to rise, but sat down as Mary Robley gently touched his arm. "It's hard," he continued, "because for one thing, you need explosives shaped just right around the fuel elements. And it has to be powerful explosives. Looks like these guys found some Semtex. Even then, the air pressure that builds up within the core tends to keep the thing from going critical."

"So how do *we* do it, I mean our bomb guys at Los Alamos?" Mary asked.

"That's something that's never been published in the open literature. They evacuate the core before arming the device. I don't know how these Arabs could have done that. But apparently they did. What's more, if these guys could build this thing, they can figure out that they didn't get all the bang they could have. And they can also figure out why. The next one will be done better; that is, if they have any more fuel."

"That's bad news for a couple of reasons," Lawson interjected. They all turned to look at the cool, well-dressed agent. "It means they figured out how to make a small device that still went critical; and they can now figure out that they just need to add some mass to the body of the next one to get a really big bang."

"You haven't said where the bomb was or how they got it there," Lara interjected quietly. "Aren't there safeguards against transporting radioactive materials?"

The Los Angeles contingent looked at each other sheepishly. "It was in the Marina del Rey pleasure boat harbor," Mary said flatly. "We don't know how they got it there, but there's a crater there now forty feet deep." The color drained from her face as she said this, imagining the force that had vaporized an entire harbor. "Now that we know what to look for, we are pretty sure we can stop any more fuel from coming into the country. But if it's already here…"

The room went deathly quiet as these conclusions were absorbed, their implications duly noted. These guys were more than just lucky one-timers. They had to be stopped, and quick.

Chapter 30

Hossein had assembled the second device as soon as the first was on its way. It had been ready even before the Los Angeles Marina blast occurred; he was certain the U.S. would not abandon her stooge, Israel, so easily. They would need a further demonstration of Hezbollah's strength, capability and determination. But the next bomb could not be a minor disturbance like the first had turned out to be. For that reason he was delighted and reassured by the information from the Most Blessed Sheikh Mughniyah. The message, from the ultra-secret "VPN" communications system developed by the Sheikh's agents at an American university, had come via the Sheikh himself, who apparently realized the importance of anything that would lead to a more glorious killing of Americans.

Their source, which he had good reason to believe was deep in the Americans' so-called Homeland Security administration, had passed on the information that small fragments of beryllium were found fused to unreacted U-235 fuel. This would seem to be inconsequential; yet, the government had released the fact that the bomb was in fact a nuclear fission device, and had been powered by Russian uranium. So why had they not revealed the fact that beryllium was found? Hossein reasoned that the beryllium covering had been effective in slowing down and reflecting neutrons, and they wanted to keep this fact from the perpetrators. This meant that the reason for the puny blast was not the fuel or the reflector, but the containment. The vessel, which had never been tested, had obviously, to Hossein's thinking, been too weak to hold the critical mass together for the twenty or so milliseconds needed for complete fuel utilization.

He had little time to redesign the bomb; but he could jury-rig a containment enhancer. He had previously purchased a carton of super-strength steel straps, those used to hold together multi-ton loads of pre-formed concrete slabs during transportation. Though working alone, he was still able to wrap the straps around the bomb, winching them as tight as possible. In this way, he could put the bomb's steel container into compression. Then, when the uranium went critical, he would gain a few more precious milliseconds before it blew apart. The concept was similar to that in pre-stressed concrete, a concept utilized in the construction of the great concrete bridge road spans, Hossein had learned in college.

The resulting package was crazy-looking indeed: a rounded gray cylinder, held together with a bunch of steel straps. He wouldn't win any creative design awards, but he might well blow the hell out of the next target city.

Khallad had promised Hossein one man to help him transport the bomb, but the destination was not revealed until the last possible moment to avoid any chance of a leak. Then one day Ramos, the head of the Mexican crew that had transported the first bomb, showed up without warning at Hossein's shack. He arrived in an ancient Ford sedan that had been re-painted several times. The engine coughed a couple of times, and the Mexican exited the tired vehicle.

They had never met, but Khallad had briefed Ramos on how to find and identify Hossein. "The fish were biting," Ramos said, smiling, as he reached out his hand to the startled Arab.

"Salaam alaykum," Hossein replied, and let the young Mexican into his small fishing shack, connected to the large repair shed.

"You speak English?" Ramos asked.

"Yes, of course. Here sit at the table and I will give you some lunch. Have you been driving long?"

"I left yesterday, as Khallad ordered," he said with a large smile. A perfect set of gleaming white teeth was in sharp contrast to his clothing: baggy shirt and pants, covered with red clay, typical of an immigrant farm laborer. Hossein was astonished the man knew Khallad's name, but he did not show any reaction. "So, where are we headed?" The Mexican relaxed in the rickety chair

Hossein had provided. He seemed much more confident than his outer appearance suggested.

"I'll send word that you have arrived." He brought the new arrival a meal of seafood fresh from the market, and a cold soda to quench what must be a terrible thirst. The Mexican ate heartily, unconcerned that Hossein did not join him. "When you're finished, I'll show you around. I have a bed for you in the back."

Ramos quickly finished the simple meal and indicated he was ready for the tour. Hossein cleared the dishes and led him to his workplace, where the new device lay on its lumber cradle. "Wow, that's different from the last one," he exclaimed, as his eyes traveled the length of the sinister metal cylinder.

Hossein was taken aback by this remark; he hadn't known the contents of the last "package" was known by the laborers. Ramos immediately saw Hossein's reaction. "It's all right, I'm the only one Khallad told. He figured I should know since I'm putting my life on the line here. Oh, and before we get going, I'm supposed to be paid in advance." Ramos smiled, once again showing not the least apprehension with his aggressive behavior.

Hossein approved of this pre-payment; he had the funds, in U.S. dollars, waiting. Money, of the sort they were talking about here, was of little consequence in comparison with the job at hand. "Here you go, $25,000 now, another $25,000 when we get back." He handed the Mexican five bundles of one hundred dollar bills, along with a plain envelope he could use for mailing.

"Right you are," Ramos said, his eyes huge with anticipation. "You don't mind if I take care of this now?" He produced a box used to mail books of bank checks, into which he placed the stacks of hundreds. They fit perfectly. He also had the plain brown shipping box with his address already printed on it. Hossein quickly glanced at it: a Post Office Box in El Paso. Ramos could easily just walk into the Mail Box store in El Paso, pick up the package and walk across the pedestrian bridge into Mexico. There was no customs guard in that direction, only on return to the U.S. This man was a planner, Hossein thought to himself. No wonder Khallad thought so highly of him. "I saw a mailbox in town. Do you mind if I take this down there?"

Hossein gave him a little shrug of agreement. He was glad of the opportunity to be alone for a few minutes. As the Mexican left in his ancient Ford, Hossein quickly tore into the man's scarce baggage. There was little to examine. Some underwear, socks, jeans, heavy jacket, a pair of tennis shoes and the briefest of toilet kits was all he could find. Nothing there to suggest Ramos was anything but what was advertised.

Ramos arrived back shortly."So, when do we leave, and where to?"

"I'll let you know soon. Sleep well, my friend." He showed him to the simple cot he had prepared for him.

Hossein had arranged the next few days carefully. He would use Ramos as a hand on his fishing boat to eliminate any suspicion his arrival might have caused. Each day, while Ramos was out cleaning up the boat, Hossein checked the websites for news and instructions. One day, less than a week after Ramos' arrival the word came: Go. In two days time they were to rendezvous with the other operatives at the target location. This news meant the initial threat to the U.S. government had not been successful; a further demonstration was needed. That was fine with Hossein, even if it meant martyrdom.

When Ramos came in and cleaned up for dinner, Hossein gave him the news. "We're on our way, I just got the word. Let's load up." They went to the shack where the strange package lay waiting and loaded it carefully into the truck.

As they finished, Ramos said with his usual smile. "I hope you have the rest of my fee ready."

"Don't worry about that. I've been straight with you all the way, haven't I?" Ramos nodded, albeit without enthusiasm. "We'll take off right after dark," Hossein concluded, picking up the last of the materials they would need for the trip. Ramos did the same, collecting his meager belongings. At dark they entered the panel truck that sat waiting outside, its incredible cargo safely latched in place.

Chapter 31

Sarah's parents were never found. During the agonizing days following the blast, Sarah was distraught almost to the point of incoherency. Fortunately, their friends came over in a near constant stream in an attempt to console her. Walid went through the motions; somehow, he managed to disconnect himself from the person who had done this thing. His office had not been damaged by the blast, and his job was still there for him to retreat to during the day. It was the nights he feared. At night, the truth came back to him in vivid nightmares. He would awake screaming, bathed in sweat.

The dreams had a common thread: he would find himself in the middle of a mushroom cloud, with flames surrounding him. There would always be a figure resembling Kaaba, the granite figure that, in real life, served as the devil in the annual Islamic Feast of Sacrifice, or "Eid al-Adha," when the devout would pelt it with stones. In some years the figure would be dressed as "Uncle Sam," George Bush, or Benjamin Netanyahu. But in his dreams it was always him, Walid, who incurred their wrath. Then suddenly the scene would change, and there were Sarah, Josh and David along with other Americans, some in Jewish prayer clothes, raining rocks and debris from the ruined Marina down upon him. After two days of this torture, he was ready for anything else; he couldn't stand this any longer.

Thankfully, Sarah's Aunt Sylvia and Uncle Herb, who lived in the Valley, invited Sarah and him to come stay with them as long as they liked. Sarah didn't want to go, but Walid talked her into going; however, he would stay at the apartment, at least for a while, as it was close to his job, and traffic was understandably horrific in the days following the tragedy. They agreed to talk on the phone every day, and get together the next weekend.

Two days after the bomb, Walid was at his computer when he saw an email from a familiar name from Pakistan: Rashiv, the friend who had helped him get the job. Theoretically, Rashiv had no knowledge of his involvement with the bomb; yet, he knew of Walid's pro-Hezbollah leanings. Could it be possible that Rashiv had been recruited, and then induced to send this email as a test to see if he had survived? He was reluctant to even open the message, for fear this action alone would set off a search for him. He found himself bathed in sweat. He was now hunted by both sides, but the Sheikh knew his identity and would not hesitate to eliminate him.

He checked one of the most secure web pages, to be used for only extreme situations. It was doubly secure. After going through Opera and using the appropriate chapter and verse in the Quran, he was routed to another site. Here he saw instructions for him, and only him; instructions that would require his immediate action. So the Sheikh did know of his survival; or at least he strongly suspected it.

He abruptly left his office and walked around the block. He found himself at a convenience store, one of the few places left with a pay telephone. He considered his options over and over. He knew that he could never return to Sarah and his life in the U.S. There was a chance that he could simply disappear, make it across the border into Mexico. He might have been a martyr by now, he reasoned, dead and gone in the flames of Los Angeles. He could start a new life, with a new name.

It didn't take him long to realize the futility of that scheme. His disappearance from Los Angeles would trigger a search by the FBI. Hezbollah who had used him so effectively, would certainly not let him live with the information he had, if he did not follow their instructions. On the other hand, if he did exactly as told, he would either be extracted by Hossein and his operatives, or die in the next blast. He would be a hero or martyr. Which side could he trust? Which side would find him of more use? What was the right thing to do?

There really wasn't any choice; he picked up the phone, dialed toll-free information, and made the call.

Mary Robley had sent Zach Johnson, one of the best at interrogation, to squeeze this guy they had just brought in. Zach appeared mild mannered and friendly when he wanted to, sort of the "good cop." He was slight of build and unimposing. He wore unrimmed glasses and his thinning hair and soft brown eyes gave him the look of a kindly psychologist or guidance counselor. The suspect looked scared to death, but not crazy like the loonies who showed up after every disaster. Walid Jahangiri was the name he gave; he had no identification on him when they picked him up in the Valley. But his claim of being a recent graduate of UCLA had borne fruit; they were able to download a copy of his picture and transcript provided by the campus police. It was a service instituted after 9/11, for use with students in the U.S. on J1 educational visas. It had been a tough fight to get this access to school records; the ACLU had gone ballistic when they found out about it. But Homeland Security had compromised with the assurance that it would be used only in cases of national emergency.

Now Mary and Steve Lawson, from Homeland Security, watched through the two-way mirror and listened through earphones. If this guy was for real it was a sensational development; the Hezbollah ultimatum was soon to be released world-wide by Al Jazeera.

"Tell me again, who exactly are you, and what do you know about the event at the Marina?" Johnson asked calmly. They had treated Walid with extreme courtesy; after all, he had come to them, and they didn't want him to go sour on them. Zach was skilled at defusing the most jittery of suspects.

"My name is Walid Jahangiri; I'm a Pakistani citizen here on a valid work permit and I'm an employee at Vcomp in Van Nuys. Please don't bring them into this; they don't know anything about it."

"All right, no one is doing anything at this point, we're just getting information." Johnson was impressed with the guy's English and lack of accent. "Now, how exactly did you get this bomb into the Marina?"

"I didn't—that is I didn't do it myself..." He paused, trying to figure out how best to proceed.

Johnson sensed what was going on. The loonies typically had a crazy story all ready to go, and would blabber non-stop as soon as they got into the interrogation room. They lived for this kind of attention. But this Walid guy seemed sincere and intelligent; just scared. He would have to take it easy on him if they were going to get the whole story. "OK, just start from the beginning, there's no hurry." Except, Johnson thought, there's an incredible hurry; they had only a matter of days, perhaps hours.

Walid was getting more comfortable; he had made his decision and there was no turning back. The easy-going nature of the interviewer made him relax; he was going to be able to go through with this. He began with the lectures at the madrassah, his education in Pakistan and then at UCLA. He told Johnson about the meeting with the Sheikh, but hesitated when asked for names and specific places. He didn't want his friends in Pakistan to suffer for his actions.

Johnson knew better than to push for those details yet. They could always come back to them after they had gotten the important facts from him, facts that could be invaluable. "Sure, that's OK, we'll just stick to the main points."

Walid told him about the circuitous journey that had been used to get the homemade bomb into the Marina. Johnson wasn't taking notes; he knew all this would be on tape. Oh yeah, the Coast Guard and Homeland Security were going to have some explaining to do. "Let's go back to the bomb itself," he said calmly, "Who made it, and where did they get the parts?"

Walid hesitated just a bit; he knew this would be coming. He had to tell them about Hossein or they wouldn't believe he was part of it. He explained as much as he could about the construction, but, after all, he didn't know all the details. When he got to the part about the stolen Russian fuel elements, Mary Robley, in the next room, sat straight up in her chair. This was exactly what McElroy, from Hazmat, had told them. This Walid was golden, and Washington would have to be told immediately. She wrote a note to Steve Lawson to get Lara and Uri over here.

"All I know is that this guy Hossein built the thing in his shop somewhere in Alabama, on the Gulf Coast, I think.

Everything but the fuel he bought in the States, online." Mary and Steve both shook their heads. The land of the free.

"How did you communicate, the timing and things like that?" Johnson was still outwardly calm, but his pulse had just hit 120. He knew they were on the right track and headed for the finish line.

"We use the internet, you know, the web? We have some fake college websites and a kind of code we set up. Only a few of us know all the rules, so it's pretty secure."

"So it's an Arabic language website, just for the troops?" Johnson was making a final test of the guy's credibility.

"No, English, we…I mean they, figured the FBI would be monitoring the Arabic language sites a lot closer."

Mary was practically beside herself with excitement. Where was Steve? Did he get hold of the Washington agents?

"And can you still get on these websites, I mean now that the bomb's gone off?" Johnson was maintaining his relaxed demeanor; inside, however, he was on fire.

"I haven't tried, but I guess so," Walid replied uncertainly. What if they had changed the main codes, now that Walid had his instructions?

"Look," Johnson said, standing suddenly, "Maybe you want to stretch, have a drink of water?" He needed to see where Mary wanted to go with this. Should they let him on to a computer? The risk was that he could alert the whole network; how could they be certain of his loyalty? How would they know if the information he obtained for them was genuine?

The results of the polygraph test they had given him when he first arrived at the Federal Building were ambiguous. This sometimes happens, the examiners said, when the subject is either nervous or suspicious. Well, this guy was certainly nervous. Johnson had noticed his hands trembling from the time he had been delivered to them. The fact remained that *he* had come to *them*. Why would he turn himself in except if he were changing sides? Only if he were being used as a Judas goat to lead the FBI into one of the greatest intelligence disasters of all times, Johnson thought with dread.

Johnson stepped out of the room, locking the door behind him. The tape, of course was still rolling, recording every reaction of the subject.

"What do you think?" Johnson asked Mary and Steve, searching their faces for reaction to the interrogation.

"I think he's for real," Steve offered, "What have we got to lose? Let's let him on the computer."

"I don't know," said Mary. "It seems a little too easy. The guy walks in, says he blew up the Marina, and offers to break into the Hezbollah computer network for us." I'm afraid he could be setting us up big time."

"How do you figure?" Steve looked at Johnson for support.

"Well, let's say this is all part of the plan. Hezbollah knows their ultimatum is going public tomorrow, and the reaction will be 'Let's catch these bastards, now!' So they figure we'll bite on anything they throw at us. This guy's all set to be a martyr anyway, so they throw him to the wolves. When it turns out we've gone on the wrong track and they blow up another city, we look like shit again."

"What can go wrong if we just let him search the sites, but not respond? Is there any way the bad guys can tell that he's seen their postings?"

"Theoretically, if they had a really sophisticated server, it might be possible. But one of the security features in Opera is a guard against hit identification. That way, if the site ever got compromised, at least the users would still be anonymous."

"Very clever, but it could turn against them here."

Mary looked at the two men. "All right, let's let him at it; just make sure he doesn't hit the 'send' key. Go on in and get him," she said to Johnson, "We'll let him on the computer in my office."

Zach went back into the interview room and got Walid. "You need to use the facilities?" he asked, nodding at the men's room. Walid stretched as he stood for the first time in two hours, "Yes, that's a good idea." Zach went in with him. Walid washed up and splashed water on his face, drying with paper towels.

As they returned to the corridor, Zach introduced Lawson and Robley. "We've decided to let you search your web sites, in here." They headed into Mary's office and sat Walid down at Mary's computer, which she had perched, not on her polished walnut desk, but on a small table against the wall.

Walid hesitated for a few moments, gazing at the machine, as if uncertain about his next move. It was then that Steve Lawson gave him the "bad cop" act. "If you don't come up with some real answers real fast, buddy, things are not going to be as nice for you as they have been. There's no limit on interrogation procedures in national emergencies, you know, and Guantanamo is not a pleasant place to vacation." He stood there threateningly, hovering right beside him, loudly cracking his knuckles. Lawson's well-muscled neck bulged over his starched white collar. His voice was low but firm, leaving little doubt about the depth of his threat.

The blood drained from Walid's face as he started to slowly type in the web address. He'd better do this right. Mary and Zach watched on another monitor. Steve was ready to pounce if he tried to send a message into the site. "I need a copy of the Ho…, the Quran," Walid said hesitatingly. "The messages have to be translated using the correct chapter and verse, based on today's date."

"Where the hell are we going to …" Steve started to lose it, but Mary rose and gave him a look that told him to cool off, quick.

"We have a copy in the staff room," she said, "for just this kind of emergency." She picked up her interoffice phone and spoke rapidly to a clerk. In less than a minute the book appeared at the door. "All right, let's go."

As Walid typed in the address, the others watched in the spare monitor. "What's today's date?" Walid asked Zach, the only agent he trusted at all. Zach told him, and Walid thumbed quickly through the Quran to the appropriate page. Zach wrote down all the particulars as Walid scrolled through the entries on the web page. "I have to hit on the right entry to access the plans," he said to Lawson, fearing a blow to his head if he were to press the "enter" button without permission.

"It's all right, let him," Mary replied, "We'll get all the code information from him later. Right now we need to know the target."

Walid waited for Lawson to nod in agreement, then he entered into the correct blue-underlined address. "This is it," he said gravely, "And they are asking me to show up, if I'm still alive." He wrote down the city and directions to the bomb site on a piece of plain paper, while the jaws of those in the room collectively dropped.

Chapter 32

The ultimatum broadcast on Al Jazeera had met with a mixed response from the public, if the immediate, on-the-spot polls could be believed. Forty percent or so wanted the government to quickly accede to the Arabs' demands. Another twenty was ready for a full-scale attack on every Muslim country in the region. The remainder either didn't have an opinion or were willing to leave it up to Homeland Security. One thing was clear: there was widespread terror, exactly what Hezbollah wanted.

The President's spokesperson had gone on television almost simultaneously with the publication of the ultimatum. She tried to calm the public with assurances that the terrorists were under surveillance and their capture was imminent. The President himself would be addressing the nation, and in fact the whole world, later that night. What wasn't made public was the frenetic activity at all levels of government that had gone on during the last five days. There were factions that had wanted the White House to go public as soon as the private copy of the ultimatum was received. This option was countered with the reasoned response that it would be imprudent to publish such a threat before it could be authenticated. The information that the Los Angeles event was due to a nuclear device had been announced within hours of the blast.

In order to avoid pandemonium, the spokesperson assured the people that they should carry on their lives as normally as possible. However, travel should be limited to the most necessary of business. This announcement had been made after serious consideration. But the thought of a nation in panic mode, she said, was anathema to the President. That was exactly what the terrorists wanted, he reasoned, to the dismay of his Secretary of State and military advisors. They would have preferred a complete shutdown, followed by a house-to-house search by the Army, police and National Guard. But the heads of Homeland Security and FBI argued, quite logically, that such a Nazi-like approach would play right into Hezbollah's design. A small group of plotters could easily masquerade as part of the hastily-assembled interdiction force and proceed as they pleased. They would be more visible if the country functioned normally.

It had been a tough call but, in the end, all but the most radical of the right-wing fringe had agreed with the decision. A few hundred of these gun-toting fanatics headed for their well-stocked bomb shelters shouting "I told you so!" In the end, they hardly had time to dress in their jungle fatigues.

Demonstrations sprang up all over the country, with signs proclaiming: "Down with the Zionists" and "Save America, Dump Israel."

The Israeli embassy in Washington was surrounded by police, fearing an angry mob attack. Surprisingly, no demonstrations were seen outside the Arab embassies. Whatever discussions going on in the White House were done in complete secrecy, though officials from all countries in the region were seen scurrying back and forth.

The President and his advisors were aware that in Tel Aviv, the Israeli cabinet ministers were meeting in emergency session. The reaction in the U.S. was very much as they had expected. Now, as reaction from around the world hit the news, a different scenario emerged. European countries with large Muslim populations, like France, were solidly in favor of quick accession to the demands. Russia, too, with problems of its own with its Muslim neighbors, the old Soviet member nations, urged American surrender. In fact, only Australia and New Zealand, who could see their own fate in the balance, fully supported resistance.

The Arab countries were surprisingly muted in their public statements. They politely suggested that it was in the best interest of the U.S. and the world at large to "be more even-handed" in their support of countries in the region. This meant that by shifting military aid from Israel to the Palestinians and their protectors, as demanded by the terrorists, the region was less likely to experience hostilities. Even the most naïve of the American media saw through that ruse.

The media had treated the issue with a broad range of response. Most of the commentators were furious that the information had been withheld. Beyond that, there was widespread accord that the demands be met, at least publicly. That way, it was argued, a search for the terrorists could proceed while the official support for Israel was dismantled, and financial aid to the Palestinians begun.

The talking heads on the television networks occupied all their air time. It seemed as if only the Weather Channel continued with its normal schedule. All attempts to pry specific information from Homeland Security and the FBI were met with stony silence. Hourly briefings from the White House remained ambiguous, detailing neither the expected time nor place of any anticipated attack. The press corps was told repeatedly, however, that there were clear leads being followed up and that arrests were expected momentarily. The president's office stuck fast to the government position that "there would be no negotiation with terrorists."

The speculation on the news shows ran rampant. Their switchboards and email sites were flooded to a degree never seen before. The calls seemed to confirm the instant polls: most people wanted to write off Israel. But presidential advisors from some past administrations, in hastily arranged interviews, argued forcefully against any capitulation to the terrorists. First, they pointed out, no Muslim government was publicly supporting Hezbollah. Thus, the attacking group would probably be small and disorganized. Second, any agreement with such a demand would bring about more of the same, from every quarter. No country would be safe.

There seemed a clear consensus from the career diplomats that, after the surprise attack in Los Angeles, the nation's vast security system, set up after 9/11, would quickly stop this gang. Homeland Security officials did go so far as to point out the huge array of border patrol agents, armed with the latest in radiation monitors, that now protected every port and border point. Now that the bomb material was known to be U-235, their radiation monitors would be set to detect the specific emission from that material. What wasn't stated was that the radiation consisted mainly of "alpha" particles, which were easily shielded. Only the exposed fuel would give an unmistakable signal. It was like looking for a burning match through a steel door.

Nowhere but at the top echelons of the government, was it known that the fate of the country lay in the hands of two young agents.

Chapter 33

December 2013

General Itzhak Weiss picked up the jangling phone. He was filled with dread every time the damn thing rang this past week. "It's the red bird, Izzy. Turn on CNN." Weiss's face drained completely of color.

"This is it?"

"Looks like it. But no 'go code' yet." The PM hung up.

Weiss leapt up and turned on his small office television. In the background, he could hear the commotion in the rest of the building. Everyone had already gotten the news.

"...and this, as you all know, is the same threat that was transmitted to the government last week..." The lovely, blond announcer was scared to death. As well she should be, Izzy thought. On the split screen, the Hezbollah letter was scrolling, slowly enough to be read by the viewers. While the demands had been made public earlier, the exact text had not. Even he, Izzy, had not been privy to exact details of the threat before this. Now he recognized the brutal language of the Hezbollah gangsters, as they were known in the IDF.

The Israel Defense Forces had been established officially in May 1948, succeeding the Haganah, the makeshift group of hardy volunteers who had defended the tiny country up to that time. Now the IDF was generally considered to be the finest fighting force, man for man, in the world. Their might in the field of open warfare was as formidable as was Mossad in the underworld.

The television coverage switched to a live broadcast from the White House, where the stoic, firm-looking American president sat at his desk in the oval office. It was late at night in Washington, early morning in Israel. The United States, and, in

197

fact the entire world had been anxiously waiting for his official response to the Hezbollah threat.

Dressed impeccably, in a dark blue suit, white shirt and bold red tie reflecting the colors of the large American flag, standing next to his desk, "My fellow Americans," he began somberly. "We face a unique crisis today, one not of our making. A group of worthless thugs, calling themselves 'Hezbollah,' or 'Party of God,' has threatened the free world with nuclear terror." His face had a hint of disgust as he said this, conveying the loathing he felt for people who would misuse the name of God in this way.

"This gang of terrorists has tried to blackmail this country, in fact the entire free world, with the menace of unwarranted nuclear attack. Their demands, as you know by now, include the abandonment of one of our closest allies, Israel. To those of you who feel that this kind of action on our part would somehow guarantee our safety, I urge you to consider its consequences carefully. The Muslim extremists who issued this threat have nothing less than world domination as their goal. We can no sooner give in to them than we could to any other sort of gangsters. Though this particular gang is somewhat different from the bunch of criminals who destroyed the World Trade Center on September 11, 2001, their ultimate goal is the same. Whether these misguided religious zealots are called 'Al Qaeda' or 'Hezbollah' makes little difference. The United States has never complied with the demands of blackmailers, and we will not do so now. Let everyone in the free world and elsewhere be clear on this: we do not negotiate with terrorists.

"The government has instigated the most far-reaching search for the perpetrators of the Los Angeles incident, and in concert, their colleagues who would be involved in any future attacks. We are making remarkable progress in this effort, and I personally want to assure the American public that we will not cease until we bring this entire matter to closure. In the meantime, I urge you all to maintain your lives as normally as possible. For the next few days, limit your interstate travel to only that necessary but otherwise continue all activities.

"I have the promise of the FBI, the Department of Homeland Security and the nation's defense forces that these culprits will be apprehended soon, without another attack. Do be on the alert for strangers, and unusual, unattended packages, anywhere, just as you would at an airport. Report any suspicious behavior to your local police, who are working hand in hand with the federal authorities. I have, for the first time, raised our threat level from 'High' to 'Severe,' the red, or highest level."

The camera slowly closed in on the President's somber, but confident, face. "My friends, this is a critical juncture in the history of this great country, and in fact the world. Will the forces of evil plunge us into another Age of Darkness as they did fifteen hundred years ago? Or will we stand up to them and bring about a new sense of freedom everywhere. The stakes are great. I ask your understanding and cooperation at this time of utmost crisis."

The camera backed away to a full shot once more. The President's face relaxed somewhat, though his gaze was fixed directly into the lens. "We will survive this threat, my friends, because we are on side of Right. There will be no mercy shown to the forces of Evil, I give you my word. God bless you and God bless the United States of America."

The world's news organizations had already taken instant polls of viewers' reactions, both after the public announcement and immediately after the president's speech. In most of the world there was widespread antagonism for any action by the U.S. other than capitulation to the demands.

But in the U.S. after the president's speech, there was a noticeable shift in popular opinion, if the instant polls were to be believed. Although there was still a solid twenty percent who would have preferred to see America cut its ties with Israel and proceed from there, he had apparently convinced a substantial part of the populace that matters were in hand, and the threat was going to be eliminated before any more destruction occurred.

At the same moment, Ambassador Doring sat in the prime minister's office with Weiss and his deputy, Ari ben Nathan. They were glued to the television set, as were hundreds of millions of others around the world. No speech in the history of time had garnered such attention. They had all been briefed ahead of time, just after Al Jazeera went public. It had now been four hours since that momentous announcement.

Weiss felt his hands relax; he hadn't realized how tense he had become. His entire body was bathed in sweat. He wondered if the American president was any calmer. He also wondered if the president knew more than he did about the "forces of Right," consisting entirely of a young Israeli assassin and a young American internet expert.

The PM sighed wearily as the three of them watched and listened to this ongoing drama. "There really is no way to stop replaying history, is there?"

Doring was more optimistic. "We're getting our chance. That's all we can ask. We have the forces of the American intelligence agencies going all out. And it's happening on our soil. Sure, there are some dyed-in-the-wool doves, those who wouldn't lift a finger even as the guns were pointed at their heads."

After he said that, he realized the impact on the two others, to whom the Holocaust was not just a footnote in history. There was a widespread feeling of shame throughout the world's Jewish community at the lack of resistance to the extermination of six million of their relatives. To those who made it safely to Israel, the words "Never Again" were more than just a slogan. Never would they allow aggressors like the Nazis, Hamas, or Hezbollah strike them down with impunity. Doring saw on the faces of the PM and his deputy the determination of the last remnants of two thousand years of the Diaspora.

He was not completely aware of Israel's defensive strategy. He knew they had some sort of "Strangelovian" countermeasure, but he didn't know its extent. But to the PM and his staff, Ekdikeo was more than a possibility, it was a reality. The grim look on their faces was more than just determination; it was a grim presage of a fiery cataclysm.

Chapter 34

They were already at LAX, headed for the military terminal, when Lara's pager buzzed. This number was known by only a few people, all at the FBI headquarters, so the message must be urgent. "Hold on, sergeant," she said as she tapped the driver on the shoulder. "Pull over and stop for a minute." She pulled out her federal satellite phone and dialed in the number that appeared on her pager; she knew it at once: Trotter. "Edmond," she said quickly as he picked up.

"Right, good. Listen, you need to go back to Fed 3, pronto." Fed 3 was the Federal Building on Wilshire.

"What is it, has something happened?"

"Can't talk about it, even on this line," he replied, "just get back there. Now!"

Lara and Uri had been scheduled to return to headquarters on an overnight flight on a military jet to plan their next move. Something serious must be up to cause Trotter to alter their return. It wasn't another terrorist attack, they were certain, or they would have been alerted at the military check-in, and presumably on the televisions that were scattered all through the terminal. That must mean there was a break in the case, something of a secure nature, unknown to the public, or even to the local authorities. They turned around and headed back to the main terminal building; the Army limo had been alerted to their arrival and was waiting to whisk them back to Wilshire.

With the aid of flashing lights and siren, in less than twenty minutes, they ran into the Federal Building, where they were met by Mary Robley. "We've got the guy and he's talking. It's the real stuff; we need you to corroborate." Mary was more excited than Lara thought possible for her. Her face was livid, her hands shaking.

"What is it, who is he, what is he saying?" Uri was beside himself as he peppered her with questions.

"I'll get to all that in a minute," Mary replied as they headed up the elevator. "Meanwhile, do you think there's any chance at all that any of those newspaper plants could have paid off yet?"

"Well," Uri said, it's less than twenty-four hours since the notes were supposed to appear. Can we check the online editions to see what's been printed first?"

"Sure, here, use my computer; it's accessed to all the major newspaper online editions. You won't have to register."

Uri sat at Mary's machine, while Lara took the other. They each logged onto browsers and began searching and quickly found the stories in the Tampa, Houston, and Chicago papers. All were in the "City" or "Metro" sections. As requested, all three stories concerned potential traffic delays due to construction work. The most creative, Lara thought, was in the Houston paper, saying the delays were due to graffiti removal from some downtown freeway overpasses, being done by crews consisting of convicted juvenile offenders. Significant delays were expected from rubbernecking commuters.

They were disappointed that no story appeared in the major San Francisco paper; perhaps the city editor didn't get the word in time or he didn't feel it deserved space. Lara made a note to tell Trotter, and try to get it into the morning edition.

That was the easy part; now they had to comb the suspected Hezbollah web sites for reaction messages to the terrorist networks. They first checked out the site that Walid had identified earlier. Mary hadn't yet told them what Walid had apparently discovered; she had just said that they had some significant information. She wanted to check out their resources first, then see if they got a match. Lara was a little miffed that they weren't being told everything at once, but Uri was used to this kind of individual "blind" investigation. It gave much more credibility to a match.

Walid's site proved of no use; without the codes he had used, they couldn't find anything. They were gong to have to do this entirely on their own, using the sites they had independently identified. They slowly made their way through the various false college web pages, looking for anything relating to the four cities, and tomorrow's date. Then they realized that the date would be coded, so they asked Mary for at least the date coding provided by Walid. Mary was reluctant, but gave in when she agreed that if the cities matched, Walid's information was probably valid. They had about thirty potential "Riemann" sites to check, but about halfway through nothing had appeared regarding any of the target cities.

Suddenly Lara, glancing at one of the suspect web pages dated the day before the first bomb, noticed a message regarding "the Rule of Riemann." It was posted on a site that was supposed to be attached to a non-existent Political Science class at Loyola Marymount University. "Uri," she said, "Unless I'm terribly mistaken, there's no mention of any 'Riemann' in Political Science. Do you think this is significant?"

"That sounds like a German physicist or mathematician to me. Do you think there's anyone around here who would know?" Uri asked Mary.

"We've got more than our share of those kinds of guys in the Analysis Branch, I should be able to come up with someone." She picked up her internal phone, dialed a number, and had a quick conversation with someone she called "Bud." Two minutes later a thin young man with very bad skin and worse teeth appeared at the door, hesitating before he entered.

"Jared, come on in," Mary said cheerfully as the young man looked fearfully into the room where two strangers sat at computer screens, and the anxiety in the air was palpable. Jared was clearly not used to Special Ops type atmospheres. "Lara, Uri, this is Jared Goldstein, one of our math specialists. He has a PhD from Princeton, works on…God, what is it you work on?"

"Mostly statistical analysis of digital data acquired from…" He hesitated, apparently not knowing if he was allowed to go any further with these strangers.

Mary picked up instantly on his reluctance and said at once, "Jared, Uri and Lara are from FBI headquarters. They're working on the Marina blast. You can tell them anything relevant; I'll stop you if I think you're drifting into a red zone."

Jared, looking a bit more comfortable, went on. "We get a lot of digital data from the satellites, and a lot of it looks random. My job is to look for significant patterns..."

Lara interrupted: "Do you know anything about the 'Rule of Riemann'?"

Jared looked a little startled at this nonsequitur, but recovered after a few seconds, looked at Lara, evidently impressed, and said simply, "Yes."

Lara then showed him the web message and explained about the nonexistent Poly Sci class. "Could this be some sort of message; it was posted the day before the blast?"

Jared studied the message, pushing his glasses back up onto his nose. "Riemann rules deal with integrating complicated formulas, getting the areas under complex curves."

"What could that possibly mean in this context?" she asked.

"Well, if we assume that they are involved with the terrorist attack, and the posting agent knew some nuclear physics, it could refer to summing up the effects of all the radioisotopes released. Yes, it's possible he was signaling the upcoming event."

Mary, Lara and Uri looked at each other simultaneously. This had to be it. This site was golden. "Thanks, Jared, you just saved us a lot of useless searching." Mary shook his hand heartily.

"If you need anything else…" Jared was thrilled, and rightfully so.

Uri and Lara got back on the computer, searching this and some other closely related sites they had previously identified. Then Uri bolted straight upright in his chair.

"Look at this one," he exclaimed, "We've never seen a reference to the University of Chicago before."

"They don't teach engineering there," Lara pointed out, "Weren't most of the so-called courses on this set of pages technical ones?" Lara pointed to the batch of pages that "Opera" had identified as suspect.

"That's right!" Mary almost shouted, "What does it say?"

"'Civil Engineering 233 homework may delayed because be difficult.' My English may not be great, but this looks terrible." Uri said.

"That's got to be it!" Lara jumped up in excitement. "That's how the page got into the Opera-suspect system in the first place: the terrible English."

"Let's check this site out for late postings, entries after the newspaper announcements," Uri was already scrolling through the internet, as the others looked over his shoulder. In a few minutes, he found an entry posted just hours ago, on the same "University of Chicago" site. It read: "For Bridge Construction problem due tomorrow, avoid structure similar to Wabash bridge."

"Holy Toledo," Lara yelled, her Ohio roots showing up.

"Well, you have a definite match," Mary said with a grim smile, "And Chicago's what the Walid guy said. And he says he's got instructions to go there. I'll get him up here to confirm the spot."

"Even better," Uri said, "He can come with us."

"Hold on a minute," Mary said, "Who said anything about you guys running this thing down?"

"Call Trotter, he'll clear it."

"You know what time it is there?"

"Doesn't matter, he's sleeping in his office."

Mary called on the secure line and found a very alert Deke Trotter on the other end. "They confirm the suspect intel?" He was brief and to the point.

"The city is a match. We'll have to go with his particulars on the location and time."

"That's a go then, we'll get a team in there. Just give me the coordinates."

"Maybe you better talk to your people, they a have different idea." She handed the phone to Lara.

There followed a heated discussion between Lara and Trotter. He finally gave in to the "continuity" argument; the Bureau would let the field agents in charge take a case to the finish unless there were severe reasons against the action. But he insisted on a major backup, with both military and civilian forces on site.

As soon as the conversation ended, Mary got on the internal phone again and gave instructions for Walid to be transferred to O'Hare airport in Chicago ASAP with full military "escort." He'd be held there until Uri and Lara could get there and proceed to the location. Mary did not want them all on the same plane. If, for some terrible reason, Uri and Lara failed to arrive at O'Hare, at least Walid could lead a team to the proposed blast site.

Furthermore, he would be a perfect decoy, allowing the team to close in on the terrorists. "You can have your pick of these; I have a feeling you're going to need them." She pointed to an open suitcase, with padded compartments containing an assortment of government-approved handguns, each with several clips of ammunition. "I understand your own weapons were confiscated for the flight out here." They eagerly accepted her offer, choosing weapons they were familiar with and skilled in their use.

The same car that brought them from LAX was waiting as Lara and Uri exited the Federal building. They rocketed back to the airport, lights and sirens blaring as they tore down I-405, traffic reluctantly yielding the right-of-way. Both were absorbed in their own thoughts as they made it to the airport in less than 10 minutes, a new record.

Chapter 35

Walid sat in the holding cell at Los Angeles FBI headquarters. He hadn't been told what would happen to him next. The cramped little room was eight feet by ten feet; it was furnished with a simple cot with thin cotton mattress, a hospital-type pillow, but no linens. He was attired in a blue prison jump suit and medical slip-on cotton shoes. There was also a small, pull down desk and metal chair, metal toilet and sink. Residue from the previous occupants was apparent everywhere. There were no mirrors or other amenities. The lack of privacy was humiliating to Walid; never before had he been exposed to other eyes while on the toilet.

He had plenty of time to consider his fate; it was impossible to sleep. He had realized that once he told the FBI of his complicity in the bombing he would be at their mercy. Sometimes he wished he had been killed in the blast; at least then it would be over and he wouldn't have had to make any more decisions. But at other moments, he thought of the thousands of lives he had taken, and how many more were yet to come. It was amazing, the depths of feelings that now coursed through him. Even he could not totally explain it. For years, he had fully accepted the commitment to Jihad. It seemed so natural that the infidels must be eliminated in order to bring Islam to its proper place as the ruling force. It was meant to be, it seemed, and he wanted to be a major factor in the revolution.

The other part of his brain urged him in a completely different direction. Something had happened to him. It had been a gradual awakening that had spread from the inside. He had operated externally for months, exactly as he had been instructed. It was only when he saw how he had been manipulated and used, that the growing questions that had been gnawing at him had come to the surface.

There were the little things, of course. There was the unwavering love from Sarah and her parents; the acceptance of his friends and colleagues. But then there were the views of *Sharia* that he saw in the relatively uncensored Western media. At first he had thought that the incidents portrayed on television were fabricated by the American press. But then the visual feeds he had witnessed were too accurate to be anything but the truth.

Most prominently were the crimes against women. At home, in Pakistan, women were treated decently, he had believed. But, of course, equality with men was unheard of. There were no published reports of atrocities against women. It was only when he came to the U.S. that he read and saw the penalties Pakistani women suffered. He studied the fully documented reports of the young woman who was gang-raped in 2002 by court decree for something her brother had supposedly done. Of course, that paled in comparison the treatment of women under the Saudi version of *Sharia*: An English woman publicly flogged for being so brazen as to offer a drink to a Saudi. Another stoned to death for permitting herself to be raped by a gang of young Arabs. These incidents were reported almost weekly, yet no action seemed to be taken, or even demanded by the various so-called Human Rights groups.

When Walid lived in Pakistan, the shrieks of outrage that these groups constantly made against the West, were prominently posted for all to see. It seemed that these groups, all Western-based, with access to atrocities worldwide, focused almost entirely on the alleged crimes that the U.S., Israel, England, and other democracies, carried out against their minorities. If an Arab, living in Israel, had the slightest grievance against the government, it was played up for the maximum coverage. Of course, this same Arab, if living in an Arab country, would have far less in terms of standard of living or "human rights." But that, he now realized, was not newsworthy, even in the West. It was now clear to him that the reason for the predominance of Western "indignities" was the free access that these governments gave to journalists. He was always amazed, not only at how gullible these "Human Rights" committees were, but also how much impact they had on a large fraction of the people.

He had also researched the writings of the late Senator Daniel Patrick Moynihan, the source that the acne-scarred David Grossman had quoted at one of the parties he had gone to with Sarah, at Josh Green's house. David had vainly argued at that party, that the "liberal" Moynihan had seen through the rantings of the United Nations, a body that had begun its life so promisingly after World War II, but had turned into a hopeless sounding board for the dictators of the many small African and Asian countries. In keeping with "Moynihan's Law," vast numbers of imaginary atrocities were ginned up against Israel and other open democracies, while real violations were ignored. At his computer in recent weeks, Walid had learned of the genocide occurring in the Sudan, and the genital mutilation of young girls in much of sub-Saharan Africa. They called it "circumcision." It was meant to diminish the libido of the girls, so they would be more likely to be loyal to their husbands. When he thought of his own family, and, of course, Sarah, he was sickened to the core.

These horrors had been unknown to him when he lived in Pakistan, where he and his friends had only heard of the cruelties committed by the Americans and their allies. As he now learned, almost all of these were fabrications of the radical Islamic press.

He sat there now, in his cell, and compared the accusations from the two sides. One side, the Jihadists, based their arguments on fear, ignorance, prejudice and hatred. The other side, while not being blameless, seemed to argue with evidence and judiciousness.

He also had access to uncensored accounts of the Israeli-Hezbollah fighting in 2006. Contrary to the inflated stories he had read in the Islamic press, the outcome had been more of a stalemate. The outrage the Israelis felt at the unhindered rocket attacks against civilians in their northern towns and villages now made sense to him.

He had read the Western accounts of the peace overture made by Israeli PM Ehud Barak during the Clinton years. Virtually all the demands made by the Palestinians had been met, yet Yassir Arafat, the recognized head of the Palestinian people, had not even bothered to respond. His "bluff had been called," to use the American parlance. The Islamic press had reported a much different version of the peace proposal. For instance, Walid had not known, or else had dismissed, the offer Barak had made regarding Jerusalem. Against the wishes of many in his cabinet, and certainly among the citizenry, Barak was willing to allow the new Palestinian state to use Jerusalem as its capital. The city that had been the object of the bitter fighting in 1948 and again in 1967, would be shared as capitals of the two States. Over 97 percent of the West Bank would be under Palestinian rule. It was more than anyone familiar with the region could have hoped. Israel, which had beaten back the military assaults of the Arabs for over sixty years was now ready to trade all their hard-fought real estate for peace with its neighbors. It was truly astonishing.

Yet Arafat walked away from the agreement without so much as a comment. The reason now appeared clear to Walid: the Arabs had never wanted peace, under any circumstances. They wanted rid of Israel and all its citizens. But, his other side argued, wouldn't this be best in the long run? Hadn't he embarked on his life's journey to bring about a new world, one of Muslim dominance and submission to Sharia? He was now in a unique position to bring his people to world dominance. He would be celebrated forever. But his misgivings continued.

On the one hand there was the hypocrisy of the entire radical Islamic culture. He saw *Sharia* as a means to control the minds of millions of people, to the benefit of a few ruthless dictators. He had witnessed, in the Western press, the heroic actions of some Muslim women who were trying to bring the world's attention to the plight of their people.

On the other, was a path to fame and everlasting pleasure. Paradise, filled with lustful young virgins living only for his pleasure, and glory-filled immortality had been his dream. Now it was at his fingertips. He had only to carry out the orders sent to him by Sheikh Nasrallah.

His decision had been made, yet he could still change his mind. One way or another, Walid Jahangiri would go down in history.

210

Chapter 36

Among all the statements made by Walid in his interrogation, Mary Robley was especially impressed with his identification of the operative named "Hossein." Walid made it clear that his name was spelled "Hossein" and not the more usual "Hussein." He was not sure, however, whether that was his first or last name. Hossein was the one who manufactured the Los Angeles bomb, he was sure, and he was also the one who would be making any additional weapons. He also knew that Hossein was an Iranian who went to graduate school somewhere in the U.S., and studied Nuclear Science or Nuclear Engineering.

After quick discussion with everyone on the team, it was agreed that Reynolds Macarthur must be immediately informed, so that he could take action toward identification and arrest. Homeland Security was in the best position to handle this situation; they had the most effective manpower and resources. It was too late in the game to worry about their clumsy attempts to be super-sleuths; this guy had to be brought in with any means possible.

On getting this information, Macarthur immediately called Carter Fredericks into his office. "This is it, Carter," Reynolds said with about as much excitement as he was capable of demonstrating. He briefly went over the information Los Angeles FBI had gotten from Walid concerning the bomb-maker named "Hossein." He told Carter to instigate an immediate and all-encompassing search of U.S. engineering schools for an Iranian national with "Hossein" in his name.

Fully two hundred agents were assigned the task of combing the rolls of all, not just the elite, universities with nuclear engineering programs. There was no stealth about this investigation. Within the hour, the registrars at all these universities were told in no uncertain terms that Homeland Security needed the names and full information, including pictures, of any and all students from Iran with the name "Hossein." It was abundantly clear that the request was intimately connected to the Los Angeles bombing.

The search went back to 1994, and by the end of the day, they had twenty-seven suspects. This was a smaller number than Carter expected, but it turned out that many nuclear engineering departments had been shut down during that period due to the high cost of the program combined with dwindling employment opportunities.

Of the twenty-seven, fifteen were found to be working in Iran, Jordan and Egypt, in various industries, none connected with nuclear science or engineering. Because the U.S. had no formal relations with Iran, the diplomatic services of other friendly nations had to be employed. Britain and France were especially helpful, the latter country having lately had a decided shift in attitude toward Muslim extremists. They quickly verified that all these fifteen graduates of U.S. nuclear engineering schools were, in fact, residing and working outside the U.S., and had been for more than five years.

Of the remaining twelve, ten were found to be permanent residents of the U.S., with clean records, employed on the East or West Coast. None had connections with any Muslim group, radical or not. That left two "Hosseins." One of these was reported deceased five years ago, and the other had willfully departed the U.S. ten years ago for Iran. However, no trace of this last suspect, Hossein Souriani, could be found. He was not apparently working in any Muslim or Western country that had records of such persons, and he had not legally re-entered the U.S. His academic advisor, one Hogarth P. McAfee, a full professor of Mechanical and Nuclear Engineering at North Carolina State University, was immediately contacted, in person, by a local FBI agent, who made what was called a standard check for security clearance. Professor McAfee checked out Hossein's picture and record, agreeing that he was indeed his student, graduating with a Master's degree over ten years ago. He was a good student, according to the Professor, and had been invited to continue toward a PhD. Hossein had refused, saying he wanted to return to Iran to aid his native country in their quest for domestic nuclear energy. Hossein had been a loner, according to McAfee, never gathering with the other graduate students for drinks and pizza on Friday afternoons, as was the custom in his research group. Instead, Hossein had spent long hours in the library, which held a depository of declassified information on all subjects nuclear.

Armed with this information, the agent, a long-time fed named Frank Conigliari, immediately contacted Carter Fredericks in D.C. It looked like they had found their man. A loner, expert in nuclear engineering, who left school voluntarily ten years ago to "help his country," had vanished from the engineering community. Carter ran to Reynolds Macarthur's office with this hot story. Macarthur agreed that this looked decisive and brought Carter up to date on some new information that had come out of Los Angeles Hazmat. A piece of highly radioactive material the size of a pea had been found on what was left of Lincoln Boulevard. On examination with standard and electron microscopy, there was found, along with other trash, a tiny bit of a circuit board incredibly identified as being a piece of a Radio Shack garage-door opener.

"How in the world do they know that, and how do they know it was part of the bomb?" Carter was understandably amazed.

"From what I understand there were about one hundred microns of an ID number on the chip and that was enough. And the radioactive material stuck to the thing had to come directly from the detonator. Let's get the picture of 'Hossein Souriani' out to every Radio Shack in the country."

"Right! What about the beryllium and polonium?"

"Already done. Our 'Public Affairs' office has contacted the twenty suppliers of beryllium sheet metal, asking about orders from unusual customers. There's not a lot of call for beryllium, it's terrifically poisonous. And there's only one internet supplier of radioactive polonium. Wouldn't you know it, it's totally legal to order that stuff over the internet."

"So what do we have?" Carter could hardly contain himself. After being shunted aside by Trotter and his FBI goons, he really wanted to break this one by himself.

"The polonium supplier was very helpful. Gave us a list of customers over the last five years. Most are straightforward: Argonne National Laboratory, Oak Ridge, and a few universities that he's been dealing with for a long time. But he had one customer he was suspicious of right away. A Post Office Box in southern Alabama."

"Holy shit!" Carter was uncharacteristically profane. "And the beryllium suppliers?"

"Lots of standard customers. Golf clubs, for one thing, if you can imagine, and other metal crafts. But one supplier, in Tennessee, who normally deals with military hardware, found us a P.O. box guy in another city in southern Alabama, about a hundred miles from the polonium customer. This guy ordered several small shipments of thin plates of beryllium-copper alloy that are easy to form into other shapes. Small enough packages to fit into one of those large P.O. boxes."

Carter hustled back to his office and told his ten assistants to send out Hossein's picture to all the Radio Shack outlets within two hundred miles of the P.O. box locations. "Tell them this is a national emergency, to get right on it!" He then sat down and reviewed the information they had. Grudgingly, he also contacted Mary Robley in Los Angeles and told her what they had discovered in this short time. She was as excited by this news as he, and quickly got the word to Uri and Lara, who were planning their next move.

In less than half an hour, one of Carter's assistants, reported a positive ID from a Radio Shack employee in Mobile. "The clerk says he's sure this Hossein guy had been in several times, bought some electronics and paid in cash. There's not that many Arabs in the area."

"Actually, he's Iranian, but it sounds like the guy. Get back on the horn with the local FBI guys down there and have the clerk brought in, see if he can remember anything else at all."

Carter raced back down the hall to Macarthur's office with the news.

"It has to be the guy! What do you think?"

"I think we saturate southern Alabama area from Mobile to Pensacola with our guys, and have them plaster Hossein Souriani's face everywhere."

"You're not worried about spooking him?"

"Too late in the game to worry about that. We need to grab him as fast as possible, before he can set off another one."

"How many agents can I have?"

"We've got access to four hundred. Contact Jerry Boudreaux at the Mobile office. Let's get them on the road."

"Done." Fredericks jumped to his feet to get the ball rolling.

"There's something else, Carter. I think the city is Houston."

"Why do you think that?"

"Think about it. Of the four targets, Houston is by far the closest. Less than a day's drive. If we can't get him at home we can hopefully get him before he gets to the ship channel."

"Why the ship channel?"

"It's so similar to the Los Angeles geography. A harbor right near the city center; second busiest in the country. I'll call Buzz Jackson at FBI headquarters downtown Houston; they've got more boots on the ground down there than we have."

"Wait a minute. It's nothing like Marina del Rey," Carter argued. "That was a pleasure boat harbor. Houston's a commercial port."

"Alright, you got a point. But if they're headed west on I-10, and Houston's one of the four target cities…Got to be it."

"You don't think we need word from the top to set this up?"

"We've already got the authority to move as fast as necessary, so long as we don't need major firepower. That we'll use with our guys in Alabama, if we can trap him. I'm sure Jackson can round up five hundred or more, counting the local cops and State Police."

By seven A.M. the next morning, Houston commuters were astonished to see patrol cars everywhere. The normally agonizing trip into the city was made even worse than if a tornado had blasted through. The ship channel bristled with Coast Guard cutters. The two airports had delays of over two hours as all arriving passengers were subjected to intrusive searches. News radio stations told everyone that a major manhunt was on, and for everyone to please be patient. Local gossip quickly arrived at the fact that the Arabs were loose in town.

The South Alabama coast was dreary that morning, a typical winter day. A slight onshore breeze pushed the waves along the white shell beaches. Several layers of clouds hid any view of the sun, and the air was damp and unpleasant. Jerry Boudreaux's hordes descended onto the area like a hurricane. He was so excited by the call from headquarters that he himself headed up one of the teams that worked their way along the coast. Other teams fanned out from the locations of the P.O. boxes, hitting every General Store and Wal-Mart within fifty miles.

But it was Boudreaux's team who found one Mr. Lo Nguyen in a hardware store in the little town of Coral Shoals. The town could optimistically be called a fishing village; a few stores and a dismal array of bungalows, 1940's style. All were built on tall, weathered wooden pilings, sinister warnings of what the Gulf might do, if she had a mind to. One wooden shack had a sign that boasted in large letters: "Fresh Shrimp All Year." In the window a tattered cardboard sign read: "Peel and Eat—$2.50." Underneath that, as if an afterthought, was printed "Cold Beer."

Off in the distance, a long pier stretched out into the Gulf. The pier was home to a few shrimp boats, rocking gently this morning at their moorings. Apparently the weather was not conducive to fishing. In fact, the barometer was low and headed lower, a distinct harbinger of a bad day to be at sea. Jerry had a bad feeling as he looked around the sleepy village. The cold wind and sky filled with dark, swirling clouds did nothing to improve his spirits. Boudreaux was a superstitious man and felt the weather was a predictor of the day ahead.

Mr. Nguyen, who liked to be called "Wen," identified Hossein's picture after only a few moments. "Sure, you mean 'Seine,' he runs shrimper and boat repair, down by pier." He pointed south, toward some pine thickets.

"Stay here, Mr. Wen, don't say anything to anybody."

"He in trouble with law?"

"We just need to talk to him, but we don't want to scare him. So just stay put, ok?" Nguyen nodded agreeably and trotted up the steps to the hardware store porch. "What's his building look like?"

"Can't miss it. Sheet metal. Say 'Fresh Shrimp and Boat Repair.' He overhaul motors."

Boudreaux went out to his black government-issue Ford Crown Vic and sent word to his troops to assemble at Coral Shoals. He then called Fredericks on the secure satellite phone. "We got him, Carter, I'm pretty sure."

"Where?" Fredericks jerked upright at his desk, where he had been dozing, unshaven and unkempt. He hadn't left in over 24 hours.

"Down here in South Alabama, just like you guys thought. Got him a fishing boat, goes out into the Gulf. Machine shop, too, looks like."

"Pick him up if you can, but don't spook him. Lay down a perimeter."

"I been doin' this a long time, Carter, don't you worry none."

By eleven o'clock the little town was bristling with black-and-whites, but with no sirens and no flashing lights. The residents looked out from their clapboard houses at the eerie scene. Off in the distance, two helicopters pawed relentlessly at the misty morning, keeping safely detached from the town. One was off to the north, where the only road out of town led to a four-way stop sign. The other chopper was off to the west, across a small inlet, in case Hossein should try to flee by boat.

Boudreaux had sent a four man team on foot to a cluster of pine trees about two hundred yards from where Nguyen had located Hossein's shop. It looked like a good spot for surveillance. The team leader, Andre Doucette, now called in, hoarsely whispering, "Looks like he's there. There's wheels out front, boat at the dock." His team, all dressed out in deer hunting fatigues, were invisible to the people in town.

"OK, Andre, that's great. Spread out as much as you can and keep your boys trained on that building." They were all armed with 30-06 deer hunting rifles with soft-point magnum loads. Anyone hit with one of these rounds would be down, if not killed outright. All the rifles had BSA 3-10X44 telescopic sights, purchased at the local Wal-Mart, calibrated up to 175 yards. The day was windless. "I'm sending out the wagon."

The "wagon" was an all-terrain vehicle that could come in on the opposite side from the assault team, over the hard shell beach. It carried four men, all with Army-issue vests and Uzi attack rifles.

In their helmets and camouflage fatigues and protective vests, they might have come from another planet.

There was no avenue of escape. Boudreaux had only to check in with Carter to get the final approval for the attack. "Carter," he spoke quietly over the satellite phone. "We got him completely covered. We're goin' in."

"Be sure to give him a chance to come out easy. There's no news nosies out there yet, is there?"

"No, just the locals, and they're stayin' tight."

"Won't be that way for long. Those choppers will have CNN down on you pretty soon. We have to make sure it's not a My Lai," he said, referring to the My Lai episode in 1968, a frightening reminder of what could happen if trigger-happy gunmen shot up unarmed civilians.

"We'll give him every chance. We got a loudspeaker on board and the whole thing's bein' videotaped."

"Alright, that's a go. Feed the video into Channel 42 on the FBI network. You got that, right?"

"Sure do, should be comin' in already."

To be sure he contacted the team leader in the Pinzgauer High Mobility All-Terrain Vehicle that was now crawling into position. Lieutenant Odie Hebert had served in the first Gulf War and had SWAT training with the Alabama National Guard. Boudreaux was totally confident in his nerve, confidence and ability under pressure. "Odie, you set?"

"Team Leader, this is Mobile One, over."

In his excitement, Boudreaux had forgotten his own orders to use standard assault talk, even over the secure phones they were using. "Yeah, OK, Mobile One, this is Team Leader. You got your video rolling, Odie?"

"That's a positive, Team Leader, over."

"Well, patch it into FBI 24 right away. Give them audio, too."

"Uh, Roger, Team Leader, do we have a go? Over."

"Get on down there, to one hundred yards, then squawk 'em, Odie."

"Roger, Team Leader, we're rolling and so's the video."

Boudreaux contacted Andre, down in the pine trees, and told him the wagon was going in. "They're going to be on the speaker any second here. Be ready in case he springs out of there."

"You got it, Chief," Andre replied, his voice shaking. They all knew how big this thing was going to be.

The silence of the morning was shattered by the incredibly loud voice from the Pinzgauer ATV: "*You in the boat shack. Come out, hands high. You're surrounded. This is U.S. Homeland Security talkin'*" Hebert had decided at the last second he better identify himself.

It was then that the first news van came screeching into town. Area reporters and cameramen tumbled out into the street in front of the startled, if somewhat bemused, residents. Much as Boudreaux hated to, he diverted a couple of his men to keep them out of the way and out of the line of fire.

"He's not answerin'. Should we go on in?"

"Shoot him in some smoke first."

"The windows is covered with some sort of metal slats, can't see in."

"That's all right, them tear gas grenades will go right on through. You copyin' this Andre?"

"Uh, Roger that. We got the doors covered, both house and shack."

Five sharp reports rang out, and the sound of tearing sheet metal tore through the air, followed by the muffled explosions of tear gas canisters going off inside the house and attached hut.

"Andre, you see anything?"

"Yeah, lots of smoke comin' out, but no personnel."

"OK, have your boys move in a little, form a perimeter. I'm bringin' the choppers in close." He switched over to the frequency the helicopters alone were privy to and gave them the order to "come in tight."

Hebert began maneuvering his ATV toward the house, all their firepower trained on the doors and windows. They would not mind at all being able to pour some lead into this guy. *"We're moving in, so come out now, this is your last chance!"* Hebert shouted loud enough to be heard in town.

Jack Winnick

The television crews were transmitting live shots and sound to their stations, which were then being shared with CNN and Fox News. The whole nation—and perhaps the world—were watching the scene playing out at Coral Shoals.

"We're up tight on the place, no sound from inside. Maybe he ended it himself. Should we take a look-see?"

Boudreaux had to decide whether to take a chance with his men's lives, or blow the place to smithereens. With the world watching, he decided to send a team in. "Andre, you go in the back, and Hebert, send someone in the front. The rest of you guys, be ready to hit anyone comin' out. And for God's sake, don't shoot each other." Boudreaux figured there was less chance of a messy "friendly-fire" incident if only two of his men entered the structure. There was no way anyone was coming out of there unseen.

The two chosen warriors slipped on their gas masks and waited for the signal to go in. Their hearts were pounding so loud they could barely make out the orders from their headsets. Twenty slow seconds ticked by, then Boudreaux gave the signal to go, as he prayed for a clean resolution to the affair. Video feed from the helicopter showed the two men charging into the building, one through the shattered front door, the other through a hole blasted in the vehicle entrance at the back of the Quonset hut. Thin trickles of tear gas slid out the holes in the structure as the two men searched the premises. Doucette kept in touch with Boudreaux as they quickly, but carefully looked through the premises.

"House is empty, coffee on the stove, place is a mess. Somebody sure left in a hurry." A few seconds went by. "Repair shack is full of old diesel engines, lots of spare parts, oil spots on the floor. All kinds of machine tools: big lathe, drills, mills, the works. Block and tackle on rollers, could carry a good size engine. Big wooden cradle in the middle of the floor. Maybe for a small boat, or maybe somethin' else," Andre reported darkly. "Empty now."

Boudreaux wiped his face with his handkerchief. They were too late.

"Lots of electronics stuff and sheet metal around," Doucette said.

"Alright, let the place air out, and bring the rest of the boys in. Don't touch nothin' in here. Just keep a list of what you find. Watch out for boobies."

"What the hell you doing down there, Boudreaux!?" It was Carter Fredericks on the secure line.

"Looks like he got wind of us, beat it out of here." He wished he had never heard of this mission.

"Well, wait for an evidence team to check out the place. Just get your troops out of there."

One of the locals, an older man who had been silently watching from the street, walked cautiously up to Boudreaux, took off his cap and asked, "Can I tell you something, Officer?"

Nearby, a woman anchor, Shelby Boliver, was still broadcasting, and looked keen on getting in on this conversation. Boudreaux, torn between telling her to move away and hearing what this guy had to say, opted for the latter.

"Sure, but keep it brief."

"Well, we seen them two guys head off early this morning, north toward the interstate."

"What were they…wait a minute, *two* guys?"

"Yep, the Asian guy, Seine, who ran the boat place and the Mexican who drives that heap out there." He pointed vaguely toward the ruined shack. "Drove off in the Asian guy's van."

"Asian, you mean like Chinese?"

"No, kind of like the Vietnamese around here, kind of dark, lean, keeps to himself, fixes engines, goes out shrimpin' like all of 'em."

"You sure this guy Seine wasn't Middle Eastern, like Arab?"

"Could be, I guess; didn't have no beard though."

Boudreaux showed him Hossein's school ID. "This look like him?"

There was a long pause as the man studied the picture. "Maybe, looks a lot younger, though."

Boudreaux turned immediately to his satellite phone. "Carter, you there?"

"Yeah, what you got?"

221

"He's gone, headed toward I-10, and he's got help, a Latino."

"I-10, you mean as in the road to Houston?"

"If he's headed west, it is. New Orleans first, though."

Carter broke the connection and raced over to see Macarthur. They had been right all along.

At the command center, Shelby Bolivar was wrapping up her coverage of a manhunt gone terribly sour.

Chapter 37

An utterly embarrassed Reynolds Macarthur broke the news to Trotter. He felt it an obligation that he deliver it personally, even though it had already been transmitted to the Director of Homeland Security, the President, and Secretary of Defense. It had then gone immediately to the heads of the FBI, CIA and Joint Chiefs. Of course, many of these people had seen the fiasco on CNN, so it was already "old news." That included Trotter; so he could at least avoid having to hear all the humiliating details.

"Deke, my boys did the best they could. There was a lot of bad luck involved, you have to admit. But this Hossein guy did get past us. We still ought to get him in Houston, or maybe even before he gets there."

"Reynolds, I know you did your best." Trotter wasn't sure if the thinly-veiled sarcasm had made it through. "If he's headed to Houston, you should get him."

"If, what do you mean, if?"

"Like I told you yesterday, we think it's Chicago. We're headed up there now."

"What do you mean—who's we?"

"I gave them the go ahead, my girl and the Israeli, along with the snitch we picked up in L.A."

"You can't believe that Arab is going to give away the target. Are you nuts?"

"He passed our best polygraph, and his story checks out with the info on the web sites. The Boss has agreed; it's our best shot at the moment…assuming you don't get him in Houston. We've got to go for it. Now that the Letter is public we don't have a choice. They're going to strike tonight, we're pretty sure. We even have the location."

There was a brief pause as Macarthur considered the situation. The president had clearly gone over his head in allowing this suicide mission by a couple of mismatched young agents. If they failed, which was likely, Reynolds would regain his standing. Of course, a major city would suffer a disaster somewhere unless his troops got the guy in or around Houston, but that was not his fault now.

"Alright, Trotter, I hope to God you're right, and they get there in time." Macarthur, an extremely religious Christian, born-again just five years ago, had kept his fingers and legs crossed as he said this.

"We'll know soon enough. Keep the line open, Reynolds."

"You got it. Over and out."

Walid had been given some jeans, a sweatshirt, white socks and sneakers for his trip to Chicago. He had also been given a parka and gloves, in case outdoor work might be involved. The two military policemen sent with him as escorts were not totally briefed on his status or the mission. They only knew he was a prize package that needed to be delivered to the authorities at O'Hare.

Chip Brent was a muscular, career Army sergeant from West Plains, Georgia. He had been an MP for about five years. His usual duty was to transport drunken enlisted men to and from the county jail. He had a brown buzz cut and talked with a southern drawl so thick no one from north of the Mason-Dixon line could understand him. He usually had to repeat himself a few times. On duty he was deprived of his "chaw" of tobacco, and this irritated him no end. Off duty, he could be found with a glass jar, which he spit into regularly, a sickening stream of thick, brown juice.

DuWayne Lincoln, was a young black man from Philadelphia. He had chosen the Army after several of his entourage in Philly had been gunned down by rival drug gangs. He figured he would have a better chance of making it to thirty if he were in uniform. He was lean, dark and mean, with a shaved head. He was often paired with Chip, a seemingly strange combination, but they got along. DuWayne liked hearing stories about South Georgia, and Chip the same about life in the inner city.

They had never been on an assignment quite like this. They knew that there was a terrorist plot afoot, but knew of no direct connection with Walid. He was not in any sort of restraints, which was unusual. That had been part of the deal the FBI had made with him. They were supposed to escort him everywhere, no exceptions. If he went to the bathroom, the door was to remain ajar. They sat on either side of him in the grayback sedan to the airport, and in the small, unmarked jet that left from LAX. On the plane with them were a plainclothesman named Lawson and a Marine lieutenant without a name badge. They were seated about five rows back, on the other side of the aisle. The Marine was carrying a very visible sidearm; it seemed to be a standard issue Colt .45. Lawson also appeared to be armed, with a slight bulge under his left arm. Neither of these men spoke to Walid. Walid remembered Lawson from the Los Angeles FBI office; he was very self-assured in his tailored suit and extremely shiny shoes. Walid noticed those more than anything; he was unused to seeing anyone wearing expensive clothing, here or in Pakistan.

The Marine lieutenant was occupying himself with a magazine; Walid saw, as he turned his head, that it was a copy of "Guns and Ammo." Lawson on the other hand, was engrossed with his laptop, an earpiece stuck in one ear as he typed away.

After about an hour in the air, Walid asked Chip, who was in the aisle seat, if he could have something to drink. Chip rang the call button, without saying a word to Walid. A young male Marine sergeant appeared a few moments later, and Chip asked him to take Walid's request. The attendant told him he could have a soft drink, peanuts and Oreos. Walid asked for just some sparkling water; his stomach was doing somersaults. As the young Marine left, Chip turned to address his charge. DuWayne was engrossed in the view out the window, even though it was dark.

"So, you involved in some sort of federal sting operation or something?"

Walid was startled out of his reverie. He had been going over his alternatives so many times he was becoming self-hypnotized. "What, no...I'm, uh, helping in a crime investigation in Chicago. Sort of a witness." As he spoke to Chip, he turned again to the men behind them. They seemed to be unaware or uninterested in any conversation the Arab was having with his keepers.

"They goin' to put you in the Witness Protection Program, you better think about it long and hard," DuWayne offered.

"No, I don't think it will come to that." Walid was becoming a little sweaty.

"Is this about the nuke shit?" DuWayne's curiosity was definitely aroused.

Walid turned his head again to see if the other members of the strange assembly were listening; if they were, they showed no sign of alarm. "Actually, yes, I'm going to help stop the terrorists, in Chicago."

"No shit!" DuWayne was clearly excited. He saw Walid's apprehension. "Oh, don't worry about us, we're cleared for anything. We brought some real bad guys to Leavenworth a while back, no problem. So you goin' to stop these fellas, huh? Part of a plea deal?"

Walid had not expected this sort of interaction. Hezbollah operatives, he knew, were always under strict instructions not to talk to prisoners. Chip, meanwhile, just sat there waiting for the attendant to return with their snacks. When the young Marine returned with the drinks and cookies, Chip thanked him in an accent totally foreign to Walid. It sounded like he was calling to some sort of domestic animals. "Whoee, thankee there, we's about to turn real dry an' blow way."

"You look like you could be one of them A-rabs you'self."

"Actually, no, I'm a Pakistani, by birth, anyway."

"And you helping' us, hey you all right! How you connected with these bad dudes, anyhow?"

Walid, though initially hesitant to talk to these American military men, now saw it as an opportunity to release himself from his endless self-torture. "Well, actually I knew about them, what they were up to, and after the L.A. bomb, I figured I owed it to the government to help stop them if I could." He went on, detailing his life in the U.S., his college days, and his job in the Valley. He didn't mention Sarah; no use getting her involved.

Five rows back, Steve Lawson listened carefully. He had installed an FBI "micro-mitter," the latest in tiny microphones, into the headrest of Walid's seat. It was now broadcasting the conversation directly into his earpiece. It was also going into his laptop, where the latest in voice stress analysis was taking down every word, testing patterns and wavelengths, checking them against his voice record in the Los Angeles office. Lawson was getting an instant analysis, just like watching a political debate on TV, where audience members keep a steady flow of electronic response going to the network, which then broadcasts it to the viewers. Everything's getting like a football game, he mused, as he watched his computer screen. There was a black line across the center of the screen that indicated normal behavior, a red area that indicated lying and a green area that showed hesitancy of response. A fine blue line tracked the voice. The green area was supposed to be an indicator that the subject was aware or wary of surveillance. Chip and DuWayne had been instructed to get Walid to talk as freely as possible. The pair was as innocuous as any the Bureau could come up with. The less intelligent they appeared, the more likely the suspect was to reveal himself. At least, that was the theory.

So far, Walid had stuck pretty close to the black line. Lawson noticed that occasionally he turned to look back at him; at those points his speech veered sharply into the green. Well, that much works, he thought. But a couple of times there were excursions into the red, as when Walid was talking about his involvement with the terrorists. It looked like he had more to do with the blast than just peripheral involvement. He hoped the escorts would lead Walid into more details of his part in the plot. Almost as if they had heard his thoughts, Lawson picked up Walid's voice again.

"I just came here to go to school, and I guess they got hold of me through some of my friends back home, in Pakistan." He had surged into the red zone, big time. "So I was afraid, for my family, that if I didn't help them…"

"Yeah, I knows what you sayin', sometimes you gotta think of your own first." This was DuWayne talking. "Cepten' when a whole lot of folks may get hurt bad, then you gotta think again, right?"

"Yes, that's it, exactly!" Walid agreed eagerly. He was back on the black line. "That's why I came to the FBI, on my own."

Lawson considered the situation as Walid continued on what looked like a truthful path. It appeared his actual cooperation with the terrorists was stronger than he was admitting to the two men. He had already admitted that back in Los Angeles. Perhaps he was trying now to backtrack; he must realize that Chip and DuWayne would relay any pertinent information to the authorities. At any rate, it seemed he had no reason to abort; he would simply report in to FBI-Los Angeles and deposit Walid with the authorities waiting at O'Hare.

Chapter 38

Lara and Uri sat next to each other in the first-class cabin of the small military jet. With them, but several rows back, were their escorts, three young Army lieutenants and an Air Force Colonel. Mary had explained that it was necessary to include as many of the Armed Forces as possible in an operation that was almost certain to wind up very prominently in the media. Even with their credentials, it took close to thirty minutes to clear the airport security at LAX. It didn't help matters that both of them carried handguns. Uri had the 9 mm Sig Sauer with its thirteen round magazine that he had chosen from the selection offered at FBI-Los Angeles, plus two spare magazines in his jacket. Lara had taken a .32 caliber Walther PPK with one full magazine of seven rounds.

Mary Robley had carefully recorded the serial numbers of their weapons, admonishing them to "not let FBI guns fall into the wrong hands." Uri was amazed at how far the bureaucracy went here in the States. They were both clad in blue FBI suits and parkas. Their holsters, specific for each of their handguns, clipped nicely on their waist bands.

Their seats were equipped with computers, accessed to the secure FBI network, as well as federal satellite phones. Actually, all Uri and Lara really wanted to do was sleep, but that seemed all but impossible under the circumstances. They were totally free to converse; the plane was guaranteed secure, and Mary had assured them they were not going to be monitored.

Both Uri and Lara realized that was fine as far as the FBI was concerned, but they were both worried about Macarthur, Fredericks and the rest of the Homeland crew. They would not like to be totally excluded on this operation; imagine the embarrassment in the press if Homeland were totally shut out. They had been humiliated enough after the disaster at the pier in

Alabama. What would be their mandate after all this? The Army and Chicago police, of course, would be part of the strike force; that was part of the deal they had made with Trotter.

This was really the first time Lara and Uri had been alone, well, relatively alone, since their night at the Beverly Wilshire; that seemed like another world now, not just a mere 20 hours ago. Lara, sitting by the window, watched the coast of California, outlined with its lights, drift away into the distance. She wondered if they would ever see it again. She had often had that fantasy, nightmare, actually; a flight that ended tragically just as she was about to successfully complete a world-saving mission. Here her fantasy had genuine roots; not the flight itself, that part was relatively secure. But after they landed, she was terribly uncertain as to what lay ahead.

She, Uri, and Walid had talked over the basic elements of their attack. They had also conferred with their military escort, and, of course with Mary Robley, who was taking direct local responsibility, even though the mission had been approved by Trotter. Homeland Security had been quietly accepting of the plan, especially after the disaster at Coral Shoals. It seemed clear to Lara that Macarthur did not want to be part of a plan that, first of all was not of Homeland's making, and second, had little chance of success. "Not Invented Here" was the way government organizations described the way they washed their hands of the ideas of other, essentially rival, agencies. She knew that Homeland would be quick to pounce if the mission derailed at some point; they were desperate to recover some of their image. It was a risky game, more so for the FBI than for Homeland. Trotter, she knew, was taking a huge risk with her and Uri.

Her thoughts continued to race through the various scenarios in which they could come to disaster. No matter what else happened, they were sure to be disgraced if a bomb were to go off in Chicago, not to mention any of the other potential target cities. "Disgraced," she thought to herself. What a miserably insufficient term for the humiliation, and deservedly so. If they failed at what they were attempting, she truly hoped she would perish in the blast. She could not imagine living to face the world, let alone herself. And her family, she thought grimly; how could they live with a scar like that, after all the heroism in their generations past.

Again and again, she went over the strategy of the plan, as well as the tactical details. It had to make sense, she argued with herself, otherwise they could not possibly have gotten the go ahead. The time element was the key; there simply wasn't enough to gear up an effort that would be certain to stop the nuclear device, if it were active, from triggering. The only hope was the surprise a small, dedicated team could spring upon the conspirators. And key to that was Walid himself; there was no way the Hezbollah operatives could know that he had been turned.

Her thoughts revolved, as they had several times in her fretful state, back to Walid. Could they be sure of his loyalty? He had passed the FBI polygraph test administered in Los Angeles by one of the agency's best technicians. He had based his "pass" primarily on Walid's performance on the GKT, or "Guilty Knowledge Test." In this they tested him on subject matter only a guilty person could know. Detractors often point out that this test can be "beaten" by a skilled liar, or simply by the subject knowing facts that are unknown by the test administrator.

Then Lara countered herself with the implications if Walid were lying. The worst case would be a blast in another city altogether. The alternatives of action in this scenario consisted mainly of "interrogation." Walid could be subjected to the latest in torture techniques, including "waterboarding," but the risks of this strategy outweighed any benefits. For example, if he maintained his story after the torture, would he still be motivated to help the team capture the bombers and defuse the bomb? On the other hand, if he were, in fact, lying, how could the Bureau generate a substitute strategy in the minimal time remaining? They would have killed their only canary before going into the coal mine.

"All right," she argued with herself, "Say Walid was telling the truth. Was there a better tactical plan than the one they had come up with?" Again, the plan pivoted on the need to defuse the bomb, no matter the cost in team members. She and Uri were the logical raiders. Both were dedicated to the task and ready to risk certain death. And both had the training necessary to carry out their objectives. Lara had mastered the four-month FBI course at

Quantico. Uri was a graduate both of the Mossad's and the CIA's lethal training academies.

As she had already reminded herself, death would be a blessing if they failed. Walid was their only bait, and Uri the only Arab-speaker ready to carry out the physical attack. She knew that once the bomb was defused, she had the entire Armed Forces ready to tie up any loose ends. Every time she went through the story she reached the same conclusion. Her head ached with the effort, compounded by lack of sleep. Only her superb physical condition kept her awake, alert and ready for action. At least, she thought so.

Then there was the man sitting next to her. Never in her short life had she been so attracted, in all senses of the word, to a man. They had shared so much in the past few months, physically and emotionally, she felt an unbreakable bond. She could not imagine what destructive forces she would feel if he were to be killed while she were spared. That simply could not happen. Occasionally, as they sat there, their hands or feet would briefly touch. An unimaginable spark of electricity flowed through her whole body at these moments, and she longed to hold him close. Only the presence of the troops a few rows back kept Lara from reaching out to him.

Uri sat quietly in the plush first-class seat. He had eaten sparingly, even though the young, military flight attendant had offered them a wide assortment of food. His adrenalin was pumping so hard his hunger had disappeared. He was used to this feeling; his system churned every time he embarked on one of these kill-or-be-killed endeavors. As he sat there, mulling over the rapid escalation of events that had led to this flight, he felt the warm presence of Lara, seated beside him. The release of passions stronger than any he had known in years still reverberated in his system after the brief, but thrilling encounter last night. Was it just last night, he wondered? His sleep deprivation had not yet caught up to him; he was used to missions requiring up to 36 hours of wakefulness. Actually, sleep was the last thing he was worried about at the moment.

He, just as Lara beside him, went over the plan of attack, as well as they had been able to detail it. He knew, as a member of the elite Kidon branch of Mossad, that he had far more latitude in his actions than did Lara. There were no congressional committees to worry about, no investigations as to the "correctness" of their attack. In Israel, these eliminations of terrorist threats were accepted as necessary, if unpleasant, duties vital to the continued existence of the State. He recalled the words of one of the true heroes of Kidon, Rafi Eital. Eital, over eighty years old, now a member of the Knesset and once Operations Chief of Mossad: *"I always tried to kill when I could see the whites of a person's eyes. So I could see the fear. Smell it on his breath. Sometimes I used my hands. A knife, or a silenced gun. I never felt a moment's regret over a killing."* Eital, who looked more like a kindly grandfather than one of the world's most potent assassins, was one of the reasons Israel had survived the past sixty-odd years. Uri fully intended to continue his tradition.

Uri pondered the hours that lay ahead with a grim foreboding about the coming venture. There was still something about Walid that he was unsure of. He had passed the FBI lie-detector test, but Uri's keen eye recognized some ambivalence in Walid's eyes, in his manner. It seemed that Walid held their only hope to intercept the bombers before they did more damage. He knew, perhaps better than the Americans, how well these people could lie. Walid could easily be leading them to their destruction along with his own martyrdom. Even if he had misled them as to the target city, Walid would be a star in the Arab world, as another city was annihilated.

Uri always set out on these operations with the knowledge that death might result. There was no question in his mind now that death, violent death, was in store. He hoped it was not his, certainly not Lara's, and God forbid, not the citizens of Chicago. As did Lara, Uri hoped to die if their mission failed. No, this foreboding was different from that which he normally felt. This was an operation that would either terminate or irreversibly alter his life.

Chapter 39

They had headed north and east through the southern Alabama flatland until they reached interstate 65, heading north toward Nashville. The famous "Auto Alley," that got its nickname from all the trucks loaded with autos and auto parts that traveled the highway, was a perfect cover for the transport of the bomb. "So where are we actually headed?" Ramos could control his curiosity no longer.

In answer, Hossein pulled off the highway at a rural intersection and headed to the back of a small gas station. Here he pulled off the heavy wrapping paper that covered both sides of the truck. Underneath was stenciled "Lakeside Plumbing" along with a phone number beginning with the area code (312). "That mean anything to you?" Ramos shook his head; he didn't know anything about American area codes. We're headed to the Windy City, my friend, and we're going to make it even windier."

Ramos was still in the dark. "Windy City?"

"Chicago! One of the biggest ports in the country. This will make them sit up and take notice." It was then that Hossein noticed just a trace of fear in Ramos' demeanor.

"Are we going to make it out of there before this thing goes...?"

"Of course," Hossein slapped the Mexican on the back. "Do you think I've come all this way for nothing? I want to see the result of all my hard work, and yours too, of course," he added. "We've got a remote trigger; we'll be long gone and on our way home before anything happens."

Before returning to the road, Hossein brought out from inside the truck, a thin paper package. It held two Illinois license plates, which he then used to replace the Alabama plates on the truck. Ramos looked at him questioningly. "You can buy anything on the internet, my friend," Hossein informed him. "There is a site that is supposed to sell 'souvenirs,' but actually you can get plates from any state, and even other countries."

Now that the dam had been breached, so to speak, and Hossein seemed to be willing to talk about their mission, Ramos was not satisfied with just being along for the ride, despite his enormous payoff. Fifty thousand dollars would go far in Mexico, perhaps set him up for a lifetime. "So can you tell me why we're doing this? Understand I have no love for the Gringos, they look at us like we're dirt."

Hossein pondered this a few moments; he had no reason to tell this man anything. Yet the trip would be long, and he had not discussed the Jihad with anyone for a long time. He began the discussion easily, "What exactly about the Americans, the Gringos, is it that you don't like?"

"Man, you have to be kidding, right?"

For the next few hours the two men exchanged views on their hatred of America and Americans. Finally, having talked themselves out, they traveled on in relative silence, only broken by the radio with its endless Country and Western music when, Hossein tuned to a news channel.

"...helicopters over the fishing village with video show no sign of the men. Homeland Security is being very tight with the details. We don't know at this time what caused them to raid this particular location, or exactly who it is they're looking for. What is clear is they missed their targets, maybe by just hours..."

Hossein smiled at Ramos. "Allah is truly with us. If we had waited any longer they would have caught us and the whole mission…"

He stopped talking as the radio announcer went on: *"...traffic on I-10 headed west toward New Orleans and Houston has slowed to a crawl as road blocks have been set up. All entries into Houston itself have been blocked as this manhunt seems to have focused..."*

The two men looked at each other with obvious delight. They were home free. At night, they would pull into one of the many truck stops, park, and get a room and shower, then up early to begin again.

As they reached northern Indiana, the weather, which so far had been of no consequence, took an unhealthy turn. A cold northeast wind whipped down across the highway, carrying nearly horizontal sheets of rain and sleet. The scenery had been mainly endless fields of dead corn stalks, bent over in the force of the driving rain. Now it turned to the "skyscrapers" of oil refineries and steel mills, belching clouds of steam and smoke into the already gray sky. It was so far from the beautiful blue skies of home; it truly looked like the hell that they were about to inflict on the infidel West.

That damned East Wind, he thought. At home it brings the hot desert wind, the dust and despair. Here, in this foul country, it had already decimated his first potential triumph, in Los Angeles. What further misery did it have in store for him? "Khamsīn," he muttered under his breath, his teeth clenched.

"What's that; what did you say?" Ramos was startled by this growl emitted by his traveling companion.

Hossein had not realized he had spoken aloud. "An East Wind. In my country, it is usually hot and dry, but always troublesome."

"What do you mean, what kind of trouble?" The Mexican had a boundless curiosity; Hossein had to give him that.

"In the desert, winds from the East bring dust, plague, famine. It is told in the Holy Book how the East Wind brings the locusts, wasps, and other vermin, ruining our crops and killing our children. It even parted the Red Sea and allowed Moses and his ragged bunch of Hebrew slaves to escape from Egypt a long time ago. But it won't help them again."

"Wow," Ramos thought to himself, "This guy is definitely *loco*, I better keep my mouth shut, get my money and part company, *pronto*."

As they approached Chicago, the wind intensified and became more easterly, stinging the windshield with the mixture of rain and sleet. Fortunately, the roadway remained free of ice, at least for the time being. Hossein, who was driving now, cursed the weather but dreamt of the glory ahead. They entered the Loop, Chicago's downtown, and headed, as per the detailed directions he had found on an internet map, to the maze of streets and parking areas directly under Wacker Drive. This drive, with its fashionable shops and upscale office buildings, ran alongside the south bank of the Chicago River just west of the inlet from Lake Michigan. The streets wound back and forth as they dropped ever lower under the Drive. They passed the loading docks of the elegant buildings above them, perched along the River. Finally, as they proceeded to the lowest level, there were only repair and maintenance facilities evident in the now dim light. They were nearing the end of their journey.

Hossein noticed they were about an hour beyond their prescribed meeting time, but this weather, he thought, must surely have delayed the others. The subterranean street was now at or even slightly below the level of the river, and they could hear the rush of water as well as the slashing of the rain and sleet on the black river. Then, after a few more turns, he saw an SUV with two men standing beside it, both dressed in workmen's clothes. He flashed his lights, twice short, then once long. The men responded with cursory waves. It was them.

Hossein parked his truck next to the SUV; he noticed a circular opening in the concrete wall just beyond, with a chain across it. An official-looking sign hanging from the center of the chain warned: *"No Access—Construction Crews only."* The two men approached the newcomers. One of them was definitely Arab, the other a large American. The Arab came up to Hossein, thrust out his hand and said in Arabic, "Salaam Aleikem, you must be Hossein, we finally meet. I am known as Khallad."

Hossein took the man's hand and shook it warmly, "I've heard so much about you," he replied, also in Arabic. Then they switched to English to introduce the others. "This is Ramos, who has done such good work for us, first in Los Angeles and now here." He clapped the Mexican on the back as Khallad gave him a warm greeting.

"Now you must meet our friend; let's call him Uncle Sam," Khallad offered. The large man hesitantly took Hossein's hand; it was clear he was not thrilled to be here. But the introduction made it clear that he was the inside person who had delivered the crucial information they had needed to produce and place the bombs. He was probably from the FBI, he reasoned. But Khallad must have an awesome hold on him to get him to this dangerous spot. For that matter, the fact that Khallad himself was there spoke to the immense importance of what they were doing. "We're a little late, but never mind, let's get the package in place. I'm afraid we're going to have to carry it from here."

"Where is Walid, isn't he supposed to be here?" Hossein glanced from one man to the other.

"If he survived, he will be. Like you, perhaps he is just late," Khallad said reassuringly. "Let's get started; he knows where to find us."

Hossein opened the back of his truck, exposing his wonderful creation. As he did so, he brought out a small knapsack and threw it on his back. Khallad and the American looked at silvery machine in a mixture of awe and disbelief. "And this thing will really do the job?" It was really a rhetorical question Khallad posed.

Hossein did not even bother to reply. Instead he said, "We can carry it with the wooden cradle." Khallad gave him a brief glance, then dropped the meager chain from the entrance to the access tunnel. Each of the four of them grabbed a corner of the bomb cradle and entered the tunnel. Before they proceeded, Khallad went back, closed all the doors to the vehicles, and reset the chain. "Just in case there are any visitors. I like the sign on your truck, and the plates" he said smiling, patting Hossein on the back. "You seem to have thought of everything." The group then resumed their trek, sloshing through rain and perhaps river water, the squeal of rats accompanying them.

They followed the tunnel as it gently curved to the left, staying in the center of the wet concrete floor. In less than twenty minutes they arrived at the prescribed location: At this point the focus of the blast would do the maximum damage to the locks and dams, as well as the downtown infrastructure. The radioactive rubble would be carried for miles, wreaking death and destruction to hundreds of thousands of people and buildings. At Khallad's signal, they set the bomb down, all of them admiring Hossein's handiwork. The control panel he had bolted onto the exterior had a series of lights, some on, some off, some flashing. The controls seemed to be mirrored in a remote control device that Hossein produced from his knapsack. "We'll be able to set it and forget it," he said, paraphrasing a popular television commercial. The joke was lost on his comrades. "Or we can leave it in the pause mode and use the remote. The trouble with that idea is that I'm not sure how far the signal will carry down here."

"Let's set it now," Khallad was eager to get going.

"I think this is the end of the road for me," Ramos said smiling, though not with his usual confidence. "If you'll give me the rest of my—wages—I can make it out on my own. Not that I don't trust the timer, you understand."

Khallad smiled in return. "A fine job, as usual, Ramos, I look forward to the next time." He reached into his overall pocket and produced a packet of neatly stacked hundred dollar bills. As Ramos turned to take the money, Hossein produced a small, .25 caliber pistol from his pocket, placed the muzzle at the base of the Mexican's head and fired once. Ramos dropped like a sack of meal. The small caliber slug would not exit the man's head, Hossein had reasoned, but rather would travel around inside his skull, scrambling his brain. This way there was no danger that a ricochet could damage man or machine in the close quarters of the tunnel.

Khallad nonchalantly pushed the Mexican's body to the far side of the tunnel, and Hossein proceeded to enter some numbers into the keyboard on the control panel. "One hour enough?" he asked Khallad.

"Better make it two, I want to be sure to get out of here in one piece. No one's going to stumble on this thing, especially after we move the cars."

The large man, who had been silent during all the preparation, suddenly put his finger to his lips. "We've got company," he said in a hoarse whisper.

"It has to be Walid," Khallad said hopefully. "No one else knows we're down here. The sound of feet, human feet, echoed quietly in the tunnel. The three men looked at each other. There was more than one person coming,

Chapter 40

After four hours in the air the plane approached O'Hare in a mix of sleet, rain and what appeared to be blowing snow. For the first time, Lara noticed Uri's green face and white knuckles. What a color scheme she thought to herself. Here's a guy who has taken on the worst of the worst in hand-to-hand combat, and is scared to death in a perfectly safe airplane. It's typical for someone who is used to being in control, to totally lose confidence when placed in someone else's charge. Well, at least there wasn't anyone forcing them to "raise their seats to the full, upright and locked position."

The weather was typical for this time of year: multiple cold fronts had caused the small plane to lurch violently every few minutes. Uri realized he must be about the color of the khaki military uniforms he saw around him; flying was not his preferred means of transportation. He turned his mind to what lay ahead of them. The information they had seemed airtight; it was consistent with what they already knew about the threats from Hezbollah. Chicago had been one of three possible target cities, and the verification from Lara's team left little doubt. The fact that Walid had independently confirmed the target site as the downtown sewer system sealed the deal.

The Chicago police had been alerted that there was a potential terror threat, but had been told that the details were still vague, and that no action was indicated at this time. Trotter had been adamant that the citizens not be sent into panic mode, and that even "Chicago's finest" be kept at the ready, but not be dispatched to the scene. The last thing they needed was to have some trigger-happy rookie cause an avoidable disaster. They had to promise the CPD that they would be alerted as soon as the site was safely approachable, so that the police could get the credit for the arrests. But it occurred to Lara that if they were under several feet of solid concrete, their cell phones would be as useless as if they were in a mine.

The plane hit down hard, then taxied to a remote area of the airport, where they were met by an Air Force bird colonel and his entourage and led across the tarmac to a small out building. "I'm Ken Blake, Air Force Special Operations," the colonel spat out, clearly not thrilled with his assignment. "Are you Levin?" he asked, looking down at a sheaf of papers in his left hand. Uri nodded, noticing that Blake didn't give Lara a glance. The guy was all business, and apparently didn't want to have to deal with women. He thrust out his right hand and peremptorily shook Uri's. "This came for you, 'Eyes Only' " he informed Uri as he handed him a sealed plastic pouch with "Top Secret" stamps on it and a tag requiring Uri's signature before release. Blake was the consummate career military officer. He had close-cropped gray hair that stood as ramrod straight as did Blake himself. He was about six foot one with not an ounce of fat on his lean, muscular frame. His steel blue eyes showed not a trace of humor; he was strictly by-the-books.

"Thanks, Colonel," Uri muttered as he signed off on something he knew instinctively was not good news. He took a few steps away from the military group, Lara following, and ripped open the package. He immediately recognized the light blue stationery peculiar to the Mossad, and saw the seal of the Israeli government at the top.

"What is it, Uri?" Lara wondered aloud.

Uri read the message, written in Hebrew, quickly, then re-read it before answering Lara. "They're wishing us luck, and telling us we're the last line of defense. The U.S. government won't be able to help Israel if there's another nuke. The public reaction is just too strong; they would rather take their chances without us on their backs; Israel, I mean."

"Could we really do that, Uri, to our only ally in the Middle East?"

"Like I've told you before, people value the immediate over the important. If Hezbollah can show America they can strike at will, there's enormous pressure to alleviate the primary threat.

Later, we can talk about avenging the losses; but without having to take care of the problem-child, Israel, at the same time."

It was then he noticed Walid, clothed against the cold in a colorful ski jacket, standing behind the military assemblage, guarded by two plainclothes officers.

"We'll take this man," Lara said to one of the officers. She noticed the reluctance in his manner and posture.

"I don't know, lady, this guy's supposed to be high priority. I don't know what you folks got goin' on here, but I got the whole city of Chicago to worry about."

"It's Agent Edmond to you, officer," she replied icily, flashing her FBI credentials at him, her stare leaving nothing in doubt about who was in charge of this operation. "I think you'll find my name on the signature release form you have in your hand there."

The beefy, red-faced policeman looked down at the form grudgingly. "I hope to hell you know what you're doing." His badge identified him as Lieutenant O'Leary; he gave Walid a little shove toward Lara.

"You're not the only one," Lara thought to herself ruefully, as she signed the form, then took Walid by the hand, flashing him a little smile. We need to get all we can out of this guy, she thought, and he's got to think we trust him, totally. Actually, Lara and Uri both had their doubts about Walid, despite the assurances from the Bureau following his exhaustive debriefing and polygraph examination. At this point, they really didn't have any alternatives; they had to proceed using his information. It was Uri's decision to bring him along on the attack. If things went to pieces, it was his neck along with theirs on the line. Lara had pointed out to Uri that Walid was once willing to be a martyr; but again, they had no real alternative.

"We got you a vehicle, as instructed," O'Leary said, his face flashing disapproval. O'Leary clearly had not missed many meals; his uniform bulged reproachfully in both the belly and seat. O'Leary and Blake were unhappy with the way this situation was being handled. Lara knew from experience what must have transpired for things to have proceeded to this point. Trotter had to have pulled all the strings he could, all the way to the President, to get the military and the civilian authorities to allow the two-person Bureau team to take charge. She also knew it meant the Bureau would take the full brunt of blame if things didn't go precisely as they had planned, an awesome task…; well, there was no sense worrying about that possibility now.

Colonel Blake held up his hands to stop the little group from heading out to the car just yet. "We have all the backup you can possibly need just outside the Loop. As instructed, all entry and exit points are sealed to any but emergency vehicles, and they have to be code-approved. It's a lousy night anyway, so the civilians won't be out partying too hard. Where you're headed there's no foot traffic, but we have police officers stationed around just in case. The cover story is that there was an El train accident in the Loop, and the emergency teams are keeping everybody out until at least 1 A.M."

O'Leary looked on impatiently, his face even redder than before. He clearly was not happy to be delegated to the role of assistant to the military, here in his own city. He was about to say something, but Lara quickly smiled and took Blake's hand.

"That's great, Colonel, and we appreciate your help on this, Lieutenant," Lara said, turning to O'Leary with a smile and nod. He didn't react at all. "As you know, we're going to be in an area with limited signal strength, but we'll contact you as soon as we can."

"That's why we got you this secure-band radio," O'Leary said finally, handing Lara an electronic device the size of a Blackberry. "Hit that red button, and if we read you, this other button will flash green. We'll find you. Oh, and there's a couple of heavy-duty Maglites on the seat. You're packing, I hope."

"You got it, Lieutenant," she said, "And thanks."

Lara, Uri and Walid were escorted out the door to a gray Crown Victoria that almost shouted "Police!" Lara noticed that, at least, it had a civilian license plate. There was an updated GPS with color display on the dash, which was going to be essential, as none of them were familiar with the Chicago streets. Lara slid in behind the wheel; she *was* familiar with the Crown Vic; Uri got in the passenger side and Walid the rear.

As soon as they cleared the airport perimeter, Uri asked Lara, "What in the world is the "Loop" and the "El train?" She laughed at this little diversion. "The Loop is what Chicagoans call their downtown; it's a couple of square miles bounded by the Chicago River on the north and west and Lake Michigan on the east. The 'El' is the elevated commuter train; it runs in a loop around the downtown. If the police can stop traffic on the El and all the bridges over the river, we will have them trapped, on three sides at least."

"If their bomb does go off in the Loop, what's the potential destruction?"

"Chicago has a high population density around downtown. We might be talking about five hundred thousand people or more, depending on how well they've managed to build this one. I just hope they haven't figured out what they did wrong the first time."

"What about wind direction?"

Lara thought for a moment, then said, "The Lake's on the east, and it's about fifty miles across. But there's a lot of population to the west, north and south." She looked at the driving sleet outside; it was blowing almost parallel to the road, and straight out of the east. She and Uri looked at each other for a second.

"An east wind again, only this time it's big trouble," he said.

"But not if we get there in time," she replied.

For the first time, Walid spoke up. "We will get there in time," he said determinedly. "We have to. My people will suffer even more than yours if we don't." Walid didn't believe the U.S. would meekly bow to the Hezbollah demands; he imagined an enormous retaliatory blow to several Muslim countries.

"Listen, Walid, we might need you to distract them, assuming we get there in time. Are you sure of the directions?"

"I'm certain. They were on the web site. They want me there; why would they give me wrong directions?"

Lara and Uri mulled this over silently, as they entered the freeway, headed for downtown. After what seemed like hours, but was actually only a few minutes, Uri said to Walid, "Look, you'll have to go in first. You'll be unarmed. Do you have any idea why they want you there?"

"I imagine they want to eliminate me," he said bluntly. "I'm a loose end."

"OK, but why would they think you would come? Wouldn't they think you would be suspicious?"

"Ordinarily, yes. But you have to understand, to them, this is a God-driven mission. We are to be together, all of us, to celebrate the victory over the infidels of the West. The escape is planned, this bomb is to be timed to go off after we have fled."

Uri thought about what Walid was telling them. He recalled the interviews and books from jihadists who had left the movement, then revealed the machinations of the leaders. Hezbollah, Hamas and the other Islamic radical groups were much like other cults, who could demand anything of their followers, even pointless suicide. These cults weren't limited to the Islamists; he recalled Jonestown and Ruby Ridge, among others. He considered what Walid might have to gain by drawing them into a trap: two agents more would be killed, but he would have alerted the whole government to the scheme.

The other option was that all this was a diversion, and the real attack was at another city altogether: Tampa, Houston, or San Francisco. Yet, for this to be the case, all of Lara's intelligence, all they had gleaned from the web sites, had to be wrong. It was possible, of course, but they would have expected, if the plotters suspected penetration of their network, some false leads to have appeared on the web. Yet none had. The clue they had planted had confirmed Chicago as the target. There was no alternative available to them at this point; they had to go ahead with their counter-attack, and Walid had to be believed.

They exited the freeway near its end, at the lakefront, and headed north, eventually finding Wacker Drive, a multi-level street that parallels the Chicago River. In this area of downtown, Wacker Drive runs under the city, past hotels and office buildings that border the short river as it carries water from Lake Michigan on its man-made journey toward the Mississippi River. This stretch of riverbank was notorious for flooding during the rainstorms that are typical for Chicago at any time of year, and had necessitated the outlay of hundreds of millions of dollars in sewer construction over the decades. Tonight, with this driving rain and sleet storm, the sewers would be running full tilt, and they dreaded heading into them with little idea what was in store for them.

Following the directions given by Walid, they crossed Water Street, their tires sliding on the wet, slippery pavement. They followed signs toward the lower levels of Wacker, all the way down to the Service Level, and finally the "Bottom Level." Here the dimly-lit tunnel led them to an apparent dead end, where a sign warned "No Access—Construction Crews only." An SUV and an old panel truck sat at the chained-off entrance to a twenty-foot diameter concrete pipe, leading down and to the left. Water was draining off the walls and ceiling, and as they left their Crown Vic and walked through the tunnel, the squeals of rats could be heard, washed out of their lairs by the rushing water.

The passage was lit by only the barest of light bulbs strung along the wall. Uri led the way, with Lara and Walid closely behind. They walked for about twenty minutes, keeping as quiet as possible, as they sloshed through the water.

As they moved along the gently curving wall, sticking to the outside, they heard the sounds of metal tools and equipment up ahead. The water at their feet was now a steady stream, headed for one of the main drainage sewers. They caught sight of three men wrestling with an oblong, dull gray object about three feet in diameter and six feet long. Several metal straps were wound around its circumference. They could also see an electronic box with red, yellow and green lights; the yellow light was blinking slowly. Uri motioned for Lara to stay where she was, which was at one of several insets in the wall, with a dim red bulb over it. He and Walid crept slowly along the wall toward the unsuspecting, frantically-working men. The men were in green coveralls, with "City of Chicago" lettered on their backs; because they were bent over the sinister-looking object, he wasn't able to recognize any of them, even as he got within about twenty feet of them.

He motioned to Walid that he must proceed on his own, and do his best at distracting them. Finally, he realized he could get no further undetected; he motioned for Lara to stay put, and he joined her, squeezing into the small inset. They waited for agonizing seconds, as Walid approached the men, who were standing next to the gray, strangely-shaped object that they concluded must be the bomb. The three men appeared to stop what they were doing and look in Walid's direction. This was it. Lara thought to herself. Let's hope we've done the right thing.

"Hossein," they heard Walid exclaim. Then there was some excited talk in Arabic that was too fast for Uri to interpret above the rush of the water. To Uri's surprise, there were then a few words in English. He heard Lara sharply inhale; she had recognized at least one of the voices. He glanced at her, and saw horror in her eyes.

"Jim," she whispered. "Oh my God, it's Jim Turner!" They looked at each other for a few seconds as they tried to absorb the impact of this betrayal. Had he been part of this all along? Lara searched her mind as she tried to remember if Jim knew about Walid's conversion. How much of their plan had been compromised? But there was no time for reconsideration; they had to go forward. If Walid had held to their plan, as it appeared that he had, and drawn the conspirators' attention away from Lara and Uri's location, they had to proceed.

Lara followed Uri as they crept along the outside wall of the sewer. She could now clearly see clearly two Arabs and one Caucasian: Jim Turner. Walid held their attention as Lara and Uri approached. When they got within about twenty feet of the men, both raised their pistols to the firing position, released the safeties, and Uri yelled: "Stop, put your hands in the air!"

The three conspirators stopped what they were doing and turned to face Uri and Lara, clearly surprised to see them. Hossein put it all together first; he grabbed Walid around the neck with one arm and held a knife to his throat with the other. "One more step and this traitor dies," he shouted, totally in control.

"What good do you think that will do you?" Uri answered in Arabic. Hossein showed no surprise; so he knew about Uri and his Mossad connection. Of course, if Jim had been communicating all this time…

"The bomb is set, you can all die if you want. It doesn't matter to us," Hossein shouted back in English.

"I don't believe you, you were planning to get out of here alive, otherwise you couldn't have talked this guy into coming down here," Uri said, indicating Jim. He glanced at Walid, he was supposed to know what the blinking lights on the bomb meant. But he looked so frightened with the knife at his throat, Uri couldn't detect any signal.

"Put the guns down and I'll reset the timer. We can all get out of here," Hossein replied.

"And let you blow up the city? Forget it," Lara said. For just a moment Hossein was distracted by this new voice; he was not accustomed to women speaking without permission. In that instant Walid tried to spin away from him, but the knife tore at his throat, a thin stream of bright red blood issuing from the wound. "Walid, get down," she yelled, and fired at Hossein. He clutched at his side as he dropped to the wet concrete. Both the other men dropped down behind the bomb, as Uri took a shot at the other Arab, drawing a groan of pain.

"Jim," Lara shouted, "Come out and I'll try to get you a deal, if you cooperate. Otherwise you're dead meat and you know it."

A shot rang out, and they saw the muzzle flash from under the bomb. The bullet ricocheted around the concrete walls as Uri fired at the flash. There was another sound of pain from the men under the bomb. Uri figured at least two of them were now injured. He couldn't afford to have them all dead, leaving Uri and Lara with no way to turn off the timer. Then another shot came from the trapped men, taking out the nearest light bulb with a secondary pop. The area was now in near total darkness, the only remaining light coming from a bulb near the bomb. Uri whispered to Lara, "Stay here and turn on your Maglite if you see anyone come out. I'm going on in."

As Uri crouched down and raced in on the right side of the bomb, Lara fired a burst from her Walther at the left side, the rounds ricocheting off the floor and walls. Uri rolled under the bomb and immediately encountered Hossein, the Arab's knife at the ready. Hossein swiped across Uri's face, aiming at his throat, but, in ducking, the knife struck the orbit of Uri's left eye, plucking it from its socket. The shock of the blow caused Uri to drop his Sig Sauer, and, in the near darkness, he didn't even think of looking for it. Hossein headed for the kill, thrusting the knife in his right hand again toward Uri from his blind left side. "This

Jew…" Hossein thought as he plunged the knife toward Uri's rib cage, "… I will have the satisfaction of killing myself."

In the split second he had, Uri instinctively anticipated Hossein's move: always place yourself in the enemy's position, he had learned over and over in his hand-to-hand training. He rolled under the knife thrust, grabbing Hossein's right wrist and pulling him over his own shoulder, digging his elbow into the Arab's side. A rush of breath mixed with fear and pain issued from Hossein's throat, as Uri twisted his right hand, breaking it at the wrist with a solid snap. The putrid smell of garlic, sweat, and stale breath caused Uri to gag, but Hossein's knife fell from his hand, clattering to the concrete. Even in the dim light, Uri could just see the gleam from the blade with his remaining eye, and he snatched it up. At the same time he twisted the Arab's hand even more, causing a scream that echoed through the tunnel. Uri rammed his knee into Hossein's groin, this time causing only a grunt from the nearly exhausted Arab.

Uri now had a split-second decision to make: He could let Hossein live and hope he could somehow get him to defuse the bomb, or he could kill him and hope that Walid was still alive and could do the job. In that split second, Uri realized that Hossein would never disarm his own creation, no matter what the consequences were to him. There was no perceptible pause as Uri plunged the knife into the Arab's solar plexus; he didn't want him to die without the knowledge that he had failed. The bundle of nerves at the center of his chest was pierced, so that he was not even able to scream. He fell helpless, his eyes full of hate, visible even in the dim light of the single bulb, as his life trickled away. Uri recalled the words of Rafi Eital, the Mossad legend, as he watched the man suffer in the jaws of a painful and certain death. He knew what Eital meant, the satisfaction of terminating a monster, and knowing that monster was aware of his fate.

"Bring your Maglite," Uri yelled to Lara. "I think we're clear." Lara hastily climbed around the bomb with her powerful flashlight. Jim lay dead, his eyes open but unseeing, a bullet wound visible in the side of his head. The exit wound was also clear: a mass of blood and gray matter was splattered on the side of the tunnel. The other Arab lay dead beside him, the victim of one of Lara's blind shots.

"Help me!" There was a weak voice from directly under the bomb.

"Walid?" Lara cried out as she directed her flashlight beam at the sound. He was barely moving, his face pale. "Can you hear me?"

Walid nodded weakly. Lara reached down and felt for his pulse. It was difficult to find, and then it was barely a flutter. With one hand he held a piece of his shirt against his neck; the shirt was totally soaked with blood, and a slight trickle still issued from the wound. It was amazing that he had any life at all. "Walid, listen to me, we're going to get you out of here, the backup is on its way right now, you're going to be all right," Uri said to him, vainly trying to comfort him; both knew it was hopeless. Lara stared at Uri in horror; he had forgotten, in his adrenalin driven state, about the empty eye socket that stared back.

"Walid, listen, I need you to tell me how to disarm this thing, can you do that?" Uri was in a near panic mode; Lara was already there. Walid had a glazed look on his face, a look that gave both agents little confidence that he was able to do anything at all. "If we prop you up, do you think you can remember how to stop the timer?" Uri was at the point of total desperation. This man had little-to-no time left to him on this earth. He motioned to Lara, in her near catatonic state, to help lift Walid to a sitting position, while Uri kept pressure on the mortal neck wound. "The lights and buttons, Walid, do you remember how to disarm the damn thing!?"

The three green and two red lights were blinking, Walid saw. Then, to his horror, he realized that one red light was not blinking; it was steady. The bomb was set to fire in less than thirty minutes, perhaps much less. How long had it been since the attack began? He couldn't remember. Desperately he scanned the control panel; it was much the same as the one on the boat in the Marina, he realized. Then he saw the toggle switch under the crucial light; it must have been added as a safety feature by Hossein, in case he had to delay the blast. It was his only chance: Walid flipped the switch with his last remaining energy, and saw the red light begin blinking again. He smiled at Lara and Uri, and then his eyes closed, his face showing calm and relief.

Just then, the cavalry arrived. Summoned by the beacon activated by Lara, the police and military rushed into the tunnel. A bomb specialist, obvious from his heavy protective clothing and various electronic devices, hurried directly to the sinister gray object. Medical technicians hurried to examine Jim, Walid, and especially Uri.

"Your eye," Lara wailed.

"I'm afraid it's gone, sir," the med tech announced gravely.

"I sort of figured that," Uri replied with a grim smile. "But I'll be the next Moshe Dayan, even the same eye."

The light finally dawned on Lara as she remembered their dinner-time conversation; it seemed so long ago. She smiled at him and gripped his hand tightly.

Among the horde of people flowing into the area was a large black man: Wash Neil had been advised of the operation and had demanded to be with the first of the troops sent in. "The bomb crew says it's ok, the thing is disarmed. Apparently it was just a simple Radio Shack garage door opener. They killed it pretty quick. But if that guy," he pointed at the now-dead Walid, "hadn't stopped the timer, I don't think we would have made it here…" The group fell silent for a moment.

"We'll have to let the world know what a hero he turned out to be," Lara stated simply. "He could have saved himself and no one would have known."

"What happened with Jim?" Uri asked. "Do we know yet?"

"Internal Affairs had been tracking him, but we didn't have anything until a few days ago. They had him, well, pictures of him with a young man…" Wash didn't elaborate. "Trotter couldn't believe it of him, after all his service. I guess those are the ones…" "But it looks like he's been sabotaging our plans for a long time. That's how these guys got away with it so long. But now we have the link to Hezbollah, both in Iran and Lebanon, and from here on, let's just say Nasrallah and Mughniyah have some pretty big targets on their backs."

"Sir," the med tech pleaded with Uri, "We need to get that wound tended to before there's any chance at infection. And don't worry, they have some great prostheses, glass eyes, I mean, they look like the real thing."

"Glass eye? Forget it, I'm going with a black patch. " The med tech, who probably never even heard of the Six-Day war, looked at him blankly.

"It's all right, I'll see that he gets to the hospital," Lara interjected as she hustled Uri over to one of the waiting military SUV's. She saw that the surge of adrenalin that had kept him going the last hour or so, was wearing off. His sudden pallor scared him; she grabbed an Army doctor by the sleeve and pulled him over to the vehicle. "This man just saved the city of Chicago; he needs some quick attention." The doctor took one look at Uri and laid his seat back, propping his head up on a rolled-up jacket. He shouted some instructions to an assistant who was standing nearby, who then brought two loaded syringes to him.

The doctor injected Uri and listened to his chest as the assistant took his temperature and blood pressure. She murmured something to the doctor, who smiled and said to Lara, "He'll live to fight another day. Hopefully not like this one. You guys had us all going nuts out here."

Colonel Blake and Lieutenant O'Leary approached the SUV, beaming, if somewhat sheepishly. "I never would have believed it," Blake said. "We were ten minutes away from alerting the whole city."

"Ten minutes?" Lara asked wryly. "That's more time than we had. If that bomb is what I think it is, the whole downtown would have been leveled." Blake and O'Leary looked skeptical. Wash Neil and another man sloshed up through the water. This is Stephens, the head of the bomb crew," he said.

"We've got it pulled open, just to make sure," Stephens said. "There's enough uranium fuel in there to blow this city sky-high. I don't know if they could have actually held the thing together long enough, but I'm glad we didn't find out." He glanced briefly at each of the assembled group, then strode quickly away.

"He's not kidding," Neil added. These guys, crazy as they seem, knew what they were doing. Let's get you guys out of here. Oh, and nice job, by the way."

Chapter 41

Lara sat nervously at Uri's bedside. The little group included Neil and Trotter.

Uri looked directly at Trotter, as best he could with his remaining eye, and asked, "How long have you known about Jim?"

"Not long enough. I suppose the signs were there, but…It's easy enough to see things in hindsight. Actually, we were more worried about you, Wash."

"You had me tailed, right?"

"Just for the last couple of weeks. One of the guys noticed your Friday getup and sounded the alarm."

"You're tailing agents now?"

"Actually, we weren't tailing you; one of our guys recognized you in your robe, or whatever you call it, going into that mosque. He was going to say hello to you, then decided to call Internal Security instead, knowing the mosque is on our list of 'at risk' locations," Trotter said. "You're lucky we spotted you when we did. Did you know your Imam is part of the Arab Homeland Society? They're the ones distributing the 'hate' textbooks to all the Arab grade schools around D.C."

"I had already figured out they were a little crazy. Believe it or not, I'd been doing some digging on my own. Most of the Muslim leaders around the U.S. are dead set against the extremists, and aren't afraid to speak out. But they don't get the press the nut jobs do."

"We know you filed a security report on the mosque. That's why you weren't brought in. We figured you were in a good spot to get more information."

Neil grinned, "I should have known nothing's secret around the Agency. But what's the deal with Turner?"

"That's a sad story. I've talked to his wife. He apparently had a thing for young boys and one of the Al Qaeda operatives got him hooked. They got video tapes of him…well, let's just say it's pretty bad."

"What a thing for his family." Lara said.

"The good part, if there can be a good part, is that we had a tail on him near the end, and we've picked up the main guys in the Al Qaeda cell. Funny, our guy was sure Jim had spotted him, but he went ahead with the meetings anyway."

"How did they get him to go to the Chicago site?" she asked.

"We got into their website, thanks to you. They had promised him all the tapes and two million U.S. if he would go with them. I guess they wanted to be sure he didn't all of a sudden blow the scheme."

Trotter shook his head and hesitated, "Listen, Uri, we've got a place for you, either at Homeland Security or FBI. The thing about FBI, we've got this nepotism policy…" He glanced at Lara and raised an eyebrow. "But the job at Homeland would be at GS-13, that's a great starting salary. And now that they can claim some of the credit in tying up the loose ends, there's no hard feelings. In fact, Fredericks sent his compliments to you two." Uri lay there, expressionless, not speaking. "OK, just think it over, big guy, we owe you." He patted Uri on the arm, rose and he and Neil left the room.

"You can't imagine how much I want to be here, with you…" Uri said to Lara after the others had left.

"But you're not, right? Danielle?"

Uri tried to grin, but it looked more like a grimace. "No, that's over; I knew it when you and I were first together. But Israel, it's in my blood. I feel like a tourist over here, even now. I know they need me, and I need to be there, doing what I know best."

"You know how high you are on their list now right, the Jihadists?"

"And you think they couldn't get me over here, and you along with me? The guy with the eye patch. I might as well paint a bull's eye on my back. With me around, you'd be as big a target as I am."

"Not hardly." She turned her head away from him for a moment and pretended to get something out of her eye. "Will you at least visit? Once in a while?"

"Wherever they send me, that's where I go. I have a feeling I'm going to be at a desk for a while."

"Somehow I don't see you behind a desk."

"Neither do I, right now, but let's face it, my life has changed."

A military orderly came into the room with an armful of newspapers. The Chicago Tribune was on top, with a front page poorly-lit photograph of Uri and Lara. The headline screamed in two-inch letters: "Terrorists Foiled!!" Then, underneath, the sub-headline added: "FBI Agents Disarm Nuke at River Site." The lead article went on to heap praise on the two agents, whom the FBI refused to name. "Their safety is our number one concern at the moment," an FBI spokesman was quoted as saying.

"Thanks for small favors," Uri muttered. "No names but our picture blazoned on the front page."

"I notice the Mossad is not mentioned," Lara said as she scanned the rest of the article. "And the picture is blurry enough to keep us sort of unrecognizable."

Lara cradled his head, stifling her tears. "You know," he said, "I could die pretty happy right about now."

Lara got up with a start. "Don't you even joke about that, you dope." She turned to him again and kissed him lightly on the mouth. "This isn't the end, you know."

Epilogue

It was exactly 10:45 P.M. on February 14, when Sheikh Imad Fa'iz Mughniyah left the meeting with some of his highest-ranking chieftains. They had spent the evening feasting on lamb, hummus, flat bread and boiled vegetables. Afterwards, while laying the final plans for the martyring of two young children, both girls, in a shopping mall in Tel Aviv, they sipped on some very strong, very sweet tea. The Sheikh rose, signaling the end of the meeting, and the others did likewise. They all kissed the Sheikh's ring, bowing in supplication, then kissed him three times on the cheeks. It had been a fruitful evening and they looked forward to reading of the carnage the young girls would bring about.

Mughniyah and his driver stepped out into the cool, still February night, quite common for winter in Damascus. The driver opened the door for his master, then ran around to the driver's side and got in. After seeing the mandatory nod from the Sheikh, the driver turned the starter on the black Mercedes sedan. The explosion rocked the whole neighborhood, showering it with human, metal and glass debris. Neighbors, most in their pajamas came running to the scene. Not much was left of the car or its passengers: bits of cloth, metal, blood and unidentifiable pieces of human flesh and bones. The blast had torn the windows from the meeting house as well as several of the adjoining structures. No other members of the Hezbollah pack, however, were injured. They hovered over the remains, which consisted mainly of a smoking hole, wailing and moaning, flailing their chests, and shouting Arab curses of revenge.

On a hilltop, about half a mile from the scene, two men, each wearing the standard red-and-white keffiyeh common to the Jordanians, watched the scene with night-vision goggles from a dirt-covered Damascus taxi. The passenger was a slender, middle-aged man with unusually thick forearms, thinning curly hair, and one eye that never moved. He signaled to the driver, a younger man with a full beard, to drive slowly away. As they passed into the night, the passenger removed his keffiyeh, put in place a black eye patch, covered his head with a blanket, and fell immediately asleep

Jack Winnick

Jack Winnick

Jack Winnick is an engineering professor with forty years expertise in chemical and nuclear engineering, mainly at Georgia Tech. He is the author of a widely-used Thermodynamics textbook and hundreds of technical articles. In addition to teaching and research in the fields of thermodynamics and electrochemical engineering, he has worked as a consultant in the oil and gas industry, and for the NASA Crew Systems Division. He is also a professional actor, appearing both on stage and television. He is an avid scuba diver and weekend tennis player. He lives in Los Angeles.

Jack Winnick

We hope you have enjoyed reading
East Wind

To contact the author
email: firesidepubs@comcast.net

See our web site: firesidepubs.com
For books in all genres

Fireside Publications
Lady Lake, Florida